uR

S0-AWC-664

ST. MARTIN'S

MINOTAUR

MYSTERIES

Other titles from St. Martin's **Minotaur** Mysteries

St. Martin's Paperbacks is also proud to present
these mystery classics by Ngaio Marsh

THE GREEN-EYED HURRICANE

"Martin Hegwood's crisp pacing and intimate knowledge of his surroundings make this sandy thriller a full blown delight."　　　*—The Clarion-Ledger* (Jackson)

"Hegwood's one of Mississippi's brightest literary talents."　　　　　　　　　　*—Daily Journal*

BIG EASY BACKROAD

"The power of BIG EASY BACKROAD lies in the fast action moving through the shadowy world of New Orleans and the Gulf Coast, captured in all its seedy splendor. It's a trip worth taking."
　　　　　　　—New Orleans Times-Picayune

"Readers will relish this saucy gumbo of back-country adventure."　　　　　　*—Publishers Weekly*

"Make room for Martin. BIG EASY BACKROAD is the real deal."　　*—The Clarion-Ledger* (Jackson)

"Atmospheric and action-packed."　*—Kirkus Reviews*

ST. MARTIN'S PAPERBACKS TITLES
BY MARTIN HEGWOOD

Big Easy Backroad
The Green-Eyed Hurricane

THE
GREEN-EYED
HURRICANE

MARTIN
HEGWOOD

St. Martin's Paperbacks

NOTE: If you purchased this book without a cover you should be aware that this book is stolen property. It was reported as "unsold and destroyed" to the publisher, and neither the author nor the publisher has received any payment for this "stripped book."

THE GREEN-EYED HURRICANE

Copyright © 2000 by Martin Hegwood.

Excerpt from *Massacre Island* copyright © 2001 by Martin Hegwood. Jacket photograph by Julia Sims.

All rights reserved. No part of this book may be used or reproduced in any manner whatsoever without written permission except in the case of brief quotations embodied in critical articles or reviews. For information address St. Martin's Press, 175 Fifth Avenue, New York, NY 10010.

Library of Congress Catalog Card Number: 00-028583

ISBN: 0-312-97975-4

Printed in the United States of America

St. Martin's Press hardcover edition / July 2000
St. Martin's Paperbacks edition / August 2001

St. Martin's Paperbacks are published by St. Martin's Press, 175 Fifth Avenue, New York, NY 10010.

10 9 8 7 6 5 4 3 2 1

To Linda, with love and superlatives

ACKNOWLEDGMENTS

I thank these friends and family members for their assistance: David Blount, Phil Bryant, Debra Case, Vincent Creel, Kenn Davis, Glen Endris, Judy Guice, Eliza Hegwood, William Hegwood, Hank Holmes, Kay Jerome, Bobby Johnson, Laura Johnson, Charleen Pierce, the guys at the Slavonian Lodge, Mike Ward, and Dennis Webb. Special thanks to my father, Tommy Hegwood, an expert shrimper and a great teller of stories about the Mississippi Gulf Coast.

If I could have one part of the world back the way it used to be, I would not choose Dresden before the fire bombing, Rome before Nero, or London before the Blitz. I would not resurrect Babylon, Carthage, or San Francisco. Let the leaning tower lean and the hanging gardens hang. I want the Mississippi Gulf Coast back as it was before Hurricane Camille.

—Elizabeth Spencer,
On the Gulf

ONE

Mr. Cass used to laugh a lot, but that was back when I was a kid, back before the tragedy that changed us all. After that, he became a sad and solitary old man. In the past few years some people in Biloxi had grown to hate him, and I'll admit they had their reasons. But as I lay awake in my camp house those steamy July nights, tossing and sweating with the sheets clinging to me, I wasn't thinking about Mr. Cass's enemies or anything they had done. I was the one he had trusted. And I was the one who let him down.

Casper Perinovich was like a second father to me when I was growing up. He and his wife, Marie, had one child, Mike, my best boyhood friend. Every summer vacation I visited for two weeks in the Perinovich home on Point Cadet in Biloxi, thirty-five miles east along the Mississippi Gulf Coast from our home in Bay Saint Louis.

Mr. Cass was still living in that same house several weeks ago when I drove to Point Cadet, the eastern end of the peninsula on which Biloxi sits. I promised my mother and father I would stop by to visit him since the fires I had been investigating were close to his house. I stopped by on Thursday, my last day on the last case I was working for Bayou Casualty Insurance.

It was a cloudless summer day, and the white glare off the sand and crushed oyster shells in the driveways and on the shoulders of the street at the tip of Howard Avenue made my eyes water. Waves of heat squiggled from the sun-softened asphalt, and sunlight danced like sequins on the broad inlet of the Mississippi Sound at the end of the street. The pungent ammonia smell from Acme Shrimp Company, running hard at the height of the season, blew in from up Back Bay.

As the founder, owner, and only employee of Jack Delmas Investigations, Incorporated, I was working two arson investigations on the Point for Bayou Casualty Insurance Company out of New Orleans. I handle most of their work on the Mississippi Gulf Coast at fifty dollars per hour plus expenses. I live in Bay Saint Louis and it's cheaper for them to hire me at an hourly rate than to send out an in-house guy. It's also a hell of a lot more effective, since the Mississippi coast is my turf.

The sign said Beware of Dog, so I stopped outside the gate and whistled. Not a dog or even a cat in sight. Got halfway between the gate and the front steps when five sharp barks echoed as if from an empty room, and the monster came barreling out from under the porch and trapped me.

I froze where I stood. The dog laid its ears back and made short lunges at my throat, pulling up only inches from my face. I smelled its hot breath through two inches of pink gums and three inches of ivory fangs. My heart went into overdrive, and I had to force myself to breathe.

Eye contact can trigger an attack, so I caught only glimpses of the dog's face, its blazing yellow eyes. The fur bristled and its back arched higher than my waist. It let loose with a series of earsplitting barks. I know dogs; these were no idle barks.

"MR. CASS!" I screamed. "HELP! IT'S ME, JACK DELMAS!"

The screen door creaked open. The dog backed away, still snarling and still snapping. Perinovich tottered through the screen door, shifting his weight from side to side as he walked to the front of the porch. With an underhand toss, he flipped a Milk Bone in a high arc. The dog snatched it in midflight. Sounded like finger bones crunching. It stopped growling at me and turned its amber eyes to Perinovich. Even started wagging its tail. Cass tossed a second dog biscuit, and the monster chomped it on its downward flight.

"Dat's all you get, Sweetie," he said. "Get on round back." Perinovich swept his arm toward the side of the house, and the wolf trotted to the corner of the house and crawled back to the cool shade and soft dirt under the porch.

"Jack! Good to see you, son."

"What was *that*?" My hands trembled as the adrenaline worked its way down to my fingers.

"I figure German shepherd mostly. Some people say he's a wolf. It's them yellow eyes. He might have a little coyote in him, but he ain't a wolf. How's ya mama 'n them?"

"I think my heart's about to jump out of my chest."

"Woulda got out here sooner, but I was hoping maybe Sweetie had cornered that pain in the ass, Billy Weldon."

Perinovich padded to the main front door, the one on the right, as if each step hurt, and held it open for me. He had shrunk since the last time I was there, but even at seventy-eight years old he was still solid. I hadn't seen Mr. Cass for nearly three years, and felt guilty about it. But there had never been a good time. When I called him earlier that day, he invited me to go night shrimping. My brother Neal, the lawyer, was running for the state senate and needed some shrimp for a fund-raiser he was holding in a few days. It was good that my fire investigation ended on Thursday. It's big-time bad luck to start a shrimping trip on a Friday.

"I got Sweetie to keep dem Vietnam gangs off my prop'ty, but she works just as good on Weldon. He come around here twice a week before I got my dog. 'Bout to worry the hell out of me to sell this prop'ty to him."

When my heart geared back down I felt light-headed. I was wet with sweat, so I balanced on the edge of the couch and held my face toward the oscillating fan. The breeze from the fan drew the smell of fresh-brewed tea from the kitchen and felt almost frosty against my skin.

"Guess you heard 'bout the casino," he said, "the one dey tryin' to put in here on the Point. Weldon ain't admitting dat's why he wants to buy me out, but it's gotta be. He got too much money backing him for it to be anything else."

I had indeed heard about the new casino. I was five days into a pair of arson investigations, fires number four and five on Point Cadet since the first of the year. That's eight times the normal rate, so the computers kicked out the order to investigate. There had been a lot of talk about the casino that week.

"You look a little hot," Cass said. "I got some tea cooling back in the kitchen." He took a step toward the rear of the house. He had the barrel chest and bull neck of a lifetime shrimper. He still had more black in his hair than gray, but his skin had started to hang on his frame. "So what you doing on the Point? You investigatin' some big crime or something?"

"We've had some fires."

"We?"

"Bayou Casualty out of New Orleans. I do investigation for them sometimes."

"Y'all think somebody set dem fires?"

"The company thinks it's unusual to have so many."

"I ain't trying to knock you outta work," he said, "but I can tell your Bayou-whatever company what the problem is. The casinos done jacked the price of land up sky-high. Don't even want the houses, just the land. So the folks, they sell the land and torch the house to collect the insurance. Dat casino money, it's making crooks out of a lot of folks."

"Is it the casinos' fault that they put a lot of money into circulation, Mr. Cass?"

"Didn't say it was their fault. They just supply the temptation.

The folks around here're taking it from there. I could use a glass of tea. You want one?"

He stepped into the kitchen. The living room still had the touch of Marie, Perinovich's wife. It had been thirty years since that great catastrophe had claimed her life. Faded lace doilies were spread on the arms of the overstuffed couch and matching chair. In the corner, a half-written letter was turned into the carriage of the black Royal manual typewriter. Brown earthenware lamps flanked the ends of the couch, like props from the set of *The Mary Tyler Moore Show*. It sent me back to when I came over from Bay Saint Louis to spend the night with their son, Mike, who had died with his mother. It felt as if Mike were going to walk into the room at any minute.

"You take yours with lemon, don't you?" he said. "Sure you do. I remember."

"You writing another letter to the editor?"

"I got the goods on him this time, Jack. That crook Bernie Pettus and that whole bunch. I'm about to bust it wide open."

"You might ought to go to the district attorney before you put it in the paper."

"Tried that thirty years ago," he said. "Found out you gotta make it public first. Then there ain't no way for a DA to bury it, even though Bernie's the mayor now. If I can get it printed on the front page of the paper, it wouldn't matter if he was the governor." He handed me the glass, up to the brim with sweet lemon tea and dripping with condensation.

"What kind of evidence do you have?"

He shook his head. "Got it in yesterday from up at Jackson. It's a public record, all anybody's gotta do is know where to look. I can't tell you about it just yet."

"Does it have anything to do with the new casino?"

"What I'm talking about ain't got nothing to do with casinos. But you can bet Bernie's got his fingers in that gambling stuff somehow. Too damn much money floating around for him to stay away from it. I'm talking about something that's gonna get the feds down here. Dat's the only way I can get him. Gotta get the feds in on it."

"You better put your stuff in a safe place, Mr. Cass."

On the sideboard along the opposite wall sat three framed pictures. One was a family shot, Casper, Marie, and Mike, at Mike's sixth grade graduation, just three months before he and his mama died. He wore that smile of devilment, as Mama called it, that he got when he and I were about to embark on some adventure that he had dreamed up. The second frame held a picture of Jesus in a pink robe pointing to the sacred heart on his chest. At the base of the picture, two tiny flames glimmered in squatty, red votive candle holders. The other picture was of Sheila, Perinovich's niece. Her black hair was cut in a page boy and she was holding her son who looked to be about two years old.

"What do you hear from Sheila?" I asked.

"She's doing great. Got her own hotel down in Miami and raking in the cash. She asked about you the last time we talked."

"Her own hotel?"

"Got it in her divorce." He shook his head. "You young people nowadays just don't stay together."

"I tried, Mr. Cass. I sure didn't want Sandy to go back to Memphis."

"I ain't gettin' on you. It's a different world nowadays."

I had lost touch with Sheila, but I thought of her often. Any man who spent any time around Sheila would have a hard time forgetting her. We dated one summer, the summer before I left for Ole Miss. Three hundred miles at that stage of life was enough to kill the romance.

"Sheila's boy, he's about to graduate down at the University of Miami," he said. "Marine biology. Maybe he can come up here and tell me how to find them shrimp." He held his gaze on the portrait. "Sheila, she's real busy with that hotel."

He touched her image lightly as if he were stroking her hair, and looked as if he had gone inside the picture. When I was around Mr. Cass, I got the feeling that he took such trips fairly often.

"Mighty good tea," I said.

He turned and stepped toward his chair. "You ready to get some shrimp?"

"Maybe I ought to just buy some from you," I said. "Neal needs about thirty pounds for this fund-raiser he's having."

"I heard about dat. Heard he's runnin' for state senate. Maybe I can call the shrimp a donation." He reached back and gripped both arms of his padded armchair and eased himself down.

"I'm not asking you to give me any shrimp," I said. "That's how you make your living."

"You ain't heard? I'm the richest man in Biloxi. I just go out shrimping for the fun of it."

"You don't have to take me. I'll get in your way."

"I don't sell shrimp to any Delmas. You got to work for 'em. And as far as you getting in the way? You're a Delmas, son. The Delmases fished along this coast two hundred years before us Jugas even got here. Your daddy, he's still the best I ever saw. I swear, he can smell where dem shrimp are. It's in your blood, boy, whether you know it or not."

So I decided to go. It was a Thursday, so no big curse should befall us, and clear weather was predicted.

It should have been a safe, calm trip.

TWO

A clash of breaking glass set off a barrage of barks that I felt through the floor. I jumped off the couch and bolted to the door. The neck of the brown quart bottle was the biggest piece remaining. The puddle of beer foamed as it soaked into the hot sidewalk. The car, a dull burgundy Cutlass, sped off around the corner and the huge dog galloped back and forth along the fence, barking loud enough to set off alarms.

"What was it?" Perinovich asked.

"Somebody threw a beer bottle out of a car. It busted on your sidewalk."

"Their aim's getting better. They usually hit the grass."

"You know who threw it?"

Perinovich leaned forward so he could push himself up from the chair. "It's dem Dragons I was telling you about."

"The Vietnamese gang?"

"Uh-huh. Here, let me go pick up their damn mess and then we can go down to the boat."

"They do stuff like that often, Mr. Cass?"

"All the time. That's the main reason I got Sweetie. Here, let me go clean dat glass up and we'll go to the boat."

"I can clean it up," I said.

"You sure you want to go out in the yard? You think you can get along better now with Sweetie?"

"Maybe I better hang back and lock up the house."

"I'll go pick up the glass," he said. "You be sure to turn everything off."

Perinovich's land backed up to the shore of Biloxi Bay, just south of the old Highway 90 bridge, now a public fishing pier. Green tufts of salt grass poked through the surface along the shoreline, and a black-over-white shearwater skimmed along six inches above the water, occasionally dipping its orange bill down to pluck out a minnow or a shiner. The pilings and planks of Mr. Cass's pier had faded to gray under twenty years of sunlight, but they were sturdy.

Mr. Cass had already filled the diesel tanks and ice hole on the *Miss Marie*. I opened the windows and doors to air out the cabin and studied the instrument panel to relearn the configuration of the switches for bilge pump, running lights, dragging light, radar, depth finder, and the rest of the thousands of dollars of electronic gear that adorned the *Miss Marie*.

Perinovich and my father had built the boat at our family boatyard in Bay Saint Louis in 1968. Mr. Cass put in two galvanized bolts where one would suffice. He double sealed the points where the ribs touched the hull to hold down on rot. He laid a double keel and fashioned an anchor post that would hold through any gale. In short, he built the finest Biloxi lugger that has ever been built. He named it for his wife and christened it with a bottle of André champagne and a splash of holy water from Father Hillary.

"Your boat looks good, Mr. Cass."

"You could eat off my decks," he said. He grasped a side stay with his right hand and swung down from the pier onto the deck in a smooth motion that belied his seventy-eight years. But when he landed he winced. Bad feet.

"Jack, I want you to remember something. You see those pilings there, second ones from the land? That's my prop'ty line." He pointed to a bleached-out creosoted post with a layer of sun-softened tar coating its flat top. The tide was down, below the post's barnacle line, and the water's edge had receded to the first set of pilings, exposing a six-foot strip of dark, hard-packed bottom sand. A brown fiddler crab, with its single oversized claw, scurried across the sand and scooted into a tiny hole just below solid ground at the high water mark.

"I own that twenty feet from those pilings to the solid ground where that grass is. The state don't own it. The law says that it ain't where the shoreline is now, it's where it use to be. That's why I put up dem No Wake signs. All dem boats goin' so fast washed away my land. I can prove it use to be where that piling is now."

"Why don't you fill it back in?"

"The Corps of Engineers and the EPA and the Bureau of Marine Resources," he said. "I won't live as long as it takes to get the damn permits. You probably won't neither."

The sun hovered over the pine trees to the west, still yellow and hot. Mr. Cass stepped into the cabin and flipped on the bilge pump and a stream of water gushed out the quarter-sized hole just below the deck line.

"I can't believe it," I said. "You had some water in the bilge."

"My boat don't leak, dammit. Dat was rainwater. I keep my boat up. Not like dat piece of shit coming here."

A dingy thirty-footer eased our way, white puffs of diesel smoke shooting out the vertical exhaust pipe. An unpainted plywood patch had been slapped on the side of the boat just above the decks, nearly covering the hand-painted name *Side Pocket*. A crudely stenciled, Peg-Board sign hung on the outer wall of the cabin. Bait Shrimp. The boat's pump kicked on and off at ten-second intervals, a sure sign it had skipped its yearly caulking, and a sheen of oil spread behind the boat from the bilgewater.

The man at the helm could be seen only in profile as the low sun and its bouncing reflection off the water made it impossible to see his face. His silhouette was long and gaunt and showed him to be wearing a long-billed cap.

As the *Side Pocket* approached, it edged closer to shore, maybe ten feet out from the end of the pier. When it was nearly even with us, the pilot gunned the diesel. The engined roared and the rusty muffler rattled and a plume of black exhaust shot skyward as the boat lurched ahead. The forward thrust made it sit down in the stern and kick up a wake as high as its deckline.

"HEY!" I yelled. "SLOW DOWN!"

I jumped out of the cabin and jabbed my finger at the No Wake sign on the last post of Perinovich's pier. The captain, his face hidden by mirrored sunglasses and the cap, looked straight ahead and kept his hand shoved hard against the brass throttle.

The first wave lifted the *Miss Marie* and banged her into the pilings, pushing her against the tires nailed up to serve as bumpers. The brass bell on the front of the cabin clanged as she rocked back and forth. Before the wake played out, we rose, hit the bumpers, and scraped back down the pilings three times. Perinovich glared at the scow as it passed and slowed back down and pulled out into the middle of the bay. Viewed from behind, the *Side Pocket* had a pronounced list to starboard.

"You recognize him?" Perinovich asked.

"Couldn't see his face for the sun."

"That's Lennis Belter. He's been mad at me ever since I turned in that worthless son of his for illegal dumping out in the gulf."

"When did Lennis become a bait shrimper?"

With a bait shrimp license, a poacher can drag fine mesh nets through the bayous, catching baby shrimp by the ton before they get big enough to survive in the gulf and screwing up the season for everyone else. It's big-time illegal. I wondered why Lennis was this long getting into it. I would have thought he invented it. Perinovich let out a sound that was either a snicker or a sigh and stared at the *Side Pocket*'s slow retreat up the bay.

"I might ought to pay Lennis a visit," I said.

Cass hit the ignition switch to fire up the diesel. The lid on the upright exhaust pipe fluttered as it stood wide open to let out the vortex of gray smoke. "Forget about Lennis. We got shrimp to catch."

Toward New Orleans the deep red ball of sun slipped below the edge of the gulf and left a rosy afterglow. The eastern, opposite horizon was fading to dark. The sky overhead was still light and marbled with thin cirrus clouds and that created a wash of pink.

"We'll go to Graveline Bayou," Cass said. "It's done got too crowded to go night shrimping out in front of Biloxi. If a storm blows up, I got a place over dere we can pull in."

"The weather report said it ought to be clear."

"It's hurricane season. Dem storms don't watch TV. The TV's saying ninety percent of the surface of the land and the water ain't gonna get no storm, but what if you're in that ten percent that does?"

The moon was rising over Ocean Springs, full and big, almost orange. The waves were slow swells without foam, a good forty feet between the crests, and the heavy *Miss Marie* hardly moved as they rose and fell. The decks glowed under our red and green running lights and the lights on the channel markers kicked on one by one. As we left the bay and got past the shelter of Deer Island, a breeze kicked up and pulled a salty smell through the cabin and occasionally pushed sweet diesel fumes down on us.

"Dat old evil wind," he said. "You know about it, don't you?"

"Hurricane Camille?"

"She's still out there, son."

To Perinovich, Hurricane Camille didn't die in 1969. She is a living entity that has never stopped roaming the earth and never will. Like the devil, she takes different forms, sometimes a gentle puff of air, sometimes a raging tornado, but still there, always moving. Perinovich, who prayed the rosary every morning, had no problem grafting this Choctaw notion onto his Roman Catholicism.

"Is there a good wind out there too?" I asked.

"Sure there is." He stuck his hand out the window. "This is the good wind."

We started the first drag under a strong moon, high and by that time white, and the phosphorus in the water sparkled like green diamonds. Perinovich set a course parallel to the shore three miles out from Belle Fontaine Beach, headed north toward Graveline Bayou. I loosened the heavy trawl doors at either side of the mouth of the net and secured the tie rope at its tip end. I checked the tickler chain to see that it was free of the net and pulled back on the handle of the winch slowly, with an eye to the trawl boards as they slipped down to the water, making sure they hit at the same time so the net would spread.

Perinovich had the trawl boards angled to drag high. We were going after the white shrimp rather than the bottom-dwelling "hoppers," or brown shrimp, and Perinovich said he would only keep the jumbos, the kind the restaurants love for stuffing. They command a premium price, but would be nearly worthless for the shrimp boil Neal was having for his fund-raiser. For that I needed sixteen to twenty count. Anything smaller would go into the gumbo I was planning.

I eased off the brake of the winch and the cable rolled off the heavy spool. I kept enough pressure on the cable to make the boards stand up when they hit the water so the flow of the water would push them apart and spread them wide. I watched for the strips of red cloth Perinovich had tied to the cable at fifty foot intervals. When the third marker rolled out, I eased back on the brake. When it engaged, the pull of the net and the pair of two-hundred-pound wooden trawl boards made the boat feel like a pickup truck that had downshifted too soon from fourth to second.

"Like putting on the brakes," Perinovich said as he turned the dial of the white plastic kitchen timer for a one-hour drag. He set a course of ninety degrees, due east. We had earlier rounded Belle Fontaine Point, which blocked out the lights of Biloxi, and were headed toward the yellow radiance of Ingall's Shipyard, some four miles ahead in Pascagoula. Perinovich flipped on the dragging lights, a green light over a white light set in the rigging high above the cabin, the signal to all other traffic in the sound that we were pulling a net.

Ten minutes into the drag, Perinovich stepped down from his captain's chair and opened the front window. He stuck his head out as if trying to get closer to whatever he had spotted.

"Hot damn!" he said. "Would you look at that!"

Perinovich pointed to a boat at the two o'clock position, close and at an angle to cross our path. But we had our net out and we were creeping, so there was no danger. The other boat had been moving at a pretty good clip, and I had paid it no mind since I first saw it and calculated where it was going and how fast.

"See that port light?" he said. "That's the *China Sea.*"

"You can identify a boat by its lights?"

"A lot of 'em I can. The *China Sea*'s got a hole in the globe of the port running light. Makes it look pink."

"Is that legal?"

"Probably not. But at least nowadays he's got lights. Look what the sum'bitch just did."

"What?"

"You been off the water too long, son. Take a close look."

The *China Sea* was dead ahead of us with its pink port running light. But above that port side light, high up in the rigging, the dragging lights were glowing. That meant the boat was trawling and moving south to north, the way the Vietnamese did when they first moved into Biloxi, a direct clash with the established local custom of east-west drags. It had led to a brief shrimping war with a lot of loud confrontations and a few near misses, but eventually the Vietnamese began dragging east to west and things calmed down.

"I didn't notice the dragging light before," I said.

"That's because he just flipped it on." Cass reached overhead and grabbed the mike off the VHF mounted to the ceiling. "Lu! Get that damn boat turned straight! You know better'n dat!"

Perinovich flipped on the searchlight and aimed it at the *China Sea*. I put the field glasses on it. A Vietnamese kid in jeans and no shirt was standing on the deck holding his hand up, flipping us off.

"SCREW YOU, OLD MAN!" came the electronic shout over the VHS, setting off the squelch. A tenth of a mile on the water for a set of good VHS radios is almost like having their antennas touching.

"Go back and get the rifle, Jack."

"Mr. Cass, I didn't sign on for any naval battles."

"Ain't gonna be one, long as he turns that boat."

He gripped the wheel, his knuckles whitening with the pressure. The muscles in his jaw knotted the way I had seen them do so many times in the past when he was ready to tee off on somebody or something. He glanced at the compass. "Eighty-eight degrees," he said. "I ain't kidding, get the rifle." He flipped the searchlight off.

I made a quick dead reckoning using the grain elevator next to Ingall's as my fixed point. If we both held our courses at the same speeds, we'd cross the wake of the *China Sea* too close to clear its nets if they were out a normal distance. I figured I had better get the rifle so I would have it in my hands. The look in Cass's eyes told me to keep it out of his.

The moon shone bright and the lights from Ingall's gave us a good view of the *China Sea*. The kid stood at the bow holding on to a side stay, arm raised and finger up.

The *China Sea* reached our path seventy-five yards ahead. Perinovich held his grip on the wheel. Eighty-eight degrees. Twelve hundred RPMs. I stepped to the door of the cabin, keeping the rifle ready, looking for cover in case they decided to shoot at us. I kept my eyes on the kid flipping us off as I moved to the bow.

The wake of the *China Sea* boiled before us and churned the green, glowing, phosphorus-filled jellyfish into a glittering trail, like the tail of an underwater comet. Somewhere in that glowing tail was their net and its cable, either one of which could wrap around the shaft and the propeller of the *Miss Marie* and leave us dead in the water. If we were in for gunplay, I didn't want to be on a boat that couldn't move.

We closed to twenty yards from the *China Sea*'s trail. I ran back to the cabin. Course steady, speed steady.

"Slow it down, Mr. Cass. It'll cost you more to replace a shaft and cable than it'll cost him to replace a net."

Perinovich stared straight ahead and, without moving his eyes, pulled back on the throttle and pushed the wheel hard to starboard. We cleared the trailing, unseen net as I held my breath.

"Son of a bitch," he said.

They wheeled away from us and settled on an easterly heading. I guess Lu had made some kind of point. We swung around, a full one eighty, and the westerly wind seemed stronger since we were now headed into it. I stepped to the stern and watched the *China Sea*, a dark, receding outline against the lights of Pascagoula.

THREE

I take it you've met the captain of the *China Sea*," I said.

Perinovich snorted. "All the rest of dem Vietnamese come over here without a dime. Ten years later, dey got kids in med school. It's like history's repeatin' itself on the Point. My folks come over here from Croatia to work the shrimp cannery and man the boats. Hell, I worked the cannery too. Ten years old, had me up on that shucking table. We worked our way up. Now the Vietnamese, most of 'em at least, doin' the same thing. But not Lu's sorry-assed bunch. Dat one on the deck is Sammy, Lu's oldest boy. Got him a gang called the Dragons."

"Is that the gang you got the dog for?"

"Dey sittin' on cars in front of the house one night, drinkin' dem big bottles of malt liquor and raising hell. I sit on the porch and watch 'em. Don't say nothing. Two of 'em throw their bottles in my yard. So I go inside and get my twelve-gauge. I step out in the yard, lay down the shotgun, pick up the bottles, and throw 'em hard as I can at their damn cars. I missed with one, but the other one busted against Sammy's car and knocked out a window."

"Please tell me you didn't do that, Mr. Cass."

Perinovich laughed. "Then I pick up the shotgun and fire it off into the air. You shoulda seen 'em scatter."

I almost said something about how dangerous it was to tweak

the nose of a street gang, but I figured he was old enough to know that. I had known Mr. Cass long enough to know that he didn't appreciate being told how to live his life any more than I do, and that's not one damn bit.

"And they've been throwing beer bottles in your yard ever since?"

"Kids' stuff. But dey don't hang out on dem cars no more, that's for sure. And nobody's coming in on that dog, no sir."

The timer dinged and Perinovich pulled the throttle back to where the boat was barely moving, just enough to keep pressure on the trawl boards. I engaged the winch to pull in the net. Water dripped off the wet cable as it trailed through the blocks. The trawl boards broke the surface, and I grabbed the lazy line and pulled the ball of the net forward to the pick-out box. I yanked the smuggler's knot at the tip end of the net and the catch nearly spilled over the sides of the pick-out box, releasing the pungent smell of salt water and seaweed. Crabs and jellyfish, not much grass, and lots of shrimp.

I tied off the end of the net and swung the boom aft while Cass looped the boat around to run back for another run out in front of Graveline. If you have a good drag, you go back over the same ground. When I got the trawl boards lined up, I eased off on the winch and the cable ran off the spool to the fourth red cloth marker. I set the brake and the boat sat down in the water from the pull. Cass set the autopilot and came up front to pick out the shrimp.

"Good drag," I said.

"Not dat good," he said. "When we first set the net out I saw the shrimp break on the surface. Them white shrimp, dey travel in a straight line. You follow the line and you scoop up ever' one of 'em. You cross dat line and they scatter. This is what we got when we went across the line."

Cass pushed a sting ray, its tail whipping back and forth, down the chute and over the side. He scraped through the trash fish and raked the shrimp into the corner. He saved the squid. He had lined up a charter boat captain who used them for bait and was paying a good price for them. There were fifteen pounds of mostly white shrimp from the drag, twenty to twenty-five count, with a dozen jumbos that Cass put in a separate bucket. Vrazel's in Gulfport gave him two bucks each for all the jumbos; they use them in their stuffed shrimp platter.

We iced the catch and stepped back into the cabin and rinsed our hands with rubbing alchohol to hold down on infection from the dozens of nicks and cuts from handling the shrimp. It stung at first, like aftershave on a razor cut. I hate the smell of alchohol, reminds me of a doctor's office.

"I got a buddy named Nguyen," Perinovich said as he shook the water and alchohol off his hands. "He come over from Vietnam. Got him a grocery store on Oak Street. Nguyen's grandson, he been hanging around with the Dragons. The kid's name is Huang, but when Nguyen tried to tell me the kid's name it sounded like 'Hank' to me. So that's what I called him and that's what dey started calling him. Now Nguyen, he's old like me and ain't no bigger than a minute. But tough, I'm telling you. Even he won't mess with the gangs."

"If he won't, why do you?"

"Somebody's gotta do it or they'll take over the Point," he said. "I don't blame Nguyen. He ain't like me. He's got something left to lose."

The beaches of Horn Island, six miles to the south, glowed gray-white in the bright moonlight, and the ivory reflection of the moon shimmered on the gulf. The green glow from the compass and the instrument panel cast a shadow on Perinovich's face and showed the blend of nostalgia, disgust, and a little fear in his eyes and along his lips.

"Where would I go?" he asked.

"Go?"

"I got no place to go. Can you see me in one of them big

condominiums? Those folks sit and look out at the gulf like they lookin' at da TV. Never even get their feet wet. They'd be just as happy if they lived in Missouri and had a big movie of the ocean going all the time. But not me, no sir. I'm a Juga, Jack. I can't leave the Point. 'Course Weldon, he don't care 'bout dat. He's just a front man for somebody with the money."

A cloud passed across the moon and the beaches on the island dimmed from gray to black, as did the water.

"Who do you think the money man is?" I asked. "You think it's Bernie Pettus?"

Perinovich shook his head. "He's stole plenty, but not that much. I had to guess, I'd say Stash Moran. But I don't know."

"You think Moran's made that much out of that steak house?"

"He's got some rich friends."

"Is the mob involved, Mr. Cass?"

He shrugged and breathed out through his nose. "Stash is just a Point Cadet boy who's done allright for hisself. He ain't in the mob. That's just a bunch of talk."

Perinovich rubbed his eyes and put on a pair of glasses to read the instrument panel. We rocked in the water, moving up and down but not seeming to move ahead. The only indications of forward movement were the tachometer and the hum and vibrations of the diesel and, when I'd step back to the rear apron, the churning of the water in our wake.

"You act like I'm doing you a favor takin' you out," he said. "But I can't fight with those nets like I used to. And I need your young eyes. I can't go at night no more without somebody whose got a set of young eyes."

"They're not all that young anymore."

"I know exactly how old they are. They'll be forty-two in September. You're eleven months younger than Mike. Besides, I can't hear all that good neither."

"You got a barge on the Intercoastal," I said.

The ocean-going tugboat and its nine barges, three deep and

three abreast, drifted across our bow, like a black iceberg blocking our view of Horn Island. Rafts of barges, some six barges deep, are pushed along the Intercoastal Waterway by three-decker tugs powered by twin thousand-horsepower diesels. Some of the empty grain barges, with their raised and half-round tops, stand two stories high and hide the tugs at night if you're in front of them. One red range light, maybe a hundred watt bulb, sits on the deck of the middle barge. That little bulb and the running lights high on either side of the front barges are the only lights they have.

I have many times, when looking at the shore from far out in the sound, missed that tiny range light and become aware of the barges only when the streetlights and car lights on shore are blocked out as the barges slip across my field of vision. It's as if a mountain had sneaked up, and it'll scare the hell out of you. Veterans of nighttime shrimping are keenly, instinctively aware when they are near the Intercoastal, and keep their eyes and ears peaked for those steel glaciers that can smash a boat into splinters without so much as a bump being felt by the crew on the tug.

Perinovich let me take the wheel while he set out the try net, a miniature version of the big net, for a ten-minute test to see what the big net was getting. We dragged up a lot of seaweed, one spiny blowfish, one blue crab smaller than Mr. Cass's palm, and one scrawny shrimp, a thirty-count at best.

"Looks like we spooked 'em bad on that last drag," he said. "Let's pull in and head back toward Biloxi."

We got the nets onboard, Cass pushed the *Miss Marie* up to top speed, and we headed west. We rounded the Point south of Ocean Springs in thirty minutes, and he set a course toward the neon signs and lighted towers of the Point Cadet casinos as I readied for another drag. When I went up front to release the winch and let the cable run, I felt Perinovich staring at me.

Mr. Cass once told me that when he saw me, he could see what Mike would have looked like had he lived. For years after Mike died I always felt uncomfortable in Cass's presence because, as much as he tried to hide it, I caught him looking at me. It gave me the creeps. Until I had a child of my own.

When the hundred-fifty-foot marker came off the spool, I shoved the brake forward. The pick-out box was drying in the breeze and smelled of brine and fish. I stepped back into the cabin.

"You seen your little girl lately?" he said.

"She spent the Fourth of July with me."

"How much do you get to see her?"

"Not enough. Memphis is a long way off."

God, did I say that? It sounded small and weak, and I immediately wished I could pick those words up off the floor.

"How far you think I'd drive if I could see Mike?"

"I try my best," I said, sounding harsher than I meant to.

"Trying won't get it, son."

Had it been anybody else, I would have told him off. But I swallowed my anger instead and tried to think up a comeback. Or at least an excuse. How the hell do you make an excuse for not seeing your kid to a man who has lost his only son?

I nodded and squeezed his shoulder. He patted my hand and turned away from me and looked without focus straight ahead into the night. The wind calmed and he checked the electronic gauge. He tapped it with his forefinger.

"You feel what just happened?" he asked.

"The wind?"

"It's about to shift directions and blow up a storm. You watch, it'll shift clockwise. But it ought to be calm for a while. I figure an hour. We'll make this a short drag and head back in."

"The weatherman said it would be clear. You don't believe him?"

"No shrimper listens to the weatherman. Weatherman'll either starve you to death or get you killed. There'll be a storm here in an hour."

The wind picked up, still light but now from the north-northwest. The second drag lasted thirty minutes and put us at the channel into Biloxi Bay, three or four miles south of the eastern tip of Deer Island. When the drag ended, we lifted the nets onboard and the catch, flopping and snapping and roiling, into the pick-out box. Perinovich set the wheel in a tight circle and turned on every light on the boat. He left the helm and stepped to the forward deck to help me cull the trash.

We weighed in thirty pounds of twenty/twenty-five-count whites, six jumbos, a bucket of squid, and a dozen soft-shell crabs. We iced them down and Perinovich took the wheel and headed in. Sheet lightning raced across the sky, and the wind cooled and shifted once again, this time from the northeast and stronger.

"You were a little off, Mr. Cass. You said an hour."

"It won't be no more than an hour and a half."

On the ride in I stood at the bow, one foot on deck and the other on the cap rail, and leaned against the taut, steel-cable forestay. The warmth of the gulf blended with cool air currents from Perinovich's predicted storm and smelled of brine. The old man's face, softened by the glow from the instrument panel and my forty-one-year-old eyes, looked past me to the channel before us. The smell and the blend of warm and cool air conjured up the ghosts of Mike and a young Mr. Cass and July of 1968 when the boat was new, when Mr. Cass still told jokes.

We passed under the Biloxi Bay Bridge, and a flash of lightning struck behind us. It was near enough and bright enough to burn into my eyes an afterimage of the green bank of needles on the skinny pine trees of Deer Island. The thunder boomed, strong enough to rattle the window of the cabin door, and trailed off across the gulf.

"There's the storm, Mr. Cass. Just like you said."

Perinovich put me out at the dock and I took thirty pounds out of the catch, which was nearly all of it. By the time I iced them down and put them in my truck, it was eleven o'clock and the lightning was still flashing two miles south of the bridge. Perinovich said he'd wait and see if the storm passed, and if it did before midnight, before it turned into unlucky Friday, he'd go back out. I tried to talk him out of it, but he said there was no use wasting what was left of a good load of ice. He could anchor inside Ship Island and sleep until sunrise, and make a few drags on the inside before coming back in.

At least that was the plan.

FOUR

Trish Bullard and I spent the next afternoon sailing on Saint Louis Bay on *Clockwork Orange*, her sherbet orange Flying Scot, working on jibes in preparation for defense of her title in the Coast Regatta the first week in August. She also wanted to get comfortable with her new spinnaker. The day was cloudless except for a few mare's tails of white on the horizon above Cat Island and there was a haze at the edges of the sky. The storm off the coast had lasted all night so Perinovich probably didn't make it out to Ship Island.

Trish was a few years behind me in school, in the same grade as my little sister. When I moved back to Bay Saint Louis, I didn't recognize her the first time I saw her since she was stuck in my memory as a tall and skinny kid with braces and a ponytail. She was all grown up and filled out nicely and married to this guy she had met in art school in Boston. He's gone now and she lives with her ten-year-old son and teaches drawing at Jeff Davis Community College and has a side business selling watercolor paintings of coastal scenes.

We've been thrown together for the past two years, ever since she got her divorce and her husband went back home to Massachusetts. She's still sour on men, and I'm still gun shy since my own divorce, so we provide cover for each other at Christmas parties and Mardi Gras balls and other couple-type events. Now everybody in Bay Saint Louis thinks we ought to get married. Trish got a phone call from one of Mama's friends who saw me at lunch over at Galatoire's with some other woman and figured Trish "ought to know about it."

We sailed a figure-eight course half a mile out from downtown Bay Saint Louis, close enough to see the cars and the shoppers along the beach, the tourists and the cyclists, going in and out of the art galleries and antique stores. When the wind blew just right we smelled the batter in the deep fryers of the waterfront restaurants.

Trish took the tiller and handled the mainsheet while I worked the jib. A southerly wind cleared the haze and set up two-foot waves, far enough between the crests for the boat to stretch out, but barely, and giving us too much bobbing motion to be comfortable. On the tight beats we slid down the backsides of waves and crashed the next ones and kicked up spray, which blew back on us. The sun and wind dried us and left a covering of salt on everything the swimsuits didn't cover. We rubbed on coconut sunscreen and drank constantly from the plastic gallon jugs of Kentwood water, the only refreshment Trish allowed on board when we were training.

Heading in to port Trish set up a perfect wing to wing, the sails so taut they appeared to be ironed. The wind aimed at the Yacht Club pier and slid us without sound over the waves we were outrunning, milking maximum speed out of the Scot although a sailboat never feels fast unless you pound the waves. We told each other such a perfect trailing wind would never come on the stretch run of the regatta. Such things only come in practice, like the hole in one without a witness.

Through crystal air, too far out to recognize the face of anyone on shore, I spied my father sitting the way he sits on the end of a tall pier at the Yacht Club, dangling his legs over the side and leaning back, his palms flat on the planks behind him, his dot of a red cap a tiny accent against the bank of live oaks and Spanish moss.

We entered the Yacht Club's cove, scooped out of the shore of the bay north of the highway, and lowered the mainsail to drift in with the jib. Daddy pushed himself up and arched his back and walked to Trish's boat slip. The tide was coming in but it was still low, exposing a foot of barnacles and green muck at the base of the pilings.

"Mighty fine wing to wing, Trish," Daddy shouted when we got within twenty yards.

"Poppa D!" She hollered. "You noticed!"

"The key to wing to wing is the man on the jib," I said, not so loud now that we had drifted closer.

"And bringing it in with no kicker," Daddy said. "I'm impressed. Most of these yacht clubbers wouldn't even dream of weaving a boat through this place without an outboard."

"She's just showing off," I said.

"Jack, would you please hush and toss your father a line before we drift past this pier."

"I could get it in without a motor," I said.

"Of course my little man could," Trish said.

"Well, I could."

"I'll let you do it next time. But for now, could you pop the jib sheet out of that camcleat? We're about to get pushed into the piling."

"I knew that," I said.

"What's up, Poppa D?" Trish said as she pulled herself up to the pier. She kissed him on the cheek.

"I got some bad news," he said. "Cass Perinovich got killed last night."

FIVE

Two hundred people spread around the main hall of the Slavonian Lodge. Two walls of the hall were lined with floral stands, redolent with carnations and chrysanthemums, and on a table with a white tablecloth at the midpoint of the back wall sat the urn which held Perinovich's ashes, its base wrapped with an American flag. Hilda Kosaro had sent her usual spray of pink plastic roses and grumbled about people spending so much on live flowers that died so soon. One stand was a Knights of Columbus crest with yellow pompoms tacked to the styrofoam form. One was a profile of a shrimp boat, a specialty of Back Bay Flowers.

Two stooped, gray-headed ladies wearing black dresses and pearl necklaces checked each sympathy card. I can't recall their names, but I've seen them at every wake I've ever been to on the Point. They moved from spray to spray, judging whether the estimated cost of each matched up with how close the sender was to Perinovich and how much money the sender had.

Even at seven-thirty, the clock at the Hancock Bank on the highway had read ninety-two degrees when we were driving over. The daily afternoon shower off the gulf had been a strong one and the air was heavy with moisture. Inside the lodge, the crowd overwhelmed the air-conditioner, and, God knows, I was hot enough already. The room was smoky and body heated and smelled of sweat and smoke and Old Spice.

"Perinovich should have died out on the gulf," my father said. "That wouldn't have been nearly as bad."

"Oh, sure," Neal said. "Falling overboard at night and getting tangled up in a shrimp net, now that's the way for an eighty-year-old man to go. Right, Jack?"

I was in no mood to listen to their yammering. I was trying to recall the events of two days earlier when I went on the shrimping trip, trying to envision that critical minute when I could have cost Mr. Cass his life. Did I or did I not check everything out like I was supposed to do?

"Right, Jack?" Neal said.

"Will you two cut it out?" I said. "Listen to yourselves. You've argued about everything else all day long, and now you're squabbling about which form of violent death is better."

"I know which one is," Daddy said. "I was just talking to Cass last Wednesday and he was asking about this living will business. Yeah, he woulda rather drowned in the gulf. 'Course even the way he went beats the hell outta dying hooked up to a bunch of tubes in some nursing home with bed sores all over his ass. That's probably how I'll go, not that I'm going to have any choice in the matter."

A month earlier, one week before the shrimp season opened on the fourth of June, my brother, Neal, who had decided that shrimping's too dangerous for Daddy since he's turned seventy, badgered Daddy into selling his trawler *White Dolphin* to Speedy Cline. It was a bold move for Neal, one that even Mama wouldn't dare suggest.

Daddy's been pissed ever since.

They began sniping at each other earlier that afternoon when we got into the car in Bay Saint Louis and they kept it up the whole way down the beach, through casino row in Biloxi, and right up to the front door of the Lodge Point Cadet. The only thing they agreed on all day was that it was terrible the way our old friend Casper Perinovich died.

And now they had even started arguing about that.

I eased away and snaked through the crowd to the bar in the side room. I loosened my tie, peeled my damp collar away from my neck, and rested my foot on the rail. Sam, white haired and sun wrinkled, was behind the bar. He's the lodge's only employee and is the bartender, maintenence man, painter, general overseer, chronicler of current happenings, and repository of those in the past. Instead of his usual knit shirt, he had dressed for the occasion. Black slacks, a short-sleeved white shirt, and a black tie maybe two inches wide. In keeping with lodge tradition, he was sipping a drink of his own. He hoisted the plastic liter bottle and eyeballed me a shot of Old Charter and mixed it with Coke.

"Free whiskey'll draw a crowd every time," Sam said.

"Perinovich still had plenty of friends," I said.

Sam shrugged and took a pull off his drink. "I always liked ol' Cass. But I remember him from the old days, back when he was a lot of fun, before he got so sour on ever'thing. There's a bunch of folks who ain't exactly shedding tears right now."

"Besides the mayor, who're you talking about?"

"Lennis Belter, Billy Weldon, all that Vietnamese gang. You want me to go on?"

"He had gotten a little cranky," I said. "I'll be the first to admit that."

"Could I be getting a drink?" Father Carey said. "A touch of Scotch would be nice."

"Here you go, Father," Sam said. "We'll be missing ol' Cass, won't we?"

"Dear man. He had his crosses to bear. He lit two candles every week, every week on Monday. One for Marie, one for Mike. Laid two dollars on the altar every Monday."

"We'll miss him, Father," Sam said. "Pray for his soul."

"And you also, Sam." Father Carey took a sip of his Scotch and water. "Now, remember, we're not rich like that Fleur de Lis Club that Jack belongs to. You need to go easy on the lodge's whiskey." He winked. "At least after this one."

The good father stepped back into the main hall. Sam chewed up a cube of ice. "You seen Sheila yet?"

I shook my head no.

"She was here a few minutes ago. Still looks good."

"I'd be amazed if she didn't."

"You know she's divorced, don't you?"

"Seems like I've been told that, oh, say, fifty, sixty times since I got here."

"I'd be after her hot and heavy if I was a young kid like you."

"Kid? I'll be forty-two this year."

"Yeah, but you still in great shape."

"According to the new federal guidelines, six feet tall and a hundred ninety-three pounds is borderline obese."

"Screw federal guidelines," Sam said. "Dat's where we got them silly-assed turtle exclusion de-vices on da shrimp nets. I'm telling you, Sheila still looks damn good. You know she's divor—Oh, yeh. You already know that."

"You're worse than Mama and my sister-in law combined. I got all the help I need when it comes to getting my ass married off."

He shrugged, popped another cube of ice into his mouth, and rolled it around from cheek to cheek.

"I heard a rumor she had one of dem implant surgeries," he said. "I couldn't tell." He pulled a dish towel out of his back pocket and rubbed the copper top of the bar in tight circles, staring at where he had rubbed as if looking for his reflection.

"You couldn't tell?"

"Well, dey looked about the same to me," he said. " 'Course you might be able to tell. I couldn't."

"Sam, that's the most ridiculous thing I've heard—"

"I said it was a rumor. I ain't one to believe rumors."

Two women walked up beside me and asked for two glasses of wine. One was tall and gray haired in a navy blue long sleeved dress, the other was shorter with a tint on her white hair that came off more orange than red.

"Did you see those diamonds she was wearing?" the short one said.

"Oh, she's just a show-off. Just like she's always been."

"Well, I might show those off myself."

"It still looks cheap to me. I don't care how expensive they are. And that dress! It's just plain tacky to wear something that tight to a funeral."

They got their glasses of Lake Country red and walked away.

"I see Sheila's still got her fan club around here," Sam said.

"Sam, now tell me the truth. You couldn't tell?"

Sam shook his head and went back to rubbing the bar.

"She still here?" I asked.

"She's around here somewhere."

I took a sip of my Charter and Coke. Tasted too sweet. "How about one of those beers?"

Sam set a can of Dixie on the counter and flicked a piece of crushed ice off the top with his forefinger. I traded in my Charter and Coke and he poured it down the sink.

"And you say she's divorced?"

Sam gave me a smug grin. "Got dis latest divorce about the same time you got yours. Made money on this one, too. The judge gave her some hotel her husband owned in Miami. And now that Perinovich is gone, she'll be selling his place. I hear Billy Weldon offered three hundred grand for it six months ago."

"Weldon couldn't piece together that much dough if he hit the Super Slot over at Casino Magic."

"I'm just telling what I heard," Sam said. "And you can bet Sheila's gonna beat him out of more den dat. 'Course, I don't guess you'd be inner-rested in what Sheila's doing."

I sipped the Dixie. "She still looks pretty good, huh?"

"Good as she did the first time you took her out back in high school. Maybe better. I couldn't tell."

Green folding metal chairs lined the walls below garlands of pink and white crepe paper left over from the CYO dance the night before. A couple of new mothers, still puffy from recent pregnancies, sat and fed bottles to their babies. They had removed their high heels and placed them under their chairs. In the corner, four men, their ties and shirt collars loosened, sat in a semicircle, smoking and resting their elbows on their thighs.

Neal, all six-foot-five and two-hundred-sixty pounds of him, stood out above the crowd as he zigzagged in our direction, moving from group to group shaking a few hands before he reached us. He still looks like some college class president with that big smile and smooth skin. He blew out a puff of air and plopped his palms on the bar.

"How much you think it'll take for me to buy that damn boat back?" he said.

"What boat?" Sam asked.

"Daddy sold the *White Dolphin*," I said.

"Tom sold his boat in da shrimping season?"

"It was an ill-advised move," I said.

Neal groaned and reached for the Old Charter. "I heard Sheila's here."

"I done told him," Sam said. "He ain't inner-rested."

"I never told you that."

"When you talk to her," Neal said, "ask her who's handling Perinovich's estate."

"He was a shrimper," I said. "How much estate could we be talking about?"

"A boat and two hundred fifty feet of waterfront in one of the three biggest casino towns in the United States."

"Well, well, well," Sam said, "look who just walked in."

Neal turned around, but I didn't. It might have been my imagination, but I swear the place grew quiet, and I felt like every eye in the room was on me. My pulse stepped up a notch. Would any of that old spark still be there? I pulled on the short end of my tie and pushed the knot snug to my collar. I shifted around a half turn, leaned one elbow on the bar, and looked toward the door.

It was Bernie Pettus, the damn mayor, shaking every hand he could grab and smiling like he had just won the lottery. There wasn't a soul even so much as looking in my general direction.

"Man, now, that takes some brass," Sam said. "Showing up here after all that went down between him and Cass."

"Probably checking to make sure he's dead," Neal said.

"That's what I'm gonna miss about Perinovich," Sam said. "Dem letters to the editor. He had been talking lately like he finally had the goods on Bernie. But if he did, I guess he took 'em to his grave."

"Is Bernie a member of the lodge?" I asked.

Sam shook his head no. "He grew up on the rich end of Bayview Drive. He ain't got no Juga blood but he comes over a lot. Now, Neal, you watch Bernie close. He can show you how a crowd ought to be worked. He's got hisself a real race this time."

"I thought Bernie would be a shoo-in," I said. "I mean, I don't have much for him, but the voters here in Biloxi have been supporting him for twenty-five years."

"He's gonna win, but he's managed to piss off one of the big casinos somehow. They're running Chase Randall against him."

Bernie Pettus looks like every TV preacher you've ever seen. He's half a head taller than I am, with a voice that fills a room and a tendency to get too close when he talks to you. Bernie's been mayor for seven years. I had a run-in with him two years earlier over his plan to build a bridge to Deer Island for a casino, but I'll admit the main reason I didn't like him was because Perinovich didn't.

Bernie greeted every person in the room, spending a well-timed ten seconds, give or take a second or two, on each of them. He smiled and laughed, grabbed the men by their shoulder and hugged the women, that kind of thing. I thought about reminding him that this was a funeral and not a party. But then I guess for him it was. Sam laid a dollar on the bar that said Bernie'd kiss the two babies over by the wall. I slapped a dollar on top of it that said he wouldn't. Even Bernie's not that bogus. Not at a wake.

"That's not my style," Neal said. Neal's a Republican.

"You might be right about dem letters," Sam said. "But Cass warn't no crackpot."

"Never said he was—"

"He just had a tough life, that's all."

"You got another beer back there?" I asked.

Sam pulled up another can. He wiped it with a paper towel and set it on a Killian's ale cardboard coaster. He then pointed across the room at Bernie, who had reached the babies. A few seconds later he slid the two bucks into his pocket.

"How'd you know he'd do that?" I said.

"You watchin' him close, ain't ya, Neal?"

Neal's jaw had dropped. Visions of a summer of kissing babies showed in his eyes. Bernie waved to Sam and came toward us.

"How 'bout a drink, Your Honor."

"Can't do it, Sam. I'm flyin' tomorrow. Gotta get up before sunrise." He held his hand out to me. "Bernie Pettus."

"These are Tom Delmas's boys," Sam said. "That's Jack, and dis big one is Neal."

"Oh, yeh." Bernie shook Neal's hand. "You the one running for state senate."

"I thought I'd give it a shot."

"Well, if I can help, give me a call." He shook my hand while giving Sam a good-bye wave with his left hand. "See ya, Sam."

Bernie moved toward the four shrimpers sitting in the semi-circle in the corner and laid his hands on the shoulders of two of them, talking the whole time.

"Dere you go, Neal," Sam said.

"Is he some kind of pilot?" I asked.

Sam looked past my shoulder and broke into a big smile.

"What's a girl got to do to get a drink around here?" Sheila asked.

SIX

Sheila's dress clung tight in all the right places and it rounded out the curves. It was black and shimmering and intensified her raven hair and deep green eyes. Her perfume was a little strong, the eye shadow a little thick, the lipstick maybe a little too red. But Sheila's never been afraid to stand out in any crowd.

"Jack," she said, "It's so good to see you."

"I'm sorry about your uncle Cass."

"We need to talk. If you gentlemen will excuse us." She slipped her arm through mine and steered me away from the bar.

"You don't want dat drink?" Sam called out.

"Save it for me, sweetie."

The fragrance of Sheila's perfume and the way she squeezed my arm took me back to that summer we had together when I was eighteen and she was sixteen. It ended when I went off to Ole Miss. We called each other the first few weeks, but then came the Georgia game. Sheila couldn't come up and this friend of mine needed somebody to take his girlfriend's roommate to the game and the next thing I knew I was dating the roommate. I felt bad about it. Until I found out Sheila had started dating Bobby Johansen the week I left the coast.

"Oh, there's Stash," Sheila said.

Stash and Bernie Pettus were off by themselves in the far corner. Bernie was using his hands a lot and doing most of the talking.

On Point Cadet, Stash Moran has set the standard for handsome and sophisticated for the past thirty years. He's trim with a tan he buys thirty minutes at a time. He had on a light blue poplin suit, with a monogram on his shirt collar and a red silk scarf stuffed in the upper coat pocket. Tiny glints of blue light danced off his famous diamond cluster ring, which Point Cadet legend holds to be a gift from Carlos Marcello himself. I think that story's a crock.

"Jack, I changed my mind about that drink. Can you get me a light one?"

As I walked back to the bar Sheila made a beeline to Stash. So much for rekindling our great romance.

"Let me have a light screwdriver, Sam."

"Looks like you waited a little too long."

"Besides money and looks, what's Stash Moran got that I don't have?"

"He's a good-looking guy," Sam said, "but so are you. It's just different."

"That's it. It can't be the looks. My hair is dishwater blond with flecks of gray, his is jet black. I got a nose that's been broken three times, Stash has one that plastic surgeons use as a model. I got a scar on my chin, he's got a dimple. You're right, Sam. It's got to be the money."

I could never be Stash Moran. I could never spend every waking minute worrying about my tan, whether my shirt was starched, or whether my car was washed and polished. But at that moment, I did regret that I had not at least polished my shoes.

"Yeh, he got plenty of money," Sam said. "That steak house sure rakes in the cash. And I hear he's gettin' into the casino business."

"His name's been mentioned with every casino that's been built down here. He hasn't gotten into one yet."

"Yeh, but he's really talking up this one. Least that's what I hear." He handed me the drinks. "How about it? Could you tell?"

"Tell what?"

"About Sheila."

"Maybe I ought to just ask her point-blank and put everybody's mind at ease."

"Dat might work."

I took the screwdriver and traded in my lukewarm Dixie for a cold one and walked toward Stash and Sheila. He must have a good sense of humor. She sure was laughing a lot.

"Jack," she said, "you remember Stash Moran."

"How ya doin', Delmas?" He grabbed my hand and crunched down before I got set. Jammed my ring into the side of my middle finger, which hurt like hell.

"I didn't know you and Mr. Cass were friends," I said.

"Ever'body on Point Cadet is Stash Moran's friend." he said.

"Sheila, did you have something you wanted to tell me?" I popped the top of my beer.

She pursed her lips and thought for a second before whatever it was registered.

"Stash," she said, "you'll have to excuse us." She slipped her arm back through mine, and I started easing her away from him.

"Call me later, babe," he said.

Sheila and I sat on the bench in front of the lodge under the statue of Saint Nikola, patron saint of the Croatians who came to Biloxi early in the century to work in the shrimp factories. My Delmas kin belongs to the French lodge up the street, the Fleur de Lis, where members are either of cajun descent or descendents of the sixty-four years of French rule.

The smell of wild onions from a recent mowing swept across the yard on a cool breeze from the gulf a block to the south. Night was coming on fast and the neon signs atop the towering casino hotels on the beach gave the lodge's front yard a purple cast, dwarfing the orange glow of the big moon coming up over Biloxi Bay. The breeze blew in low clouds from the gulf and they shone silver in the moonlight. Sheila reached into her purse and pulled out a long, thin cigarette and paused.

"I forgot," she said. "You don't have a light, do you?"

"Those things are bad for you."

"They calm my nerves, honey." She reached into her purse for her lighter. "This has been a hard time." She looked down the street to the twenty-story Isle of Capri Hotel and smiled. "Biloxi will look like Miami pretty soon."

I grunted and turned up my beer.

"I know you hate that, Jack. But you can control the growth, and it can be a good thing. Think about the jobs and the money the casinos have brought in. Before they came, the coast was flat on its back. It had been that way since Hurricane Camille."

"I don't want to live in an amusement park. I hear the casinos are pushing Chase Randall for mayor. Daddy always said if we let them in they'll take over."

"You think this Randall man is worse than Bernie Pettus?"

"I hate the idea of casinos taking over elections."

"All big businesses do it. You don't think Ford Motors could influence an election in Detroit? The casinos have been great for Biloxi. Roy Enberg is looking at coming here. I mean, even if you don't like the casinos, you've got to admit that's big."

"This Enberg, is he some kind of big shot in gambling or something?"

She bit at her lower lip as she smiled. Her eyes showed amusement. I couldn't tell if she was trying to decide what to say or to stifle a laugh. "Enberg is one of the biggest. He's right up there with Harrah's."

"You think he might be behind all this talk about a new casino on the Point?"

"Could be," she said. "Enberg would build a world class resort wherever he went. If he comes in, Harrah's and Bally's and all the big ones will be coming. This place could use a little excitement."

"Well, it's getting it," I said. "How's Stash doing?"

"Just fine, I guess. We mainly talked about business."

"You think Stash might be in on the deal?"

"I couldn't talk about that even if I knew anything," she said. "Believe me, I know all about Biloxi and its rumors."

I pulled my collar away from my neck. "I don't know much about business."

"That's not what I hear. I hear you've got the best detective agency on the Coast."

"Agency? I'm the owner and sole employee. I handle insurance claims, divorces, and every now and then look for a missing heir or two. Not exactly a conglomerate."

"And weren't you a vice president of some bank up in Memphis?"

"In a different lifetime, darling." Even with the breeze, a drop of sweat tickled as it ran down the side of my face.

"You know," she said, "these casinos pay a ton of money on security. One of them might be in the market for a good security director."

"I'm making all the money I need working for myself. Watching TV monitors all day doesn't do it for me."

"But you could make so much money."

I crushed the beer can and tossed it like a free throw into the oil drum at the corner of the building. It rang against the side of the empty barrel like a gong.

"Why don't we back up and take another run at this?" I knew where we were headed. I had been there every day for six months before my ex-wife, Sandy, decided I was beyond hope and took our two-year-old daughter, Peyton, and moved back home to east Memphis. Now she's dating a radiologist and working on her tennis game. And Peyton just turned eight. "You look good, Sheila. How's that for starters?"

"If you think you can sweet talk me into anything, and I mean anything, you are absolutely right. But I've got to talk to you about something else. It has to do with your business."

"I'm not interested in casino work or hotels."

"It's about Uncle Cass."

"What about him?"

She sipped her screwdriver. The ice had melted to where there was a layer of almost clear water floating on top. "I need an investigation by somebody who knows what he's doing."

"Did Mr. Cass have insurance?"

"Eastern States."

"Bart Newman does their work."

"I've already talked with Mr. Newman. He did his investigation. He also looked over what the Biloxi Fire Department and the police had written up. Eastern States is going to pay the full value of the policy."

"I'm good, Sheila, but I couldn't get any more than full face value for you."

"Screw the money, Jack." She dropped her cigarette to the concrete and ground it out with the toe of her shoe. "Uncle Cass's death was no accident. Somebody murdered him."

SEVEN

Murder?" I said. "What are you talking about?"

"He was murdered. Somebody set up that explosion."

"Have you got any reason to think that?"

"How else could it have happened?"

"Sheila, the house was built in the 1920s. It had gas space heaters. Cass was almost eighty years old. He forgets and leaves the gas running, it builds up in the closed house, he walks in and flips on the light switch, and the whole place goes off like a grenade." I told her what I had told myself a couple of hundred times. I wondered if my voice sounded as flat and weak and unconvincing to her as it did to me.

"Did you ever know Uncle Cass to take any chances? I mean, wasn't he the type who could see any potential danger?"

"I see that kind of stuff happen every day," I said. "You don't have to be careless but one time."

"Look at this." She pulled a folded, blue-backed report from her purse. "I asked Bart Newman about the space heaters. They were turned off. Clamped down hard in the off position."

"How about the stove?" The stove I was supposed to check.

A moving shadow fell across the grass behind Sheila. It gave me a start. I glanced in the direction it came from. He was halfway across the yard, coming toward us. I tensed out of reflex, but Sheila smiled and held out both arms toward him.

"Jack, this is Joey." She squeezed him around the waist. "My baby." He was a big kid, as tall as I am, thick chested with a wide neck, broad like Sheila's father had been, with the dark hair that all of the Zimariches have.

Joey shook my hand and nodded at me, but didn't hold eye contact long. He shifted his weight from foot to foot like kids at the first stage of manhood will do in the presence of adult men they don't know.

"I hear you're studying marine biology," I said.

"Yes, sir."

"He's on the dean's list," Sheila said. Joey smiled and lowered his eyes. Had a good smile. "Isn't he pretty, Jack?"

"Mama, I've got to give Aunt Caroline a ride home. Can you give me the keys?"

"Sheila, I'll give you a ride home if you need it," I said. "That is, if you don't mind riding in a pickup truck."

"It's so nice to be around a man who isn't hung up about his car," she said.

"Mom, I can't believe you're saying that. You treat that Coupe Deville like it's a member of the family."

"But I'm a woman, darling. I'm supposed to feel that way about my Deville."

"And Carlos is not supposed to feel that way about his BMW?"

"Carlos is Miami Beach, honey. Jack is Mississippi Gulf Coast."

"Hey," I said, "we get pretty emotional about our pickups. Joey, you take Aunt Caroline home and I'll take your mama wherever she needs to go."

"Nice to meet you, Mr. Delmas." He took the keys and Sheila kissed him on the cheek before he walked away.

"Good-looking kid," I said. He was Sheila's father, Ronnie, made over, but I didn't mention that.

Soon after Sheila was born, Ronnie Zimarich cleared out the bank account and ran off with a hooker from the old Golden

Nugget. Took three months for them to drink up the money. Ronnie couldn't say for sure just where the hooker went after that. He limped back into town on a Greyhound. Sheila's mama, a kind and insecure soul, took him back. So did the Cadillac agency where he worked. Sheila was six when he did it the second time.

He never came back full-time after that second time, and I've never known the deal he and Sheila's mama had, but he would sometimes move in for a week, maybe as long as a month. Mama and Daddy didn't talk about it, and I was only nine or ten at the time. But I remember Ronnie buying jewelry and expensive dresses for Sheila, and I never heard her or her mother say a bad word about him.

"He *is* a good-looking boy, isn't he? And he's so smart." Sheila followed Joey with her eyes as he walked back into the lodge. I could have pictured Sheila a lot of different ways, but doting mother was not one of them.

"You have a child, don't you?" she asked.

"I've got a daughter. Eight years old. She lives with her mother in Memphis."

Sheila sighed deeply. "It hasn't turned out exactly like either of us would have planned it, has it?"

She crossed her legs, clutched her knee with both hands and leaned back, looking up to the iron gray sky. I wondered how my daughter would feel about me when she got to be Sheila's age. If I did a count of the days, I'm afraid old Ronnie Zimarich probably saw as much of Sheila when she was eight as I do of Peyton today. And I considered Ronnie an irresponsible bum.

"Sheila, back to the explosion. The fire department, the police, and Bart Faggard all investigated it. None of them found a thing."

She reached out and stroked the side of my face and spoke in the same manner as she probably did with Joey when he was nine years old.

"Jack, honey, the Biloxi police wouldn't know a case of arson if they found a gas can with a charred rag stuffed in it."

"They've got a good arson division."

"*Had* a good division. A new man has taken over."

I nodded. The department had dropped off a lot since Johnnie Barron retired. I was fighting with them on these cases I was working. It was over petty, bureaucratic stuff.

"Well even if the police didn't spot it," I said, "an insurance investigator would."

"A sober insurance investigator might. Besides, they only look into it when they think the fire is set for profit. Bayou Casualty doesn't send you over here looking at a fire scene unless they think somebody's trying to screw them, right?"

"Not necessarily."

"Oh, come on, honey! Would they hire you at a gazillion dollars a day plus expenses to check out a house fire if twenty people saw a lightning bolt hit the house? They send investigators when they think there's a chance they won't have to pay off."

"How do you know so much about arson investigations?"

"I'm in the hotel business," she said. "But that's beside the point. Bart Newman, even when he's drunk, can figure out that if a policyholder dies when his house explodes, the company has to pay off. Eastern States might put up some piddlin' thousand-dollar reward if they suspect arson, but if they know they're on the hook they're not going to spend five or six grand on an investigation just for the sake of justice."

"That's a pretty cynical view of the insurance industry."

"Like I said, I'm in the hotel business. Don't get me started on insurance."

She took a sip of her watery screwdriver and gazed off toward the twin towers of the casinos on the beach.

"I can't rely on the police," she said. "They still haven't even questioned anybody from that Vietnamese gang. They know Uncle Cass had a problem with them. The gangs in Miami will torch a place in a second, and they have been known to blow one up."

"Sheila, the cops can't go rousting people just because they had differences with Mr. Cass. Right now BPD figures it's an accident. I do too. Besides, those gang members weren't doing anything more than picking on Mr. Cass. That doesn't add up to murder."

"Somebody could have hired them to blow the place up. I'll bet they wouldn't have turned down the money."

In the soft neon glow her skin looked as smooth as a still pond, her coal black hair took on a bluish hue. She had filled out some since I last saw her, and it looked good on her. The soft breeze blew her hair back just a bit, like she was on the set of a photo shoot for some magazine. Her eyes were moist and the purple light reflected off them, changing from green to black.

"I need to know what happened," she almost whispered. "I feel guilty that I didn't stay in touch with Uncle Cass, and I owe him that much. I mean, you're not even blood related and you stayed in touch with him."

"I wish that were true."

"You were here for him. He told me once that when he looked at you it was like seeing what Mike would have been. Did I ever tell you that?"

"Sheila, there's nothing I can do."

She tossed her hair to the side and rubbed the back of her neck. "I understand it may be a wild goose chase," she said, "but I feel so bad that I neglected him so long. But I always thought there'd be time. If only I had visited him more often, or just called."

I rested my elbows on my knee and massaged both my temples.

"Do you charge a daily rate?"

"For goodness' sake, Sheila!"

"What?"

"Look, I'll do it. I'll look into it for free, okay?"

"I'm not asking you to work for free. I've got plenty of money."

"Then don't spend too much time in those casinos over there," I said. "Right now, the only thing I need is a car. The clutch in my truck has been sticking, and I need to take it in tomorrow."

"I'll get the rental car agency to send one to your house. You'll have it tomorrow morning."

Most of the trouble I've gotten into the past few years has come when I've done investigative work as a favor. But I had to see if that damn stove was left on. As much as I hated the thought, if he had been murdered, at least I wouldn't have been the one who killed him. And if Sheila would spring for a car for the next few days and I was going to have to rent one anyway, technically I wasn't doing free work.

Neal tells me that, other than the fact that I quit the Ole Miss law school after three semesters, my biggest roadblock to being a lawyer wouldn't be brains, it would be my lack of what he calls money sense. I tell him that a lawyer's money sense is usually another word for greed. We argue about lawyers a lot.

"I'll look into it for a day or two," I said, "but Sheila, it was an accident."

"If somebody deliberately blew up Uncle Cass's house, you'll be able to tell it. You're the best arson investigator on the Coast."

"I'm not even close. Johnnie Barron is the best, retired or not."

"Well, go hire him to help you. But I want you to head up the investigation."

"Sheila, I'd be fourth on the scene behind the fire department, the police, and Bart Newman. If there's any evidence left over it would be a miracle. We've had a rain since the explosion. That washes away most, if not all, of the chemical evidence."

She touched my face and ran her fingers through my hair above my ear. "Why didn't we ever get together, Jack?"

It was how Sheila won every argument we had ever had.

"I'm trying to be serious."

"I'm serious," she said. "I don't know why I've ended up with the men I have."

I didn't tell her that that the men she was drawn to liked the things she did, the cars, the clothes, the bright lights. Men who were just like her father. Didn't say that living on the beach in a raised cabin and working just often enough to pay the light bill and buy the beer for the afternoon sail tended to wear a little thin on any woman who thought of a Lexus or a Cadillac as a birthright. Didn't mention any of that. If she wanted to know more about that, all she had to do was ask my ex-wife, Sandy.

EIGHT

A diesel engine revved up on Back Bay one block over. A deep throated sound, one of the big boats, one of the seventy-foot steel rigs the Vietnamese use. I had the windows down and heard the deckhands shouting something in English, but with the Indo-Chinese singsong inflections that told me they were my age or older. The Vietnamese kids who grew up on Point Cadet have Point Cadet accents. They say "dis" and "dat." "Upon" becomes "upoyn." I assume it's an accent brought over from Croatia. It's a lot like what you hear in Brooklyn or the Eighth Ward of New Orleans.

I still knew some people on the east end of Howard Avenue, and a few on Myrtle Street and on First Street. I needed to find somebody who could tell me what they saw or heard the night of the explosion. The scene was cold and contaminated and had been rained on. It didn't much matter if I started with the interviews or the on-scene investigation. My chances were equally bad both places.

The streets were lined with the old *Juga* houses, company houses built when Point Cadet was a company town and shrimp boats had sails, when men named Dukate, and Marvar, and Baricev saw promise in tin cans that could be sealed, and they sent off to Dalmatia for fishermen who could use the big nets, who could come and harvest the Mississippi shrimp, so bounteous that even slow trawling, shallow draft schooners could pull in enough to keep the canneries running. They were row houses, wooden and long and set at right angles to the street, straining toward what was then oyster shell streets and rubbing shoulders with each other, each structure housing two families divided by a center wall, and each structure a copy of the ones to either side of it. A wide-planked porch across the front, a saddle roof supported by square and tapered wooden columns set on squatty bases of red brick, and two front doors in mirror image on either side of the mid-point.

The street showed five For Sale signs, four of them from Billy Weldon Realty. Three of the Weldon signs had red, bumper-sticker "Sold" labels slapped diagonally across them, that gloat by real estate salesmen that they've notched another one and if you've got a place you want to unload you better get down to the office fast. Some of the houses with such signs, houses where two or three generations of Misoviches or Stanoviches or Garonoviches lived and grew up and made the transition from the Adriatic Sea to the Mississippi Sound, also had signs announcing applications for zoning changes. This meant the bulldozer was on the way. That, or a fire.

Fat Johnny started the trend. After Johnny Banko, née Johnny Bankovich, the millionaire owner of Fat Johnny's Ford-Lincoln-Mercury, Home of the Working Man's Deal, sold his mama's place to the Oriental Palace Casino, he asked what they would do with the house. They told him it would be bulldozed as soon as the Caterpillar finished some grading work across town. Fat Johnny didn't sleep that night thinking about his mama's house.

The next morning he went to the Oriental Palace with a roll of thousand-dollar bills to buy it back. He was abruptly told that a deal's a deal; they weren't selling the place back to him. When he started crying about his mama's house, the casino told him he could have it if he'd haul it off since they had better use for the bulldozer anyway.

Word spread fast around the Point about how they gave the

house back free of charge about how they didn't care what you did with the house as long as you got it out of their way. And a spin-off from the casino industry took root. Arson for profit. It wasn't long before Bayou Casualty had me over there at fifty per hour plus expenses poking around the ashes of three of the houses they insured. The casinos have been a real boost to my economy.

A white Chevy pickup, its paint dead and chalky, stuck out into the street. A broomstick propped the hood up and Randy Pohlman leaned over the engine so far that one foot was off the ground. Randy grew up a block from the Perinoviches and that's where I met him. In high school he played catcher for the Biloxi Indians and damn near killed me once when my coach called for a suicide squeeze and I tried to steal home on him.

I pulled to the curb and he raised up. I stepped out of the truck and a redbone hound, short-haired with long ears and not quite knee high, came racing out of the yard barking and snapping and chased me back into the cab.

"Get on back in that yard!" Randy shouted. He picked up an empty Coke can and bounced it off the sidewalk beside the dog. It yelped as if it had been hit and ran into the yard. The dog walked around on its toes in a circle and barked straight up at the sky. I never used to have a problem with dogs.

"Thought I'd stop by and see how the leisure class is doing," I said. "Got a little engine problem?"

"Changing spark plugs. I gave the chauffeur the day off."

He pulled a greasy red rag from his back pocket and wiped most of the oil off his fingers before we shook hands. He had the grip of the mechanic, with the effortless power of a hydraulic valve, the kind of grip you'll never develop in a gym.

"You think you could put a new clutch in my truck?"

"It's gonna take a coupla days. I'm kinda backed up."

"No big hurry. I'll drop it off this evening."

"Saw you the other night at Perinovich's wake," he said. "I was headed over to talk to you, but you cut out the front door with Sheila."

"Sorry I missed you."

"Hey, I'da cut out with her myself. She looks good, don't she?"

I smiled and nodded.

"So what's been going on?" he asked.

"I'm checking out that explosion that killed Cass Perinovich. You know anything about it?"

He shrugged and shook his head. "I was half-asleep when it went off. It wasn't all that loud, not considering what it did to the house. More like a deep boom than a blast."

A Kelly green Lincoln Town Car eased toward us. A magnetic sign on the door read Billy Weldon Realty. On the bumper was a Re-Elect Bernie Pettus sticker. The driver had a phone wedged under his right ear and his head tilted to keep it from squirting out. His left wrist lay over the top of the steering wheel. He waved at Randy by extending the index finger of the hand on the wheel and pointing it at us. Randy didn't respond. I thought the driver would stop, but from Randy's reception he saw there was no point in that. The Lincoln drifted five or six houses past us and stopped in front of the old Jannasich place, a rental unit for some five years now. The house stood out for its lack of a For Sale sign.

"There you have it," Randy said. "The most perfect specimen of the Mississippi coast buzzard species ever spotted in the wild."

"Is that Billy Weldon?"

"You mean you ain't met the best friend a carpetbagger ever had?"

"Never had the pleasure."

"I keep forgetting it's your brother who's into all that Economic Roundtable bull hockey. Weldon's vision of heaven is every square inch of Biloxi covered with casinos and parking lots. And everybody who works in a casino's gonna live in the subdivisions he plans to cover the north shore with after he's screwed this place into the ground."

"How'd you miss getting appointed to the Coast Development Council, Randy? You sound like a natural."

"Look, I ain't got any beef with anybody who wants to go into a casino. But you tell me. Once we got enough jobs for everybody, why move a million more people in here even if the casinos have a job for ever' damn one of 'em behind one of their blackjack tables? Weldon and his bunch keep preaching about how it's good for the economy, but I wonder whose economy they talking about."

Weldon stepped out of the car, flashed us a smile, and waved to Randy, who never uncrossed his arms. Weldon held his phone with its strap wrapped around his hand. He wore a powder blue shirt with French cuffs and dark blue suit pants that squeezed tight at the waist against an office paunch. He had a lot of hairspray, an indoor complexion, and an unchallenged middle-aged softness.

"What a buzzard," Randy said. "I hear he even went to the wake to hammer on Sheila about selling Mr. Cass's place."

"Sheila can handle him."

"Bad thing is, he'll win. They're gonna make this place a parking lot sure as I'm breathing. Stash Moran has done bought an option on the old Harkins store. You can bet he knows what's going down. Hell, I even heard Bernie Pettus is buying up whatever he can."

"Where does Weldon fit in on all this?"

Randy snorted and smirked and scratched his elbow. "He's buying up whatever he can for some rich dude. Whoever it is, I'm sure the guy wanted to keep it low key. But he picked the wrong agent to do that. That fool Weldon's been running around like a damn six-year-old with a secret he's busting to tell."

Weldon twisted his camera into various angles as he snapped

six quick shots of the front of the house. He pulled out a notepad. Sunlight glinted off the cap of his ink pen. He used a light touch in handling the pen, like he didn't want to scratch it. I figured it must be that latest fad among the coast business set, a Mont Blanc. Neal told me how much one of those things cost, and I still don't believe what he said. Weldon got back in his car and cradled the phone back into place on his shoulder.

"Weldon needs to lighten up on using that phone," I said. "He's going to develop a bent neck if he keeps his head tilted like that."

"He's a lot better at lookin' the part of a big shot than he is at being one. If he's the one some Las Vegas group hired to put together a deal, there must be a serious shortage of filmflam artists around this place."

The big green Lincoln drifted on down the street, like a thresher shark in warm water barely flipping its tail.

"I was on my way to see what's left of Mr. Cass's place," I said.

"Ain't much left. Whatever there was, you can bet the Belters have hauled it off."

"Some things never change."

"Only thing's changed about the Belters is that there's more of 'em nowadays," he said. "Of course there's one less now than there was, least for the next couple of months. You know about what Perinovich did to the Belters, don't you?"

"I know there was some bad blood between Lennis Belter and Mr. Cass, but that's about it."

"The Belters have gone into a new business."

"I do know that much," I said. "Bait shrimp."

"Guess again. That's what's on the side of his boat, but he's really in the hazardous waste business. Used batteries, cleaning fluid, used motor oil. Whatever the EPA says you can't just throw out, Lennis just hauls off at sixty-five bucks a barrel, no questions asked. He dumps it out in the gulf. But last month, he let Elvis, that's his youngest, take out a load. That worthless Elvis is so lazy he don't even bother to get out past Deer Island. Dumped two barrels off the side right there in broad daylight. Guess who saw him."

"Perinovich?"

"You got it. And it just so happened that Mr. Cass had Ralph Stengel on board with him. Stengel's the president of Save Our Gulf. They marked the spot and two hours later the Sierra Club sends down a diver to recover the barrels and WLOX is there filming the whole thing. Next thing you know, Elvis is cooling his heels in the county jail for ninety days. And he ain't heard the last of the feds yet."

Randy let down the tailgate of the truck and we sat on it. He wiped the sweat off his brow with his forearm.

"So Perinovich put them out of business?" I asked.

"Not by a long shot. Hell, they're probably glad to get that stupid Elvis out of the way for a month or two. This waste disposal, it's big business. From what I hear, the Viets are moving in on Lennis and trying to steal his clients. I'm wondering whether it'll be Lennis or the Dragons who get on the New York Exchange first."

"So that's why Lennis had his stinger out for Mr. Cass?"

"That's a big part of it, but I reckon the land deal had more to do with it."

"Land deal?" I asked.

"Perinovich had been telling the casinos to kiss his ass for over a year now. His piece of land has been hanging up the whole project, and the project includes Lennis's property. That means Lennis wasn't getting the chance to unload his place to Billy Weldon for a ton of money."

A window unit kicked on across the street. Its housing was loose and it rattled against the wooden window frame.

"You really think Lennis would have bombed Mr. Cass out?"

Randy let out a horse laugh and shook his head. "That's a good one, Jack."

The mailbox was missing an R, it said "Belte." The hand-lettered sign nailed to the water oak was written in Vietnamese. The house set among trees in a dank shade, a good hundred fifty feet from the road. She sat on the wooden porch in front of a box fan, painting her nails with the intensity of a diamond cutter. She wore a yellow, sweat-stained T-shirt, Elsie's Lounge printed across the front. She was thin and didn't appear to have much under the T-shirt, but her legs were long and well shaped. She wore her hair up, a concession to the heat.

The lot was a good two acres, but it was at the bottom of a natural drain field that sloped to the bay and half the land was spongy and covered with wild ferns and pitcher plants. The house, a wood frame, lapstrake structure with peeling white paint, sat under the shade of two ancient, moss-festooned live oaks, one at either end. I drove through the sparse yard along the ruts that served as a driveway and she didn't look up even though the dogs in the pen in the back of the lot set up a howl that could be heard all the way to the beach.

A pair of knee-high kids, one still in diapers, stared at me as I walked toward the house. They were brown, whether from the dirt or from the sun it was hard to tell, and the baby's nose needed wiping. They stopped playing with the toy dump truck as I walked toward the porch. They had a glum look of suspicion, a distrust so apparent that I wondered if it was possible to teach it to babies that young. Maybe it really was in the genes. I gave them a little wave and the taller one grabbed the wrist of the one in diapers and led him around the corner of the house.

"Morning," I said.

She lifted her head and looked me up and down, never saying a word.

"I'm here to see Lennis Belter."

"He ain't here."

"You know when he'll be back?"

"He don't check in with me."

She went back to painting her nails. The FM rock station blared with a tinny quality, the cheap jam box unable to handle the full-blast volume she had set it on.

"You live here?" I reached for an itch in the middle of my shoulder blades. The back of my shirt was damp and sticking to me.

"I do now."

"You lived here long?"

"I been living here too long, mister."

"Were you living here last Friday?"

"What you want?"

I reached for my wallet and pulled out a business card. "I'm Jack Delmas with Bayou Casualty Insurance Company."

"We done got all the insurance we need, which is none."

"I'm not selling insurance. I'm an investigator. I'm looking into that fire last week down the street at the Perinovich house."

Her eyes hardened. "I don't know nothin' about that."

"Were you here when it happened?"

"Maybe I was and maybe I wasn't. That ol' Perinovich bastard weren't nothin' but trouble for me. He got what he deserved far as I'm concerned."

"You knew Mr. Perinovich?"

"I knew he sent my husband off to jail on some lies he done told. That's why I'm livin' in this dump."

"Look. I'll level with you. I've got to file a report on that explosion for my company and I've got to check out the whole neighborhood."

"You think I give a rat's ass about that?"

"Don't reckon you do," I said as I reached to my back hip for my wallet, "but this might interest you." I help up six ten-dollar bills fanned out. "Any information you can give me about the fire, if it checks out I'll give a reward. Cash money. I'll lay it right in your hand."

Behind me the roar of a busted muffler came at us from the street, the valves tapping like a snare drum. The girl gathered up her nail polish and remover. The two waifs peered around the corner, the older one keeping the baby behind him with his extended arm.

"Oh, shit," she said. "Lennis's done brought that worthless Eight Ball with him."

"Eight Ball?"

"His drinking buddy. S'posed to be a welder. I ain't never seen him draw a sober breath."

The truck was rusted at the bottom of the doors and wheel wells and the rust had crept up the sides as if by capillary action, a common condition in trucks and cars driven through salt water or over roads soaked by waves when a squall blows in. It put out a white thin plume of smoke and tilted toward the driver's side. The two dogs in the bed of the truck jumped out and trotted toward the pen back at the rear corner of the lot. Lennis reached out the window and pulled the outside latch to open his door.

The passenger wore his cap turned backward, a red cap with white polka dots. He was thick chested and had a bull neck and was twenty years Lennis's junior. His pug nose and bulging jaws made him look like a bulldog. His oily hair flared out below the cap and hung over the collar of his threadbare denim shirt. He nearly fell out of the truck when he pushed the door open. He staggered to the front of the truck and rested his broad butt on the bumper, grasping both legs just above the knees to stabilize himself. He started to lean over to one side and righted himself with a jerk.

"You got them dishes washed yet?" Lennis shouted. "You been sittin' out here on yo' lazy ass the whole time I been gone, ain't ya?" He stayed beside the truck, a good fifty feet from where the girl and I were.

"I'll think about it, mister," she said to me in a low voice. "You come back when he ain't here. You come back and talk to me, but don't say nothing to Lennis. I ain't about to share no reward with him."

The girl slammed the screen door behind her. "No, I ain't got your damn dishes washed!" she shouted. "Ain't got your damn clothes washed, ain't got the beds made!" Her voice trailed off as she kept listing the things she had not done for Lennis as she walked deeper into the house.

"Mr. Belter? I'm Jack Delmas."

Lennis glared at me and stood gripping the door of the truck with his right hand. He pushed the sagging door closed, but it wouldn't latch. He took both hands and shoved it up and forward with such force that he knocked himself backward. It still didn't latch.

"Delmas? You one of them Delmases what's got that boatyard in Bay Saint Louis?"

"That's my father."

He studied my face as he spat to the side. "You come to bring me that money your old man owes me?"

"I don't know anything about that."

"I'll just bet you don't." He wiped his mouth with his palm. "Your old man sold me a rebuilt motor three years ago and the piece of shit burnt up not halfway through the season."

"You got your receipt?"

"You some kinda lawyer, college boy?" Lennis was drunk enough to forget caution and feel little pain, but still sober enough to be dangerous.

"I'll ask him about it."

"You tell him ain't nobody gonna cheat Lennis Belter."

My jaw tightened as I weighed kicking Lennis's ass against the slight chance of learning anything useful from his chip-on-the-shoulder bluster. The dude with the polka-dot cap grinned at me without showing any teeth and spit straight ahead through closed lips. I reminded myself that I was a forty-year-old professional and needed to exercise restraint, something I have to do fairly often these days.

"I'll ask my father about it."

"If you ain't here with my money, what you here for?"

"I'm looking into that explosion, the one that killed Casper Perinovich."

Lennis took a few slow steps toward me, tilting his head to one side, then the other, as he examined my face. "I don't know nothing about that. I was out in my boat the night it happened."

"Did anybody here see or hear—"

"Nobody here seen nothin'."

"So you've already asked them if they know anything about it?"

He walked around me in a wide arc, his hands in the back pockets of his jeans. "Time for you to leave, Delmas."

"Mr. Belter, I'm not accusing you of anything. I'm just trying to find out if somebody could have—"

"I done told you. Now you go on and get outta here. I got work to do."

"Please. Just a few questions."

"Listen, I ain't got nothin' to say. You wastin' your time around here. If anybody blew up that place, they got slanty eyes."

"Vietnamese?"

"You pretty smart," he said. "You really are a college boy."

"Why do you think it was one of the Vietnamese?"

"I'm going inside to get my shotgun. Don't you be here when I get back."

"There's no need to—"

He took the three steps in two strides and slammed the screen door. The man at the bumper of Lennis's pickup started whooping.

"Whooo-eeeee! You better haul ass, dude!"

I walked quickly toward my truck, keeping an eye toward the door. As I stepped up into the cab, I saw his outline through the screen, silhouetted by the sunlight filtering through the house from the open back door. It was the same outline I had seen the other day when Perinovich and I were at the dock, the day Belter had slammed the *Miss Marie* against the pilings with his wake. The too-long neck with an oversized Adam's apple, the high cheeks and hatchet face with the long thin nose over the sunken mouth, the chin reaching forward to a point, the big ears flaring out slightly, the features of the worst type of my southern white race, sprung from a two-hundred-year-simmering of recessive genes in some inaccessible hollow or swamp.

I started the engine and backed the truck around to point the nose toward the street and waited to see if he'd come out. Lennis stayed behind the screen. He was holding something long and thin. I let off the clutch slowly and crept forward.

Lennis let me get almost to the street before he opened the door. He propped it open with his foot and stepped out to the porch, resting the stock of a shotgun on his hip with the barrel pointed straight up.

NINE

The blast had ripped straight through Perinovich's living room and knocked the front door and the windows on either side of it into the front yard. The bottom half of the front wall was blown away and the top part was black with soot. Three upright frames on the east side of the house were intact, but deeply charred. All the frames on the west lay broken and scattered around the side yard not more than six feet from the house. The roof, still in one piece, had squatted down and rested at a cockeyed angle, propped up on the east side by the weakened frames.

I left the car at the curb hoping to avoid driving over any evidence in the driveway, hoping something was left at the scene that had not been contaminated. I had rented a new Mercury Sable, bright red with gray cloth upholstery. After driving around in my pickup, the Sable felt like a Rolls-Royce.

The fire axes had spread bits of ebony wood across the yard and the rain had washed some of it down the driveway to the street. I spotted a broken piece of brown earthenware in the grass at the base of the steps. I picked it up and wiped off the mud and put it in my pocket.

Every time I survey a burned house I feel like I'm reading the story of the place, especially if it has a few years on it. I imagine Christmas mornings and birthday parties, a mother tucking in a three-year-old and a father watching the game in the La-Z-Boy.

This time it wouldn't be imagination, it would be memory.

The police tape was gone, probably neighborhood kids looking for something to hang in their rooms. The yard was still rutted and water stood in the six-inch-deep tire tracks. A fire truck and seven or eight booted firemen can naturally plow up a lawn when it gets soggy from the hoses.

I had not requested nor had I seen the police report. I wanted to draw my first impressions and conclusions free from the taint of somebody else's findings.

The first thing I did was go to the remains of the kitchen window and look for the stove. The damn thing was gone. Somebody had unhooked it and loaded it up and carried it off. A hollow feeling rose in my chest. The cops must have felt the stove was exhibit A.

A rainy front passed through the night before, and the sky still hung low and dappled gray, with a dark edge to the west promising more rain. The TV said it was a long front, reaching to the Caribbean, and we had caught the northern tip. The southern end was kicking up a storm near the Greater Antilles and it was being watched as a tropical depression.

A chemical analysis would be watered down at best. And since it wasn't a Bayou Casualty case, I'd have to bribe the guys at the company's lab to get one. I owed it to Perinovich, and I had promised Sheila, but it was still a shame to waste a good bribe on such a long shot.

Hunter Perry, the heir to the Perry Sugar Company fortune over in New Orleans, met and married a showgirl when he was four days deep into a six-day drunk in Las Vegas. Eight months later, he hired me to trail her. It wasn't hard. I snapped three great zoom shots of her coming out of a Motel 6 with a Saints rookie cornerback. Those shots gave Hunter a chance to buy his way out of the marriage. It still cost him a hefty lump sum, but there was no courtroom divorce. And for reasons I can only guess, Hunter was real anxious not to go into any open courtroom.

That cornerback's still in the league, Cleveland last time I heard. He's great on supporting the run but can't single cover a wide-out to save his ass. And it's two wives later for Hunter. And since that time, I've had no problems getting into Hunter's luxury box at the Superdome. I don't abuse the deal, I pay him for the tickets. My one edge is that I pay general admission price and he doesn't question who I send up there.

Two opening-day tickets would set me back eighty, but I'd get at least three hundred bucks' worth of lab work on the sly. Sheila would gladly give me the three hundred, but it just wouldn't be the same to the guys at the lab.

I shot half a roll on the front of the house, then some on the east side, which was the least damaged, but still blown through at the windows and burned through at two places. The smoke had been black and thick, the intact portion of the outer wall was still smudged even after last night's heavy rain.

On the driveway side, the one-inch pipe that carried natural gas to the house entered through the floor a foot in from the outer wall. I went down on one knee and stuck my head under the edge of the house to see if there was evidence of explosion or fire underneath. With the overcast skies there wasn't much light to see under the house, so I pushed back and straightened up to reach into my pocket for my key-chain flashlight.

I sensed movement behind me. Out of the corner of my eye I caught an arm swinging down toward me. I ducked and rolled. I pushed myself off the ground.

He was a hard-muscled guy, Vietnamese, early twenties. Another one, barely teenaged, stood behind him dancing around on the balls of his feet. The older one lunged at me, the club raised.

I blocked with a forearm and caught his wrist. The club flew from his hand and clattered along the driveway. I spun and kicked him in the chest, knocking him back three steps. I swung the second kick at the other kid and that froze him. The third kick I aimed at the big one's jaw.

He ducked and returned with a kick that grazed my ribs. I was lucky he missed, I hadn't expected that. He kicked, spun, and kicked again in a pretty fair series.

He had some training. Not enough. I started with the MPs back when the Ayatolla had us by the short hairs. I knew his third spin kick was coming and I caught his ankle. I leveraged down and to the right and slammed him against the wall. His skull knocked against the wood.

I caught him on a rebound and grabbed his wrist. I launched him to the driveway. Whatever training he had kicked in and he rolled away from me. His street instincts took over and he ran like a shot toward the road. I couldn't have caught him on my best day, and I was a good fifteen years past that.

The little kid had been entranced watching the fight. It took a full second to hit him that his older companion had hauled ass. He wanted to run but those feet just wouldn't move. I jumped at him and trapped him, his back against the wall and an azalea bush to his right. I had an angle on him if he tried to go left.

He sprang toward the space between the wall and me. He was quick as a jackrabbit, and almost got through. I grabbed a handful of his T-shirt and threw him to the ground. I pinned him to the ground with my foot on his chest.

"Whoa! You're not going anywhere." I watched in case he reached for a knife and glanced down the street to make sure the bigger kid wasn't doubling back. "Roll over." I nudged his chest with my shoe. He tried a glare, but it came across with more fear than defiance. He was no more than five three and weighed a hundred ten pounds at the most. He rolled over and lay stomach down.

I knelt beside him, one hand on the small of his back to keep him from jumping up, the other patting down his pants legs, especially at the ankles. He wore a Sea Wolves T-shirt, khaki painter's pants, and a showroom-new pair of Nikes, the kind that can get you killed in the New Orleans projects. He raised his head and I tapped him on the side of his face, not quite a slap, but hard enough to make him flinch and wonder just how rough I would get.

"I'll tell you when you can move."

I stood and told him to sit up.

"Who was your friend?" I asked.

A veil lowered across his eyes and they became as flat as a bad oil painting.

"I know he's a Dragon," I said, "and I can pick him out of a lineup. So why don't you save us both some time and tell me who he is."

He looked past me toward where the other guy had run.

"What's your name?"

"Hank," he said.

"You're Nguyen's grandson, aren't you?"

He lowered his eyes.

"Now let me guess," I said. "That guy who just left you here by yourself, I'll bet his name is Sammy. Dan Lu's son."

Hank raised his hand to block the sun from his eyes and raised his eyebrows as he studied me, trying to remember where he might have seen me or to figure out who I was. I decided to let him keep guessing.

"Get up, Hank. We need to talk."

He stood and I grasped him above the elbow. I led him to the car and opened the passenger-side door.

"Are we going somewhere?" he asked.

"That depends on you. You tell me what you're doing attacking somebody with a deadly weapon."

"I didn't attack you."

"The law says that doesn't make any difference. You were with the guy. Tell me who he was, or you'll be arguing the law with Judge Ward down at the youth detention center. Or maybe first you'd like to explain the whole thing to your grandfather."

I motioned and he got in the car. I took one last look down the street before getting in myself.

"His name's Sammy," he said.

"Sammy didn't seem to care that he was leaving you behind."

"It's hot in here," he said. He punched the button to let down the window. Sweat was rolling into his eyes and one drop trailed down beside his ear.

"Let me guess," I said. "You and Sammy go for a walk. Getting a little fresh air. The next thing you know, you see this brand-new shiny red car. And y'all decide you want a car like this. So you pick up a two-by-four and try to knock me out and take my car. Am I right so far?"

Hank looked down at his hands and started to get teary-eyed. He looked out the window.

"If you're looking for Sammy to come back, you're in for a long wait."

"He's going to get some of the Dragons. You better get out of here."

"I've got plenty of time. Let's wait for him."

Hank looked through the open window down the street. The smell of wet earth drifted into the open windows. So did the smell of burned wood. A parking garage for a casino was going up two blocks away, and a pile driver banged out a steady beat in syncopation to the tweets of front-end loaders and bulldozers in reverse gear. I said nothing and let Hank watch for the return of Sammy and the Dragons. He sat as still as a statue, his head turned away from me. I marked the time on the car's digital clock and gave it a full five minutes.

"Okay," I said, "you can get out now."

"You're letting me go?"

"Be sure to thank Sammy for all the help he gave you."

"You're not calling the cops?"

"Don't let me catch you with Sammy again. But you tell your Dragon buddies how he wimped out and ran away from me. And put out the word that if I catch Sammy on the street again, I'm going to whip his skinny ass. No questions asked."

TEN

I cruised the streets of Point Cadet for thirty minutes looking for Sammy. I was in the mood to kick his ass, I was already dirty, and I didn't need to give him time to regroup. I drifted along at walking speed, peering down alleys and driveways and studying faces outside bars and poolhalls and coffee houses.

Three Vietnamese kids, none of them old enough to shave, stood at the corner of Third and Oak staring at me as I rolled past them. The word had spread that I was around. I know enough about gangs to realize that as long as Sammy knew that I was hunting him, there was no way I'd find him, so I said to hell with it and drove down to the beach.

Getting assaulted with a two-by-four is no way to start a day. My next two tasks were only a little more pleasant. I had to get the report on the explosion from the Biloxi Police Department. But worse than that I had to go haggle with Speedy Cline about buying Daddy's boat back from him before he sank it or let it rot. Dammit, I *told* Neal to mind his own business.

I hadn't ridden down the beach for a while—that ride to Mr. Cass's funeral with Daddy and Neal snapping at each other didn't count—so I decided to roll the sun roof back and check out the beach volleyball games.

I turned onto Highway 90 and immediately got stuck in

backed-up traffic. The lighted message board in front of Fat Johnny's Ford read ninety-four degrees. The humidity I guessed to be 100 percent. Heat rippled from tailpipes as a long line of cars, funneled by orange barrels into a single lane, inched ahead in ten-foot intervals. Heavy steam rose through the grille of a gray four-door New Yorker that had pulled off into a right-turn lane. A puddle of hot green water grew on the pavement beneath it. I finally got through the bottleneck and stepped on the gas and the Sable took off, lifting as if it had wings.

I could get used to a red convertible. I love my truck, but something about a highway along a beach calls for CD players turned up loud and wind blowing through your hair. I could roll the windows down in my pickup and turn the radio up to full volume, but it's just not the same. I zipped past the three big casinos, the Isle of Capri, Casino Magic, and the Grand, past their high-rise hotels and neon marquees. The wind whipped through the sunroof and the rock and roll surrounded me. I put on my Ray Bans and rolled up my sleeves. The car had that new-car aroma and that firm feel. I felt I had stepped off into a humid Las Vegas. I had this sudden urge to undo the top two buttons of my shirt.

"I don't reckon I got much need to sell," Speedy said. "I've had me a good year. I tell you I caught over eight hunnerd pound so far?"

"You told me," I said.

The *White Dolphin* smelled like it hadn't been washed down real well from its last trip. If you miss one shrimp or shiner or squid when you hose off the decks after a few drags of the net, you'll smell it in two days, especially in summer. At least Speedy had washed the nets. You don't wash the nets and you get the smell plus the flies. But he had not coiled the ropes. They just lay there spread around the deck like so much spaghetti.

"You can make a decent profit, Speedy. I'll give you two thousand more than you paid for it. That's not bad for a month's investment."

"I already been offered more'n that."

He grinned at me and scratched at the three-day stubble on his face and pulled at his underwear through his pants. The stump of a cigar he was chewing was the same length and in the same condition as every one I've seen him chewing on for the past twenty years. I wondered if it was the same cigar.

"So you've decided to quit the concrete plant?"

"Not just yet. Way I got it figured, I'll make enough after two years to pay off this boat. After that I can go into shrimping full-time."

"Speedy, a boat this big costs a bunch of money to operate. You're going to play hell making money running it part time. Why don't you sell it back to me and get you a weekend rig?"

"I made near 'bout two grand so far."

"You haven't hauled it up yet. It costs a wad to scrape the bottom and repaint. And you're going to have to replace the nets, and caulking that hull is a bitch, believe me."

"I keep this up, I'll hire me somebody to do all that."

This was Speedy's first big boat. He was two thousand to the good and convinced that every week would go like the last one had. My grandfather started Delmas Boatyard in 1936 and we make and repair mostly wooden boats. I love wooden boats. Nothing feels better in the water, nothing looks as good as wood. But nobody should buy a wooden boat before it goes through a springtime haul-up.

You lie underneath the boat face up in ninety-degree weather and hold your arms up until they ache. You chip off rock-hard barnacles with a Red Devil scraper and taste their grit and crunch it with your teeth. You wire-brush chalky red lead paint until the dust mixes with your sweat, and it gets in your eyes and you nearly go blind, and your face looks as if it were finger-painted by a four-year-old. You start to stink so bad you offend yourself. And that's just normal maintenance, you don't want to hear about replacing a rotten frame.

"I hope you're setting the boat money aside," I said.

"You ain't talking to some tourist. I lived here all my life."

"Think about it, Speedy."

"I got to get out on the water," he said. "Cain't catch no shrimp shootin' the bull up here on this pier."

He untied the spring lines and hopped down to the deck of the boat. He stepped inside the cabin and flipped on the bilge pump. I stayed on the dock as he started the engine and backed out of the slip. I had parked the Sable out of sight at the far end of the parking lot; didn't want Speedy thinking I had come into some money.

I watched until he got to the channel. It was like seeing a stranger in the house you grew up in. Or like seeing the mother of your child going out on a date with some damn X-ray reader. And that son of a bitch Speedy knew it. He waved at me and tooted the horn as he reached the channel and turned south.

I could have kicked myself for hanging around the pier and giving him the satisfaction.

"I figured you'd be showing up," Louise said. "Won't come around just to say hello. Gotta wait until they nearly burn the city to the ground before you come by to see me."

She had streaked her hair and lost thirty pounds. She showed off her new figure for me by standing up from her seat behind the glass and making a slow 360-degree turn.

"Louise," I said, "you're going to start some trouble around here you keep strutting around like that."

"That's what my grandson keeps telling me. He says they're wasting a lot of talent keeping me here behind this window." She hit the switch at the base of the microphone. "*Go ahead, thirteen.*"

The station had been a schoolhouse until it got too old and run down. Then the city decided it would make a good cop shop. Louise sat behind glass, one of those annoying configurations with a half-moon hole at the bottom and a circle cut at face level, always somebody else's face level, for you to talk through. The tiles in the drop ceiling were sagging and some were water stained and the room was cold and smelled like lemons. Two guys, young and pumped, walked behind me. They wore jeans and knit shirts with badges and pistols on their belts.

"You heard from Johnnie Barron lately?" I said.

"He brings me a flounder every now and then. He knows how much I love them. Spends 'most every day at the old bridge. He's been smoking a lot of mullet. You like smoked mullet?"

"We non-Yankee types call it Biloxi bacon."

She stuck her tongue out at me. "Johnnie'd love to see you, Jack. He won't admit it but I think he's getting tired of retirement." She pressed the talk button. "*No injuries, thirteen, but traffic's backing up fast. Got one car on the scene already. Call in when you get there.* I mean, he'd never say that, but going fishing every day just don't seem to be as much fun as it was when he only went on his days off. 'Course, he ain't asked for my opinion." She pushed the button. "*Thirteen's on its way.*"

"How can you talk to me and field all those calls at the same time?"

"*That's a ten-four. D'Iberville Arms. A six-forty reported.* Honey, I've been doing this so long it don't even dawn on me that I'm doing it."

"I need to see Morgan," I said. "It's another arson case."

Her smile vanished and she shook her head. "The boy's in over his head. Barron left way long before he had time to teach Morgan anything."

"I was surprised Johnnie left."

"He had the years," she said. "He could have stayed around, but I don't blame him. If I had my years, I'd leave, too."

"Louise, if you and Johnnie both leave, this place will fall apart."

"Oh, don't worry about that. Bernie Pettus will take care of everything."

Louise paged Morgan to report to the front. When he reached the lobby, she pointed her head in my direction.

"Sorry, Delmas," he said. "We still don't have those reports for you."

Louise caught my eye, rolled her eyes to the ceiling, and began talking into her dispatcher's mike.

"I need a different one. I need the Perinovich explosion."

"I thought Eastern States had his coverage."

"This isn't an insurance investigation."

Morgan frowned and puffed out his cheek. He was a stocky kid with a hard-bitten look about him that didn't go with the smooth face. His dark red hair and freckles across the bridge of his nose accented the youthful appearance. "You need to check with the fire department."

"They say the police have impounded the files."

Morgan raised his eyebrows.

"That usually means the case has been ruled an arson," I said.

"I know the policy, Delmas."

"Do you have the files?"

"It's news to me if we do."

"How about the coroner's report?"

"You'll have to check with the coroner."

"What was the cause of the fire?"

"You'll have to read the report."

I heard the front door shut behind me. It was Bernie Pettus. "Somebody helping you, Delmas?"

"I'm here to pick up a police report."

He looked at Morgan. "Police report?"

"On the Perinovich explosion," I said.

"We aren't releasing that file," Morgan said. His eyes shifted from me to the mayor and back.

"That's right," Bernie said, "it's an ongoing case."

"I went to the scene," I said. "It looks like the investigation is over. And the fire department says BPD took the files. Is it arson or not?"

Morgan shook his head no and the mayor shot him a hot look.

"We haven't determined who did what," Bernie said, "so we're still investigating."

"You telling me that until you can tell me who set a fire you don't call it arson?"

"We don't release such files," Pettus said.

Behind the mayor, Louise smirked, shrugged her shoulders, and turned toward the radio panel.

"When did you start your police career, Bernie?" I asked. "I was asking the investigating officer about his case. I thought he was the—"

"That's the policy, Delmas," Pettus said. "Unless there's something else you need, I'm sure officer Morgan has some work he needs to get to. Don't you, Morgan?"

Morgan gave him a quick, dirty glance. "Yes, sir," he said, and walked back down the hall, opening and closing his fingers into a series of tight fists.

"Bernie, why don't you help me out here? There's no use in y'all stonewalling this case. I may be able to come up with something that would help you."

"I'm sure our officers can handle it."

"Did Johnnie Barron check this case out?"

Bernie's jaw tightened. "He's not on the force anymore, Delmas. Besides, Officer Morgan has more training than Johnnie Barron ever had."

"But Morgan doesn't have thirty years' experience."

"You'll get the report when it's made public. Now, if you'll excuse me."

Bernie turned and left me standing there. He walked down the hall and went in the same door Morgan had gone into.

"This is none of my business," Louise said, "and you didn't hear this from me. But I know Morgan's been talking to Barron. The kid's scared to death. You might want to go see Johnnie."

ELEVEN

The fishing rod was bent nearly double from the weight of whatever he had hooked. He worked the spinning reel slowly, keeping the tip of the rod raised. Below the old bridge, at the surface of the water, the line whipped back and forth as the big fish tried to shake the hook. Johnnie Barron glistened in the sun, the sweat giving luster to his dark black skin and making it look as if it were oiled. He kept the tension steady as the medium-action rig strained almost to the breaking point. The fish broke the surface, a channel catfish.

Johnnie reeled it in and flipped the rod around to shake it off the hook, but that only set the hook deeper. The big cat had clamped down too hard. He pulled it over the railing and laid it on the concrete surface of the old bridge.

"It never fails," I said. "The big ones always turn out to be catfish."

"That's the damn truth. If you could eat these saltwater cats I could make a fortune selling them."

The big gray catfish flopped around on the concrete, his huge gaff fin sticking straight up. A catfish fin will slice through the sole of a tennis shoe like a carving knife. Barron bent down and clamped down on the shaft of the hook with a pair of needle-nosed pliers. He hoisted the fish over the rail and flipped it off the hook. It splashed as if he had dropped a cinder block.

"I guess you ain't gonna give me no peace," he said, "even after I'm retired."

"As a matter of fact, I was thinking about taking you on as a partner."

"Partner? It'd cramp your style to actually know something about fire investigations."

"I'm serious, Johnnie. You might want to team up with me on some cases now that you've got the time."

He reached into the white plastic bucket, and pulled out a piece of cut squid, which he baited on the golden hook. Thirty feet out over the water, a dozen sea gulls hovered in front of us, dive-bombing a school of shiners, chirping and cawing and stealing from each other when a fish was dropped.

"You ain't about to take on no partner. We're friends now. Been friends a long time. Don't need to be makin' no partnership and screwin' up a good friendship. Know what I'm sayin'?"

His cast arched and plopped onto the flat surface of the water. Two hundred yards across the bay, there was a steady whine of tires on the steel grid of the drawbridge, all of them headed to the casinos. Years earlier, the old two-lane bridge we were standing on was the link between Biloxi and Ocean Springs and was the major east-west highway for the entire southern United States. Since the casinos, even the new four-lane bridge in front of us is overloaded and overwhelmed by the steady stream of traffic pouring into the area. The interstate, four miles inland, is also stretched to its limit.

"If I can't talk you into becoming my partner, how about giving me some advice?"

"Damn," he said, "I go into retirement, I lose all the jobs they pay me for, and the jobs I don't get paid for just keep on coming. What kind of advice you need?"

"Hey, I offered to pay."

"Sometime you get off cheaper when you don't take somebody's money up front. Know what I'm sayin'?"

"What do you know about the Perinovich explosion?"

Johnnie leaned on the railing and tugged at the line. He spat into the water and grunted. "What kinda help you need?"

"The report."

"You asks the fire department?"

"They sent it to BPD. And BPD won't say whether it's being treated as an arson or not."

"Of course it is. Didn't you say they got the file?"

"They won't say if it's undetermined origin, accidental, or they're just holding off. Since this one's an explosion, God knows how long it'll take."

"If the fire department sent it to the cops, it's a damn arson. That's been the policy forever."

"Not now," I said. "They don't label it arson until they name a suspect. Bernie probably figures all these houses getting burned on the Point will raise insurance rates. If he strings them out, the companies won't be raising the rates until after the election's over."

"You see why I'm out of there? Just that kinda stuff. Know what I'm sayin'?"

"This new guy, Morgan," I said. "My guess is that he knows nothing about fire investigation. Much less explosions."

"Wouldn't say he don't know nothing. He ain't a bad kid, he just got thrown in over his head. He's been to the classes but he ain't seen much in the field. He'll catch on."

"All I wanted to do was to see the report, and Morgan acted like a horse's behind, and this was even before Bernie butted in."

"You mean he was walking around with a chip on his shoulder?"

I nodded.

"You mean he acted like he didn't want anybody questioning anything in his report?"

I nodded.

"You mean he acted like he wasn't sure about what he was

doing and didn't want anybody to know it? Like he wouldn't take nobody's help even when they wanted to help him?"

I felt my face redden as my memory kicked in. "I see where you're going, Johnnie. I wasn't that bad, was I?"

He chuckled as he shook his head. "Cut Morgan some slack. Anybody's new on the job, people figure they don't know what they're doing. Took me a long time to figure out nobody's perfect. As I recall, took you a long time, too. Morgan, he's just like you was when you started out."

He reeled in and checked his hook. Whatever it was stole the bait. He reached down for another piece of squid.

"You get Bernie Pettus out of the way," he said, "and Morgan'll be a good cop. He can't pick up and leave like I did. You tried that picking-up-and-leaving stuff yourself."

"That's right. So it can be done."

"But not everybody can pay the price like you did. The beach bum business ain't for everybody. Know what I'm sayin'? You ought to be glad. It might start gettin' crowded on that beach."

I rested my elbows on the railing and watched a patch of roiling water below us. I couldn't see beyond the surface, but I figured it was a school of mullet.

"By the time I got to Perinovich's house it had rained. The police tape was gone. No telling how many people had been in and out. In fact, I got attacked when I was there."

He put his shades back over his eyes and turned his face toward me.

"A couple of Vietnamese jumped me. They were trying a carjack."

Barron started laughing.

"What're you laughing at?"

"Ain't nobody hard up enough to want to 'jack that old blue piece of shit you drive around in."

"I had a rented car. Bright red, sunroof, shiny wheels. A carjacker's dream."

"Rented car? Well, well. You sho'nuff got paying clients nowadays. Hell, I might hafta rethink that partner business. You say these guys were Vietnamese? How can you tell?"

"Because I'm a real pro, Johnnie. I know what Vietnamese looks like. One of them, the older one, was named Sammy."

"Figured that," Barron said. "Who's the other one?"

"A kid named Hank. Can't be more than twelve or thirteen. His grandfather is Nguyen, the one who owns that Little Saigon Grocery on the corner of Oak and Howard. White-haired guy about this tall." I held my hand out shoulder high. "He and Perinovich were big buddies."

"Yeah, I know him. I never thought of him and Perinovich as bein' that tight."

"He was as tight with Perinovich as anybody who didn't grow up on the Point."

"This Sammy you say came after you, he's the American dream. The kind of dream where you wake up in a cold sweat. Know what I'm sayin'? The Vietnamese been here long enough for us to rub off on them."

"They seem to be doing pretty well from what I see," I said. "They work their butts off on those shrimp boats and most of them are making pretty good money."

"Any group's got bad apples. This Sammy, he's the worst. We've had two Vietnamese gangs around here, the Baby Viet Boys and the Royal Family. They bad enough. But this new bunch that Sammy's got, they might be worse. The Dragons. I hear they're out of Los Angeles."

A train whistle cut through the air as a fast-moving, Biloxi-bound freight reached the railroad bridge behind us. The line of box cars behind it set up a clatter that echoed across the bay.

"The Dragons," he said, "they're like grown-up versions of the Baby Viets and the Family. Extortion, stolen cars, stolen guns. You remember that home-invasion robbery over in Long Beach? I guarantee you that was the Dragons."

"Why don't I ever hear about any of this?"

"The Dragons, they headquartered on the West Coast. Ain't been in Biloxi long enough to make any noise yet. But once Sammy gets a few recruits, you'll hear about 'em. Main reason you don't hear about 'em is because they don't mess with folks outside their turf. They pick on other Vietnamese."

"Sounds like the cops don't care as long as they keep it in the family."

He rubbed his mouth with his palm. "Who're you? Geraldo Rivera? That's bullshit. The reason the cops don't bust it up is because when they respond to a call over there nobody saw nothin' and nobody heard nothin'. Hell, the *victims* won't even talk."

He yanked the pole to set the hook and cranked the reel. It was a redfish, maybe two pounds. He lifted the lid of the bucket and dropped the fish in and it flapped against the side sloshing the ice and water around.

"What the gangs do," he said, "they start the young kids running errands. Tell 'em to go into the convenience store or whoever they're shaking down and pick up a package. That's probably where this kid is. He that young, he ain't smart enough to know he might be doing something illegal. Next thing you know, he's got a history of doing errands for the Dragons and he's in it up to his eyeballs. This kid, he got any tattoos?"

"Never noticed any."

"They'd be hard to spot. Look at his hands next time you see him. Between the fingers. Anyway, the Dragon's favorite trick is to set up one of these kids on some rap they know they can beat. Then, Sammy'll take a lawyer to the youth detention center and spring the kid. And the kid, he feels like he's in debt to 'em big-time."

"So you think Nguyen's grandson is being pulled in?"

"What'd you call him? Hank, wasn't it? I'd guess he's wearing a brand-new pair of high-end sneakers and he thinks Sammy hung the moon." Johnnie flipped the rod and moved his forefinger off the line and the fresh piece of squid splashed into the water.

"You got an extra beer in that cooler?" I asked.

He tilted his head toward the forty-quart Igloo. "You say they tried to 'jack that shiny red car you were driving."

"Sammy sneaked up on me and took a swing at me with a piece of a two-by-four."

"You made him eat that two-by-four, I hope."

"He didn't hang around long enough. I caught Hank and put the fear of God in him as best I could. But I don't know how much good it did."

I leaned my elbows on the railing. That school of mullet was still churning the water and there were silver flashes from minnows breaking the surface. Johnnie yanked at the pole as the cork bobbed, but missed whatever had hit the bait, so he pulled it up. It had been picked clean.

"Just my luck," he said. "Mullets tearing the water up and I ain't got a minnow to my name." He reeled in and retrieved another piece of iced-down squid.

"This explosion," I said, "you think the Dragons could have done it?"

"Hell, yeah. Out in San Francisco last month one gang firebombed a restaurant that didn't pay up. Count on it, they do it on the West Coast and Sammy'll try it over here."

We watched the cork and I sipped on my beer. Off to our left, a tall tug, headed in and pushing a low barge loaded with coal for the generating plant up on the Biloxi River, sounded one long blast and one short one, the signal to raise the drawbridge.

"I might need some help on this Perinovich thing, Johnnie."

"I'm retired."

"I mean the police reports. I need to see them."

"You'll get 'em. I'm guessing right after the election. What's the rush? You ought to just start making your estimates, cause Bayou Casualty's gonna have to pay off on this one no matter what the report says."

"Bayou Casualty's not the carrier."

"Well, why you care about any report?"

"I got to know whether the stove was left on."

The tip of the rod twitched and he jerked it to set the hook. He reeled it up and the bait was gone again. "Damn, these bait stealers are tearin' me up. I wish I had some minnows."

"I'll run get you some if you'll go get me that report."

"You figure a bucket of minnows will cover that?"

"Hey," I said. "I offered you a partnership and you turned it down."

"Y'all must represent the company made that stove. That what it is?"

I drew in a slow breath and let it seep out. I looked out over the water. I couldn't look at his eyes. "Johnnie, I haven't told another soul what I'm about to tell you. I went shrimping with Perinovich the night before the explosion. That afternoon, before we went out, I went to his house. He was boiling a pot of tea. When we left the house, I was the last one out the door. He asked me to make sure everything was off."

"Did you?"

"God, I don't remember. I wasn't paying much attention to what I was doing. I don't think I left the stove on, but I can't swear that I did or didn't. What worries me, they took the stove out of the house." I drained the beer. "So how about it? You get the report and I run get you some minnows."

"Forget the minnows today," he said. "I'm about to pack it in. Since that front moved through, the fishing ain't been worth sitting out in this heat for. Know what I'm sayin'? It'll clear up tomorrow. You come back here tomorrow and bring some minnows and some beer, and don't get me none of that cheap shit. And bring some ice for that minnow bucket; they won't last thirty minutes in this heat without no ice. I'll see what I can do about that report."

"Johnnie, what I said about us going in partners on some cases, I mean it. I got a client on this case who can pay you."

"I get a six-pack of Michelob outta your cheap ass and I'll figure I made out like a bandit."

TWELVE

The top of the thunderhead towered fifty thousand feet above the water, gleaming white against the deep blue sky. The anvil-shaped cumulo-nimbus darkened from white at the top to slate gray toward the bottom, but not in equal gradations. The monster cloud was rimmed in black along its flat underside where sheets of dull silver rain hung below it like a veil. It was a sight that made me remember why I had bought the camp house.

When the red Cadillac turned into my yard, I rose from my porch swing and set my coffee mug on the top railing of the front deck. I had tied a pyramid sinker on one of my surf casting rigs, and was spooling two hundred feet of new fifteen-pound test monofilament on the reel of a second rig, and I didn't feel like talking. But I was trapped, too late to duck inside and pretend I wasn't there.

The Caddy sparkled with its candy-apple finish as it came to a stop beside my blue F-150 pickup. My truck has dead paint, a dent over the wheel well, and a cracked windshield. The Blue Book price on it isn't high enough for me to carry any insurance on it except liability. I got it back, complete with a new clutch, from Randy the day before. Randy's a great shade tree mechanic, but he doesn't wash the cars when he's through, so my truck came out with the same coating of dust it had gone in with. I got that feeling I get when I'm in a clothing store surrounded by new suits and I look in the three-way mirror at the clothes I wore into the store. I had been meaning to get that dent fixed.

A two-toned blast rang out from the Cadillac's horn and Sheila stepped out. She wore big round sunglasses and a yellow cotton dress with a flowered print. Her bracelets jangled as she bounced up the twenty wooden steps to the deck. Her shoulders were bare except for the two spaghetti straps on the dress. It was low-cut and showed a lot of cleavage, especially from my vantage point fifteen feet above her. I still couldn't tell. She hugged me and kissed me on the cheek.

"I just love your place," she said.

"That's nice of you to say. But as far as I know, there's never been a woman born who likes a place like this. They may tolerate it for a day or two, but the thought of living here doesn't set well for some reason."

"Oh, I don't know. This place looks like you."

"You mean a little worn around the edges?"

"I was talking about this great view of the Gulf."

She was right about that. I live in a camp house, set high on pine poles. It has a deck that wraps around it on three sides and the best view of the Mississippi Sound in Bay Saint Louis. That afternoon there was haze toward the horizon but no clouds except for the one huge thunderhead and a hazy bank of white behind it. A flock of brown pelicans was flying in formation ten feet over the surface. Tiny waves feathered along the shoreline and a steady and cool breeze came from the southwest. The clean, salt smell was pure, without the strong smell of mud and seaweed that would come when the tide went out.

"I really miss a lot of things about the coast," she said. "This is the kind of place I wish I could have raised my son. I haven't been a good mother in a lot of ways. Joey's spent so much time in boarding schools he never had the chance to have a real home."

"Joey seems to have turned out just fine."

"Oh, he has! Isn't he the most handsome thing? And just as

good as can be." She sat on the swing and reached into her purse for a cigarette. "I haven't had the best luck with my husbands. I'm sure you've heard all about that."

"No, I haven't."

"God, that's what I love about southern men. They know just when to lie. Of *course* you have. I know how gossip works in this place. You try getting knocked up at the age of seventeen and you'll get a real lesson about that."

"Don't let them get you—"

"Oh, don't worry. I've gotten over it now. It drove me out of town, but I've done all right since then. You've heard about my hotels?"

"I heard you had one. I didn't know there were others."

"I've got three. The story is that I got them through divorce settlements. That's only partly true. I got the first one ten years ago after I caught my first husband in the sack with the convention director. Actually, I filed after he announced he was moving her into our house and thought we'd make a good threesome. I had enough sense to get some of his games on film before I filed for divorce. Trouble is, that hotel was in the red so bad he was glad to unload it. But it was my chance. I've worked up to three now, all in Dade County."

"Do you have any restaurants?"

"Only those in the hotels. Why do you ask?"

"I thought maybe that was the business you've been talking to Stash about."

She reached over to the ashtray. "Have I been talking business with him?"

"That's what you told me at Mr. Cass's wake."

"We were just batting about a few ideas. That's all."

She smiled and reached for my hand. She laced her fingers with mine and I was transported back twenty years, before either of us had been knocked to the ground a few times, when the simple act of holding hands had a lot fewer implications. It felt so good, it almost made me believe she and Stash really were just talking business.

"I'm having trouble with the Biloxi police," I said. "They took Mr. Cass's file from the fire department, so they suspect something. But they're not releasing it. Usually that wouldn't matter, but I was called in on the case so late that there have been a couple of rains."

"Can you use Bart Newman's report?"

"I'd still like to see what the police came up with."

"I can talk with Bernie," she said. "He's a businessman. He'll understand why I need a report as soon as possible."

"You mean you know him?"

"Of course I do." She crushed out the cigarette. "Why are you looking at me like that? I've known Bernie Pettus for years. Look, Uncle Cass's battles weren't necessarily my battles. I've got plenty of my own to fight. What's the problem with the police?"

"They've been treating arson cases in a pretty strange manner since Bernie took over the department. He thinks that if they don't make a one hundred percent sure determination of arson and don't label it as such, it'll hold down the fire insurance rates."

"Will it?"

"Not for long. The companies aren't going to let that slide or every town in the country would be doing the same thing. But it may hold the rates down through the election."

She laid her arm on the back of the swing and looked out over the gulf. "It sounds like this might be tougher than I thought."

"I'm only saying it may take more time than it would normally. What do you know about Mr. Cass's situation with the Vietnamese in the neighborhood?"

"He was friends with an old man named Nguyen. He's got a grocery store on the Point somewhere, but I've never met him."

"I mean the younger ones. Did he ever mention a street gang called the Dragons?"

"We didn't talk much. But I hear he was almost at war with them."

"Did he ever mention the Belters to you?"

"You mean that bunch of white trash on Back Bay? I know Lennis and Uncle Cass had a history of hating each other."

The phone rang and I stepped through the sliding glass door to answer it. It was somebody trying to sell me a credit card. When I walked back out to the deck, Sheila was putting on lipstick, using the mirror of a compact.

"I want you to understand there's not much to go on here," I said. "I still can't prove it wasn't an accident, and most of what I've got is speculation."

"You'll turn up something. I just know you will."

"I can't stay with this too much longer. Bayou Casualty has me booked for a couple of other fires and I can't put them off more than a few days. I'd like to solve this as much as you would, but—"

"I'll pay you whatever daily rate Bayou Casualty would."

"—I can't lose them as a client."

She stared out at the gulf and ran her fingers through her hair as she tilted her head back and breathed deeply. She sat still for several seconds with her eyes closed before drawing in a shallow breath and blowing it out. She reached for her purse and started feeling around in it.

"Speaking of money, I want you to give this to Neal tonight." She pulled out some bills, folded and clamped together with a paper clip. The bill showing was a hundred. She also pulled out a blue plastic card. She held the money out toward me. "I hear he's having a fund-raiser for his Senate race this evening. Are you going?"

"As a matter of fact, I'm going to be the chef tonight. Neal and Kathy would love to have you come."

She aimed her green eyes at mine. "I don't have anyone to take me."

"Uh . . . I . . . I've asked Trish Bullard to go with me. I really didn't know you'd want to come."

She lowered her eyes. "You don't have to explain. I'm sure you and Trish will have a good time. Please explain to Neal why I couldn't come."

"But you *can* come. We'd love to have you."

"That's not my style," she said. "But I'm going to be in town for a while. We can see each other sometimes later." She took hold of my hand and pressed the blue plastic card into my palm. "You decide when."

THIRTEEN

There was a soft pop. A blue ring of flame raced around the burner of the propane tank as I fired up the tripod cooker. I planned to boil the shrimp in three batches, ten pounds a batch, and counting the time they'd need for cooling, it was time to get started. It was two hours before the party, three hours before sundown, and Kathy had banished me to the driveway, a few steps beyond the gate of the eight-foot-high brick fence that enclosed the backyard.

The centerpiece of their courtyard is a live oak whose longest branches touch on the carpet of St. Augustine grass. The oak is draped with gray Spanish moss and is circled around its base by a thick bed of white caladiums edged by a strip of monkey grass. The jasmine bush in the far corner perfumed the heavy air. Three straight afternoon rains gave a deep green luster to the yard and to the banks of resurrection fern on the crooked limbs of the oak.

The maid and and her granddaughter were setting up the outside tables. They worked neither fast nor slow despite frenzied exhortations from Kathy, who came outside at irregular intervals and gave them last-minute and ill-advised instructions, which did nothing but stop the work while she talked. They nodded and waited for her to leave and went back to what they had been doing at the same pace. I enjoyed this show through the courtyard's iron gate while I waited for the water to boil. As she had promised,

Kathy stepped through the gate at straight up five o'clock and brought me a Corona in a foam cooler.

"You got a pretty good crowd coming?" I asked.

"We ought to. We got membership lists from the chamber of commerce and the county bar association. We kept the suggested minimum down to fifty dollars. Heck, they'd spend more than that at a restaurant for a couple of seafood platters. Especially since we've got an open bar."

"You got any of the casino people coming? I hear they like politics."

"We've got a few."

The race was heating up. Neal was running against Biff Batson, the twenty-five-year-old chairman of the Hancock County Young Republicans. The kid was two years out of college and listed his occupation as consultant. They were running around one-upping each other, trying to show the beach crowd and the rich folks at Diamondhead who was the most pro-business. Neal, being old enough to actually have a track record, was getting hammered for suing the old L&N railroad fifteen years ago after its train, twenty miles per hour too fast on a railbed the company had not re-worked in thirty years, jumped the track and wiped out a thirty-two-year-old father of three sitting at the crossing waiting for the damn thing to pass. Suing anybody for anything is viewed with disdain at the club. Neal's main advantage in the race was that the family has been here three hundred years and we're kin to most of the county.

My contribution to the evening was the thirty pounds of shrimp Perinovich and I had hauled in. That, and a willingness to cook them, ice them down, and then blend into the woodwork. Shallow conversation with complete strangers is not something for which I have a great talent. I'm pretty good at cooking shrimp and nailing yard signs into the ground, and I'm fair at stuffing and sealing envelopes. Neal would have named me as campaign chairman, but he wasn't far enough ahead in the polls to do something that stupid.

"How's it going with Sheila Zimarich?" Kathy asked.

"Going?"

"Doesn't she have you on retainer?"

"Retainer? I told you not to be hanging around with those lawyers."

"Neal tells me you two used to date. She doesn't look like your type."

I turned the burner up a notch. "Funny thing about that. Sheila's always attracting a pack of men, but to hear the women talk, she doesn't seem to be anybody's type. Of course that's mainly those old busybodies who go to the beauty parlor every morning."

Kathy laughed and held up both hands. "Okay. I get the point. She's gorgeous, she's flashy, and she makes other women uncomfortable. I admit it. Please don't tell me I'm beginning to sound like that."

"Sheila hasn't had it easy," I said.

She slapped at her forearm. "Have the mosquitos been bothering you?"

"Not as long as I'm around this cooker."

"That mosquito truck always comes by right at sundown." She looked down the street before turning toward the gate. "One more thing and I'll let this business about Sheila drop. Have they always been like that?" She cupped her hands under her breasts and lifted them up.

"Now you're starting to sound like the men around here."

Bubbles climbed the side of the aluminum pot and a light steam rose from the water. I put the lid on and sat in a lawn chair. When the steam got strong enough to bounce the lid around, I began quartering lemons and onions. I cut open three mesh sacks of Zatarain's shrimp boil and emptied the contents into the water.

The red powder, with its cayenne and sassafras and basil, rose on the steam and burned the linings of my nostrils. It made me cough and drew water in my eyes. I dropped in the lemons and onions and the boil subsided. I was drying my eyes with a handkerchief when Neal pulled his Lincoln into the driveway.

"Kathy kick you out of the house?" he asked.

"I don't even want to go inside right now. Neither do you. Last-minute jitters."

Neal held a brown paper sack. A dark spot of wetness was forming at its bottom. "I picked up an extra ten pounds of shrimp. We can always make shrimp salad with what's left over."

Kathy stepped through the iron gate with a bottled wine cooler and a canned soft drink, both cold and both dripping with condensation. She handed Neal the can.

"Jack gets a Corona and I get a Diet Coke?"

"We can't have our next state senator greet his constituents after a couple of beers," she said.

"What about Jack?"

"They already know about Jack."

Neal glared at me. Like that's *my* damn fault or something.

"Oh!" Kathy squealed. "Look at that!"

Beneath the biggest limb of the live oak, a silver platter and two silver bowls sat on a long hors d'oeuvres table. Flower arrangements flanked the silver at either end of the table. The white tablecloth, with the arrangements of leather leaf fern and white killian daisies, stood out in sharp contrast to the lush green of the backyard. The sun, low in the western sky, seeped through the big branches spreading fuzzy blades of light through the late afternoon haze. One of them struck the platter and gave it a yellow glow.

"I've got to get a picture of that. That's a cover for *Coast Magazine.*" She dashed into the house.

"I've got to hand it to Kathy," I said. "This place really looks good. How many people are you expecting?"

"I sent a hundred fifty invitations. I don't figure any more than fifty, probably more like thirty."

"I almost forgot. Here's three hundred bucks that Sheila sent."

"Well, bless her heart. I would have sent her an invitation, but I didn't want her to feel obligated. Of course I guess it would have been uncomfortable for her with you being here with a date and all."

"I wish everybody around here would grow up. I haven't dated Sheila Zimarich in twenty years. To hear everybody talk you'd think I was taking out a different girl to the senior prom and leaving my steady at home."

"I won't mention it again," Neal said. "But I'll have to send her a note. I understand Sheila's made a bunch of money with those hotels. They say she does her own TV commercials and is a celebrity in Miami."

"That's a hell of a note, isn't it?"

"What?"

"She couldn't make it with the right crowd in Biloxi, so she goes to Miami and gets on everybody's A list."

Kathy ran out with a camera. Disappointment registered in her face. "Oh, pooh! The light isn't hitting the platter like it did."

"It'll come back," I said. "The sun is behind a cloud right now."

She held the camera pointed at the table with her finger on the button waiting for the sun to come back. "Oh, Jack, while I was in the house Trisha called. She sounded awful. Said she's sick and can't come tonight."

"What's wrong with her?"

"Sore throat. A little fever. She said she just wants to go to sleep. Looks like you're a bachelor for tonight."

I thought about calling Sheila, but that wouldn't go over so well since she knew I had planned to take Trisha. I don't think Trisha would have minded, at least that's what she tells me all the time. But a woman will lie about stuff like that. I pictured being thrown in alone with a bunch of country clubbers in a political setting.

"Have you got anybody to tend bar for you?" I asked.

"No. I figured everybody can pour their own."

"Neal, these are Republicans."

FOURTEEN

The bartender idea started out real well.

I was having an easy time of it, sipping light margaritas and not having to chitchat. The glassed-in back porch was cool enough to fog the windows, and it smelled of hors d'oeurves and boiled shrimp. The crowd was on its third round and had grown loud, lots of laughing. I had gone through half a blender, but I'm all right with tequila as long as I don't mix it with anything else. Besides, I could sleep on the couch if I needed to.

I knew most of the people I had been mixing drinks for, but not these two. I guessed they had come to town with the MagnaChem plant north of the bay, maybe with a casino. One was a fireplug, a big head with no neck, a barrel chest with a girth just as big, and short, thick arms. He barely came up to up to my shoulder but outweighed me thirty pounds. His face was florid from high blood pressure, heavy drinking, or both. The other one was taller, a white-haired patrician with a hairstyle that came out of New Orleans. I know all the hairstylists and most of the barbers in Bay Saint Louis and none of them did it. He was lean like a runner. He wore a pale blue silk shirt, French cuffs, and diamond cuff links.

The patrician was chilly reserve, the fireplug constant motion. The energy in the fireplug was visible, humming as if some motor in him was on high idle. He talked like he was from Milwaukee or Detroit. The blue blood pronounced his *A*'s like they do in Boston.

"That's the thing that floored me when I moved down here," the fireplug said. "The workers' compensation laws. You know this Neal what's-his-face?"

"Not at all," the other one said. "He does some legal work for us and Bill asked me to sit in for him tonight. I would guess we're giving to both candidates. Do you have any single malt?"

"No, sir," I said.

"Oh, well, any Scotch and water will do."

"Make it two," the fireplug said. He licked cream cheese off his finger. "I can't get used to that bourbon down here."

I pulled out a bottle of Dewar's White Label and the patrician crinkled his nose.

"We gotta talk to this Neal character tonight," the fireplug said. "They gotta tighten up the workers' comp laws. Geez, for what you get the premiums around this place are murder."

"I suppose it could be worse," the patrician said. He kept looking around the room as if searching for a familiar face. "At least they don't have strong unions down here."

"Amen," the fireplug said.

"Although from a personal standpoint," the patrician said, "I guess it would be better for me if they got the unions in."

"How so?"

"If we get unions in and have a few strikes, maybe they'll shut this plant down and move me back to Boston."

I've got some buddies I sometimes go flounder gigging with when they get off graveyard shift over at the plant. I wondered if I could get them interested in stirring up a little wildcat strike for a few days.

"Not me," the fireplug said. "I'm here to stay. This past Christmas I got a new set of Ping irons and played a round with them that afternoon. Back home I wouldn't have used them until April."

I handed them their drinks and they walked back into the crowd. By my count there were seventy people, most of them packed into the back porch. The bar was in the far corner, but it had been a hot day and a lot of the guests were drinking bottled water or draft beer from the keg Kathy had set up outside on the brick patio. It was dark now and there were fireflies under the live oak. Kathy eased toward me through the crowd.

"Jack, I really appreciate you doing this."

"No problem. I feel right at home."

"I was going to tell you earlier. I got a call this afternoon from Sandy up in Memphis. She said she had tried to call you, but couldn't reach you."

"Is anything wrong?"

"No, she and Peyton are just fine. But I've got some bad news."

My stomach tightened. I didn't want to hear what I knew was coming.

"He gave Sandy a ring, Jack."

My chest went hollow and my heart sounded like a stick banging on an empty oil drum. I drew in a breath slowly and held it. "In case you don't remember, we're divorced," I said. "She's a grown woman, she can do whatever she wants to do."

It's been six years since Sandy went back to Memphis. She loved the coast at first. But after three years the beach cabin didn't look as good as the east Memphis mansion she grew up in. She took our daughter, Peyton, with her. None of it's good, but that's the worst part. Sandy has dated this radiologist for the past three years.

It must have been the brassy taste that rose in my mouth, but the margarita didn't taste too good anymore. I tasted a sickening sugary coating on my tongue that I hadn't noticed before. I tossed the remains of it down the sink, and poured myself an Old Charter over ice. I didn't want any more sweet taste, so I left off the Coke and tossed in a splash from the Perrier bottle. Kathy stared at me and nibbled on her bottom lip.

"Don't say it," I said. "I knew this was coming." I took a big swig of the drink. It felt warm all the way to my stomach. I caught myself staring across the room at nothing.

"Jack?"

"I guess you and Neal will be going to the wedding."

"Of course we will. She'll be inviting you, too."

"I'll probably just send a gift. I figure a new tennis racket ought to come in handy up there."

"Don't get nasty, Jack. You've said yourself plenty of times, she can't help the way she was raised. Most people would think east Memphis is a pretty good life."

I nodded and took another sip. Kathy was right. Most people would. But a steady diet of golf and supper clubs, all of it with people from the office and all of it after a day behind the desk in her daddy's bank, had damn near killed me. I chucked it after two years.

At least Sandy tried it my way for a while, I'll give her that. She moved to the coast and we lived in the beach camp, the same one I'm in now, for three years.

Two and a half of those years were great.

Damn, I couldn't believe she was getting married.

I felt like I was pissed off, but I was having a hard time because I didn't know who I should be pissed off at. I never had that problem before. But let me tell you, it makes you feel like you're coming out of your skin. I'm sure the psychologists have a name for it. I tried to settle on being mad at the X-ray reader Sandy had just gotten engaged to. But that was tough, since I've never laid eyes on so much as even a picture of him. I didn't realize I had polished off my drink until I took a sip and came up empty.

"I'm sorry, Jack."

"I'm all right. You just caught me off guard."

Kathy gave me a pitying look, and glanced back at me as she walked away. I smiled to let her know everything was all right, but I didn't fool her a bit. She blended into the crowd, and I had not felt so alone in years. I poured another glass of Old Charter and put some ice in it but the Perrier bottle was empty. I sipped it and it numbed my lips, which felt real good.

"Say, you got any more of that Scotch back there?"

The fireplug and the patrician had come back, and I had not noticed them. The Bostonian had not been able to shake the fireplug and he looked bored. He rattled the cubes in his glass to let me know he wanted one, too.

"So, what did you think?" the fireplug said

The Bostonian sighed. "Are we still talking about the workers' comp laws?"

"Yeah. What did you think about what he told us?"

"Excuse me," I said. "Are you gentlemen concerned about the workers' compensation laws in the State of Mississippi?"

They went silent and stared at me.

"I agree with y'all," I said, "something has to be done. Did you know that bleeding heart bunch in the legislature has decided that if a worker in one of your factories loses an eye, you've got to pay him for sixty-seven weeks. Hell, that's like giving him the keys to a Corolla." I took another sip. "I mean, he knows the risk when he takes the job. Am I right?"

The Bostonian gave me a hard look as I handed him his Scotch.

"Sixty-seven weeks, you say?" asked the fireplug.

"That's what it works out to. And if he loses both of 'em, he gets enough for a Mercedes." I tossed back half of what was left of the whiskey. "I know it's tough being blind and all, but it's not the company's fault. These workers, they just figure somebody ought to pay and they go for the deep pockets. Am I right?"

"Damn right!" the fireplug said.

"And you got to pay the doctor bills on top of that. I mean no wonder all these plants are moving to Mexico."

"No wonder!" the fireplug agreed.

"I mean, that's the reason I'm incorporated. I was going to hire somebody to work with me. But if I send him out on a case and he gets shot, there's no telling what I'd have to pay him."

"Shot?" the Bostonian asked. "What kind of work are you in?"

"I'm a private investigator. It's dangerous work and sometimes I could use some help, but what with these workers' compensation laws, I can't afford any. So I set myself up as a corporation and took out workers' comp insurance on my only employee."

"You have just the one employee?" the patrician said.

"Hell, I *am* just the one employee. It's all perfectly legal, don't you see? Y'all need to get a lawyer to show you how to set it up. Only problem is, now I'm worried to death that I'll go out on a case and stop off in the wrong place for a beer and get myself shot. Then some smart plaintiff's lawyer's gonna come along and claim it's a work related injury and talk me into suing myself. Then I'll go broke and I won't be able to live off of what I get out of my company in the damn lawsuit by the time the lawyer gets his third. And the bloodsucker gets even more if either side decides to appeal it! You follow me?"

The fireplug, who had been apparently sipping several beers in addition to the Scotch I had given him, nodded in knowing agreement. The Bostonian tilted his head and narrowed his eyes while he gave me a cool appraisal. Bad thing was, I was beginning to think I was making sense.

"Yeah," I said, "you two need to go over there and talk about these outrageous workers' comp laws and see if you can get the whole thing repealed. I mean we're in a global economy, right? Next thing I know my clients are going to start going to Mexico to pick up their private investigators."

"There you go!" the fireplug said.

The Bostonian took a sip of his drink and eased away, watching me out of the corner of his eye as he slipped into the crowd. The fireplug started talking about how we'll have to drop wages at least down to Mexico's level or China will start beating our brains out in the South American markets. For some reason, he was particularly worried about sales to Chile. Then he told me why I better start putting at least part of my money into gold coins.

A few minutes later I saw Neal, all six-foot-five of him, coming toward me.

"What in the world did you tell Mr. Hodge?" he asked.

"Who the hell is Mr. Hodge?"

"He's the vice president out at MagnaChem. He said I had a bartender over here talking crazy."

"Talking crazy, hell! I was agreeing with him! Go back over there and tell him that you tried to fire me, but that crazy-ass legislature has passed laws that tie the hands of the employers so tight that I threatened you with a wrongful-termination lawsuit if you did. And tell him I said I'll name his Yankee ass as co-defendant!"

Neal's jaw went slack. He cocked his head and stared at me until I saw his lightbulb pop on. "Kathy told you about Sandy, didn't she?"

I killed the drink. "We're talking workers' comp laws here, Neal. Sandy's got nothing to do with it. I was just agreeing with them. You people in the legislature keep giving away the store and pretty soon all those workers on the line are going to be raking off so much of the profit that the guys in the front office won't be able to buy single malt Scotch. Oh, maybe that's what he's worried about. You didn't have any single malt Scotch. Maybe he's worried that it's already too late."

"Why don't you go out for some fresh air, Jack?"

Through the window I saw a luna moth circling beneath the mercury vapor light in the corner of the courtyard and a ragged strand of Spanish moss swaying just beyond the brick wall. I sat on the edge of the stool and swirled the ice cubes around the inside of my glass to melt them down some. Neal stood silent in front of me.

"I apologize," I said. "But you know how I feel about these corporate types when they look down their noses at anybody who gets a little dirt under his fingernails every once in a while."

"I've been told many times. But this is not the time or the place to start the class war that you seem to think is coming."

"Why don't I put these bottles up top and let folks mix their own drinks? I'm really not in a mood to stick around."

"You may not be in a mood to stick around," he said, "but you're not in a condition to drive, either. You're drunk and that green-eyed monster has jumped all over you. Go back to the den and get some coffee."

I tossed another couple of ice cubes in the glass and topped it off with bourbon. The drink was the same color as strong tea.

"For God's sake, Jack. Don't get any deeper into that bottle. Give me your keys."

"Oh, come on."

"You don't need to be driving anywhere right now."

I was about to argue with him when I remembered my rule that if I ever felt like arguing about giving up my keys, it was past time to give them up. I groped through my pocket and pulled up the ring of keys and the blue plastic card. I had forgotten the card. I laid the keys in his hand.

"I'll be in the den," I said.

I went to the den and called the Goldstar Casino and ordered the complimentary limousine, one of those big white stretch Cadillacs they send for free to pick up anybody with one of those blue cards. I sneaked out the front door. I was going to rest against this silver BMW, but when I got within a foot or two it gave me a back-off beep, so I sat on my haunches at the end of the washed gravel driveway. When the Goldstar stretch arrived, just before I got in I walked over and squatted hard on the hood of the BMW.

Man, those things have some top-notch alarm systems.

FIFTEEN

I pounded the button of the elevator two times before I figured out the problem. Had to insert the blue card before the damn thing would let me ride any higher than the mezzanine. Once I figured that out it took another two minutes to realize that *P* stands for penthouse. I would have asked the man and woman who got on at parking level three, but they didn't seem to want to talk to me. In fact, they kind of hung against the wall as far away from me as they could get. So I thought, screw 'em, and let them get off and figured it out myself.

I made a mental note to tell the manager that something was wrong with the carpet where you step out of the elevator up at the penthouse level. I could hardly keep my balance, and I bumped up against the wall. Felt like I was walking on an air mat. The carpet pad must've been too thick. Somebody's going to hurt themselves and sue.

There were bright, blinding chandeliers with those clear bulbs and along the walls silk flower arrangements sat on narrow, red mohagany tables in front of tall gilded mirrors. I used one of the mirrors to brush my hair with my fingers and check to see if I had anything on my teeth. Suite four was the last one at the end of the hall. I inserted the key and walked in and called Sheila's name.

She emerged from the back in a sheer white nightgown, the

dim lights from the living room reflecting on her coal black hair. Her smile told me that she knew I would be coming. She walked over to me, laced her arm through mine and kissed me.

She led me into the sunken living room and sat me on the couch near the picture window. The lights of the boats shone red and green, little pinpoints of color on the black ocean. The moon beamed a broad, dazzling swath across the gulf. The pastel glow of neon signs rose from below, and the long stream of car lights stretched along Highway 90 like twin tubes, one red and one white. If I stared at them for a second or two, they blended together into a pink line.

She sat and folded her legs under her as she leaned toward me. "I was beginning to wonder if you were ever going to come and visit me."

"You jus' gave me the key . . . when was it? . . ."

She laughed and squeezed my forearm. "One of these days I'll learn the virtue of patience. Can I fix you something to drink?"

". . . Was it this morning? . . ."

She eased over and kissed me, a deep, long kiss. She pressed against me and flicked her tongue along the base of my neck and my pulse began pounding in my ears. "You look like you've got something on your mind."

I shrugged.

"You want to talk about it?"

I shook my head.

She laughed and stroked the side of my face. And then she stood and looked down at me for a second or two. The moon was a soft backlight shining through her nightgown, silhouetting every curve. She was perfect female beauty under an easy blue glow. She pulled the nightgown over her head and dropped it to the floor. She tossed her hair back and knelt in front of me and reached for the top button of my shirt.

I looked around and had the start that comes from waking up somewhere other than my own bed. I lay back and closed my eyes; the sunlight hurt enough without trying to look at it. Last night's whiskey was stale in my mouth, and I struggled with nausea. Dull pains and sharp pains fought a tag-team match behind my eyes. The shower was running in the next room.

I stumbled to the window and closed the blinds and plopped back down on the bed to reconstruct the night before. I lost the thread somewhere after the time Sheila laid me on her bed. I remembered her helping me up from the couch, and I remember stubbing my big toe on the way to the bedroom. I remember how cold the sheets felt when I lay on them. I recall the coolness on the soles of my feet when she removed my socks. And I vividly recall how her breasts felt through my undershirt as she lay on top of me and pressed against my chest. Those puppies were real, by God!

But that was all I could conjure up.

I tried, I even bore down and wrinkled my forehead and clenched my teeth like a six-year-old trying to make a wish come true. But the night before faded to black with Sheila on top of me, lightly nibbling the top of my ear.

The pillow beside me bore her indentation and the fragrance of her perfume. With the room now shaded by the drapes, I took a few deep breaths and tried not to raise my heartbeat any more than the bare minimum since each beat sent a stab of hurt through my head. The air-conditioner kicked on and chilled the light sweat on my face and neck and I felt the tightness ease around my eyes. I eased back into sleep, and when I awoke the second time, the shower was no longer running. And I realized I still had my undershorts on.

Scents of cinnamon rolls and coffee drifted in from the next room. I raised my head with great care. I went to the bathroom and rinsed my mouth and used the cellophane-encased comb the hotel provided. The whites of my eyes were crisscrossed with spidery red lines, and, God, my lower eyelids looked like tiny crescent rolls. I splashed cold water on my face and drank a few handfuls and it quelled my stomach. I put on the blue terry cloth robe with the Goldstar insignia. Most of the hotels I stay in on undercover assignments don't provide such amenities. Hell, some of them don't provide towels.

I stepped into the living room and there was Sheila, her back to me, dressed in a white business suit, arranging the rolls on a plate.

"Looks like you're expecting company," I said.

She turned and smiled. "You're the company, honey. Are you feeling better?"

She stepped across the room to me, put her arms around me, squeezed me, and gave me a light kiss.

"Look," I said. "I'm sorry about last night."

"Sorry? You were great."

"I passed out, didn't I?"

"You were just tired, honey."

"Oh, God. I'm sorry, Sheila. I shouldn't have come over here."

Her hand exerted a warm, soothing pressure on the side of my face. "So you don't remember last night?"

"How did I get into the bed?"

"You really don't remember, do you?"

"I remember when you were standing beside me. I'll never forget that."

"But afterwards?"

"I'm sorry."

She smiled and ran her finger down the bridge of my nose. "You were just great, Jack. I'm glad you came."

"For twenty years I waited for last night and I—"

She put her finger to my lips. "It doesn't matter. When I went to the door and saw you there . . . Well, that was so sweet of you to come."

"Sheila, I swear it had to be those damn margaritas. That's never happened to me before."

"Passing out?"

"I'm talking about the other part."

She tossed her head back and laughed from way down deep. "Well, I've seen it happen more times than I can count! Don't apologize because you didn't perform like some eighteen-year-old in heat. If that's all I wanted, I can buy a substitute at any of a dozen shops on Bourbon Street. With batteries."

I reached out to touch her hair, but she stopped me. "Sorry, darling," she said, "I can't get messed up this morning, much as I'd like to. I've got an appointment." I guess she saw the disappointment. "Really, I'd love to stay. But I've got to meet someone for breakfast. It's business."

"I hope it's important business."

"If it weren't, believe me, I'd stay all day and now that you're feeling better, probably all night."

"Will you be coming back?"

"I'm afraid not until this evening," she said. "We didn't plan this very well, did we?"

She stepped to the mirror and put her hair back into place, checked her makeup, and stepped toward the door. She pulled it open and turned to me.

"Be sure to take your key with you when you leave."

Maybe Sandy would have reacted to the fiasco of the previous night the same way Sheila had. I'll never know. When we were married, I was still a few years from having that particular problem, drunk or sober. But it was doing me no good to think about the what-ifs. Sandy was in Memphis, and Sheila was here.

I ran my fingers through my hair and felt it stand straight up. I didn't even think of looking in a mirror. I stepped through the bedroom toward the shower. On my way, I picked up the blue plastic card off the top of the dresser, grabbed my slacks from the foot of the bed, and slipped the card into the front pocket.

SIXTEEN

H e bowed to me, really a nod of his head with no bend of his neck, a remnant of Indochina. He pointed an unsteady finger to the stuffed armchair on the opposite wall of the living room. I thanked him and declined the offer. Holding the arms of the chair, he lowered himself as far as he could before plopping onto the lumpy cushion. I sat on the couch, across the room from him but still close enough for us to share the coffee table between us. Dust motes floated in the sunlight beaming through the window behind me. My tongue kept sticking to the roof of my mouth and I could still taste lime juice.

"I remember you," he said. "I saw you at Cass's funeral."

"Mr. Cass was my friend."

"Also a friend to my family," he said. "A brave man."

"He told me about your bravery, Mr. Nguyen. About the hard times you had when you came to Biloxi."

"They were much better than the times in Vietnam."

On a round table in the corner sat a display of photographs, some yellowed with age, most showing the tree-lined streets and rickshaws of Saigon. The room was redolent of boiled rice and shrimp and a current of cayenne pepper.

If the Dragons were involved in blowing up Perinovich's house, the Vietnamese of Point Cadet would know it before anybody else.

And if any Vietnamese was likely to talk to me about it, it would be Perinovich's friend Nguyen.

"You have tea?" he asked. "Cass taught me how to make it like Biloxi. Very cold. Much sugar."

I was still thirsty and needed to chase the taste from last night out of my mouth. Wet and cold anything sounded real good. I reached in my pocket for the B.C. headache powder I had picked up at the 7-Eleven on my way over. When he came back I poured the sour powder into my mouth and washed it down with the light brown tea.

"Could you tell me about the explosion that killed Mr. Perinovich?" I asked.

Uncertainty swept across his eyes. His smile stayed but it lost its spark. Even twenty years after coming here, the built-in reflexes kicked in. To be questioned by someone you don't know about the details of a death was an occasion for terror in the Vietnam from which he came. His brain told him he was safe, but his brain was having a hard time overcoming his gut, which remembered a time and place where it was thought better to kill ten innocents than to let one guilty go free.

"I'm not with the police, Mr. Nguyen. I ask this only as a friend of Cass Perinovich."

"I did not think you were with the police." He was stiff and sitting erect. This was not going to be easy.

"Were you here the night of the explosion?"

"I was here."

"Did you see anything or hear anything?"

"I saw the red lights, I saw the fire truck."

"Did you see anyone going to or coming from the Perinovich house?"

"It was late," he said. "I was asleep. The booming woke me up."

"When you woke up, did you look outside?"

"I went outside to the porch."

"Was anyone in the street? On the sidewalk?"

He looked straight ahead, blinked his eyes, then stared straight ahead for a full ten seconds before he blinked a second time.

"The Dragons were outside, weren't they, Mr. Nguyen?"

From the next room came the creak of a coil spring being stretched. Then came the slam of a wooden screen door. The compressor of the refrigerator kicked on as someone opened it. Rock music from a radio started up and drifted into the living room. Nguyen gazed straight ahead as if he never heard any of it.

Hank took three steps into the room before he realized I was there. He froze, then ran his eyes from me to his grandfather and back.

"Come in, Huang," Nguyen said.

Hank cast his eyes down with an Oriental deference, but then he swaggered across the room and sprawled across a chair like any defiant American teenager. Nuygen's face registered displeasure with his grandson, but he kept quiet.

Hank eyed me with a movement so slight I hardly noticed it, sizing up the situation, wondering what I had told his grandfather about our earlier encounter. Even at his age, he knew not to admit anything or give away any secrets until they were out in the open for sure.

"Be polite, Huang," his grandfather said. "Stand up and greet our visitor, Mr. Delmas." Hank stood and gave me a tiny nod.

"Hello, Huang," I said. "Please, sit back down."

He slouched back into the chair and draped one arm over the side.

"Mr. Delmas is asking about the bomb. The bomb that killed Mr. Perinovich."

"I was here that night, Grandfather."

"Yes, that is so."

"Did you hear anything, Huang?" I asked. "Did you hear people talking? Maybe a car driving down the street?"

"Just the fire trucks."

"Maybe people were sitting on the cars," Nguyen said.

"There was a lot of noise," Hank said. "There were lots of firemen and policemen. I don't remember any people on cars."

"Mr. Nguyen, these people in the street, could they have been the Dragon gang?"

Nuygen assumed an impenetrable gaze, the same one his grandson had when I nabbed him at Perinovich's house. Hank tilted his head back and sighed deeply.

"Mr. Nuygen," I said "the Dragons are dangerous people."

"That is true."

"Do you think the Dragons might have caused the explosion?"

"I don't know about that," he said.

"I've got to have some help, Mr. Nguyen. Hank, what about you? Do you know anything about the Dragons?"

Hank was quick, I'll give him that. When he realized I had not told his grandfather he was hanging out with the Dragons, his eyes told me I had earned some trust.

"I've heard of the Dragons," he said. "I know some of them."

Nguyen cut his eyes in warning toward his grandson.

"Mr. Nguyen," I said, "the Dragons have committed crimes on this street."

He neither nodded nor blinked nor acknowledged that I had spoken.

"I hear that they try to get young boys to join them," I said.

"That is what they say."

"They steal from their own people. They sell drugs to their own people."

Nguyen held his eyes closed. Hank had not looked at his grandfather. His eyes pleaded to me to keep our secret.

"Bad young men," Nguyen said, his eyes still closed. "They tell me to pay them money so they let my store run in peace. I tell them I will not give them money. Other stores give them the money. Every week they give them money."

"Who comes for the money?"

"The young ones," he said.

Hank stared at his Air Jordan shoes. They were white and spotless and the soles as crisp and unmarred as if just taken from the box.

SEVENTEEN

I didn't have the ten years or so it would take to get anything out of Nguyen and Hank, so the next day I decided to drive back to Perinovich's house to resume the on-site inspection that had been interrupted by Sammy and his damn two-by-four. Maybe some of the neighbors would tell me who had been trying to buy property in the area. I was a quarter mile past Biloxi's city limit, headed east to Point Cadet from Bay Saint Louis, when a patrol car fell in behind me. It was a Biloxi Police Department car, an older one with a scrape on the bumper, driver's side. My gut tightened up a little. It always does when a cop starts following me.

My eyes shifted between the road and the rearview mirror. He lagged behind a hundred feet, following me into the left lane when I passed slow cars and pulling in behind me when I eased back into the right lane. I checked my speed every five seconds and kept it under the limit. He kept the same distance, speeding up and slowing down when I did.

My tag wasn't expired and my brake lights worked. I wasn't speeding and I wasn't weaving all over the road. Maybe they knew I was going back to Perinovich's house. That had to be it. But how could they know? Hell, I had just decided to go there an hour earlier. Besides, they didn't know I had gone there the first time.

And so what if I was going there? What business was it of theirs?

They were through with their investigation. I had as much right to be there as they did. If they thought they could back me down by tailing me, they didn't know who they were messing with. My hands tightened on the steering wheel. Bernie Pettus could try to play his little games, but I had already determined that those first two fires were arson. And, by God, I was going to find out what happened to Perinovich's place.

You'd think that with the bad history Bernie and Perinovich had, a history anybody who reads the *Sun-Herald* knows all about, that Bernie'd go out of his way to show the public that he was fair, that he wanted to get to the bottom of the explosion. But no, he was dragging his damn feet, probably just to hang up the payment of the insurance check out of nothing but pure spite. No wonder Perinovich couldn't stand him. If there's one thing I hate, its some play-it-by-the-book bureaucrat.

And if that two-bit, back-slapping windbag thinks he can intimidate me by sending one of his cops to shadow me, he's got another think—Hey, where'd the squad car go? It had disappeared from the mirror. Nothing there but a yellow Volkswagen Beetle and a gray Crown Victoria. I glanced at the blind spot. Nothing there either. The tightness in my stomach eased and the grip I had on the wheel softened.

And I felt like the biggest damn fool.

The casinos were having a big day and parking on the streets between the beach and Howard Avenue was scarce. Behind St. Michael's Church, one block in from the beach, a tight space in a long line of parked cars opened up and I parallel parked between a red F150 pickup and a silver Park Avenue with Alabama tags. I didn't get as close to the curb as I wanted to.

I leaned over to the glove compartment for my camera and sensed a car slowing beside me. It was an orange Camaro with tinted windows all around. It stopped three feet beyond my front bumper and a second car, a gray Prelude, pulled in behind it and double parked beside me, blocking me in.

The driver of the Camaro got out. He was a stocky kid, bordering on fat, with a thick neck and close cropped hair. He had the cheek bones and almond shaped eyes of the Vietnamese, but his size and coloration indicated that he had some Caucasian blood. The other kid, smaller and pure Vietnamese, stepped out from the passenger side and let out two guys from the backseat.

The driver's door of the Prelude opened and the driver stepped out. The passenger had to crawl over the console to get out because they had parked too close to me for him to open his door.

My adreneline started pumping as I imagined a scene from an old black and white Cagney movie where Chicago mobsters pulled up beside some Model A with running boards and unloaded a Tommy Gun into it.

I slid to my passenger door, fumbling along the floorboard until I found my .45. I hopped out, keeping the gun out of view, and stepped toward the front of my truck.

Of the six kids, the driver of the Camaro was the biggest, but any one of the six was old enough and big enough to be dangerous. I slipped the .45 into my waistband, unseen, and pulled my tee shirt over it.

The six spread out slowly, using their cars as cover. Two of them trailed off toward the back of the Prelude. I had to move my eyes to keep all of them in sight.

"Is there something I can do for you guys?" I asked.

"Hear you been looking for Sammy," the big one said.

"That's right," I said. "My problem's with Sammy. It's not with any of you."

"You got a problem with Sammy, you got a problem with us."

My mouth grew dry and I felt a trickle of sweat running down from my arm pits. My heart quickened as I scanned their eyes to pick out any weak links. The two directly across from me, shielded behind the Prelude and my truck, were ready to haul ass at the first sign of real trouble. Their eyes were showing full borders of white, and I could practically hear their hearts pounding. But the two to my right near the Camaro and the two stationed to my left at the rear of the Prelude all had the mean eyes of experienced gang bangers.

The guys to the left drifted back, further spreading the angle of my view so I had to turn my head to see all six. I eased my hand to my waist, which was hidden by my truck, and lightly grasped the .45, keeping it under my shirt. If they saw it, somebody would open fire. That is, if they were carrying guns.

I had to wait for some sign I was about to get popped before I dared to use my gun. I shoot some unarmed kid and the best I could hope for was a lifetime of bankrupcy. But *if* they pulled a gun, and *if* my reactions were quick enough, and *if* their aim bad enough, I would have a chance. I could fire off a few rounds at the back two and hit the ground and maybe the front pair would back off long enough for me to find cover. A tingle of apprehension and adrenaline ran up my spine to the back of my neck.

"Now listen, guys," I said. "I don't have any problem with any of you. If Sammy wants to settle this, he knows where to find me. But we all need to back off here before somebody gets hurt."

The two by the Camaro eased to the front of their car. They couldn't make a run at me cause they had double parked too close. Out of the corner of my eye I caught one of the kids to my rear flank lift up a metal object. My hand twitched, but I stifled the urge to pull out the big pistol. It was a tire tool he was holding. He slammed it against the tail light of my truck and there was a tinkle of glass hitting the pavement.

I crouched and used the line of parked cars as cover as I scooted down the sidewalk past the rear of my truck. The kid kept pounding my tail light, trying to bust out every shard of red glass.

I ducked between two parked cars fifty feet away. Kept my eyes on the kids through the windows and windshields. Flipped the safety off the .45. Lost sight of one of the kids, so I ran my eyes up and down the row of cars trying to see if he was shadowing me.

Don't shoot until you see his hands, I kept telling myself. I steeled my nerve to hold my fire if he sprang at me. *Make damn sure he's got a gun.*

My heart was thumping and my tongue felt like sandpaper. The big kid moved to the middle of the street. He shouted something in Vietnamese to the others and pointed at me. The guy smashing my tail light turned around, and he and the big kid started walking toward me. One of the other kids opened the door of the Camaro and reached down to the floorboard on the passenger side.

I eyed the spot on the trunk of the Prelude where I'd fire the warning shot. I popped up, raised my gun, and drew a bead over the roof of the car, aiming at the silver circle where the lock was.

The big kid seemed to look past me. His eyes bulged and he wheeled around and dashed toward the Camaro. The other kid turned and sprinted and dropped the tire tool clanging on the concrete. I lowered my pistol and ducked back down below the car's roof level. I hadn't located that missing gangbanger, so I didn't need to be standing up too long.

I duckwalked to the street side of the car I was hiding behind. I kept my eyes straight ahead, looking at the kids through the windows of the line of parked cars to make sure they didn't pull out a shotgun or something. I didn't need any of that shit for sure, not sitting there with only a seven-round clip to my name.

They started their engines. I stuck my head out to peek around the car. A terrific blare from a siren, point blank against the back of my head, split my damn eardrums wide open. Felt like somebody rabbit punched my young ass with brass knuckles. I flinched and dived to the side and put my index fingers in both ears and wiggled them around to get back my hearing.

The cop said something through the open window of his squad car, but I couldn't make out what it was. I slipped the gun back in my waistband, covered it with my tee shirt, and stood.

It was Morgan. He stopped his squad car beside me and pushed the gear lever into park. He mouthed something else which I couldn't distinguish any clearer than if he had been talking through water.

"What?" I cupped my hand behind my ear.

"WHAT'S THE TROUBLE?"

"Not anymore," I said. "I thought there was."

"I SAID WHAT'S THE TROUBLE."

"No trouble."

He stepped out of his car and left the light bar flashing. "That your truck up there with all that glass around it?"

I nodded. He walked to it and I followed. He nudged a piece of the broken glass with the toe of his shoe.

"You want to tell me about this?"

I pinched my nostrils shut and blew to clear my ears. "You got some disrespectful kids running around this town, Morgan."

He glanced at the bulge at my waistband. He puffed his cheeks and blew out a short breath. He shook his head and stepped over to the taillight and ran his finger down the jagged edge of broken red glass.

"I don't guess you recognized any of them," he said.

"We don't run in the same circles."

"You wouldn't be going over to the Perinovich house, I don't suppose."

"You ought to know," I said. "Y'all have been tailing me ever since I crossed the city limits."

He frowned and gave me a puzzled look. "I don't know what you're talking about."

"I've got permission to go on that property. I'm not about to back off just because some cop decides to tail me."

Morgan bent down to the pavement and picked up a few pieces of glass. "Look, Jack, just stay out of this one. OK?"

"I'm only doing my job."

He threw a piece of glass at the curb across the street. "Barron tells me you're allright, so I'll tell you this. You'll be getting a report in the next few days. It won't be my report, but it'll be the one the department is releasing."

"Any particular reason you told me that?"

"Like I said, Barial tells me you're—"

"I mean the part about it not being your report."

"I've already told you more than I ought to." He dropped the rest of the broken glass to the pavement and tilted his head toward my truck. "You need to file a report on that taillight. Your insurance won't pay off without a report."

I figured I'd start with taking pictures. They always help, even after a scene becomes cold. Sometimes a picture taken from across the street will give you a better perspective than you can get when you're close enough to touch the house. After a few long-distance shots, I would go in and check the fittings where there was a gas line leading into the house.

I had snapped three shots from outside the fence when the patrol car turned the corner. It had that scrape on the front bumper. Hey, now, maybe I wasn't as big a fool as I thought. Maybe they had really had been tailing me. They pulled in behind my truck, and the driver talked on the radio as the chief of police himself got out from the passenger side. We had met a dozen times over the years, but he never seemed to remember my name.

"What's up, Chief?" I kept snapping photos. "Not much, I'd guess, since you've got time to tail me."

"What are you talking about?"

"You know damn well what I'm talking about."

He drew in a breath, tilted his head, and blew it out. "You'll have to leave. We're securing the scene."

I adjusted the zoom lens. "Yeah, right."

"I mean it. You'll have to leave."

"I don't understand what's going on here," I said. "This scene is as cold as they get, but you won't even let me have a report. And here you are still poking around."

The driver, tall and skinny, walked up to us. "I thought you told me Eastern States was the carrier here," the chief said. "Where's Newman? This ain't Newman."

"This is that guy Morgan was telling you about," the driver said.

"What the hell're you doing around here? What business you got wanting a report?"

"God, what a zoo," I said.

"You got some kinda problem?"

"Yeah, I sure do. I got a problem with you following me all over town."

The chief scrunched his eyebrows like he was trying to figure out a chemical equation. He looked at the other cop, who shrugged and rolled his eyes.

"I've also got a problem with the way your department is stone-walling this whole damn thing."

"You keep interfering with this investigation and I'll show you a problem. I'll run you in on obstruction of justice charges next time I see your ass this side of Oak Street."

"Come on, Chief. I got a client who only wants to know if the explosion was an accident or if it was deliberately set. All you got to say is that you're investigating it as an arson, and I'll get out of your hair."

The chief turned to the skinny cop, who shook his head no.

"I ain't gotta tell you shit," the chief said. "Get outta here before I run your ass in."

"When can I get the report?"

"God, you deaf or something? I just told you to get the hell outta here. Now, if you don't get back in that truck and leave, I'm gonna put you under arrest."

The chief gave me the practiced glare of the thirty-year cop. I turned and stepped to my truck. If the cops had some reason to go back into the case, I figured I'd hear about it soon enough. Besides, I was thrown into the bull pen of the New Orleans jail once. Didn't stay in there long, but long enough to where I won't voluntarily get my ass put back into any jail. As I pulled away from the curb, the chief opened the passenger-side door of the squad car and grabbed the mike.

When I got to Highway 90 and headed west, a smattering of rain from an isolated gray cloud splattered my windshield and made steam rise from the pavement. With the cops hanging around Perinovich's house, there was no way I could talk to the neighbors about who had been trying to buy property in the area. It was as good a time as any to try to squeeze something out of Bobby Weldon. I kept the window rolled down and jammed in a Stevie Ray Nix tape. I glanced in my rearview and caught a Biloxi police car turning onto the beach drive and falling in behind me a few car lengths back.

EIGHTEEN

My heart sinks every time I see it, and I've seen it hundreds of times. That splendid, awful photograph taken from an airplane on an August afternoon that is now so many years ago. The clouds whirling around the eye are a wall of smooth plaster. The sky above it is baby blue. The sun shines from behind the plane, over the cameraman's shoulder, and ricochets off the wall of clouds. The reflected yellow light comes back through the prism of millions of droplets and comes out a soft green haze, the same moss green of a fern or a tropical harbor. It is an inviting scene, beckoning like a clear pool on a hot day. But it is the malevolent green eye of Hurricane Camille.

Billy Weldon had other pictures on the wall of his office besides the famous shot the Hurricane Hunters took. The little league teams he sponsored, the white-water rafting trips he took, a cyclorama of a dozen photographs that chronicled his visits to the trendy vacation spots of the past twelve years, each visit occurring in the year when the place was trendy. A plaque from the Realtors' Association proclaimed him as the current president, and a Chamber of Commerce certificate showed he was on the board of directors.

But I kept going back to the Camille photo.

It is Sunday morning, August 17. The eye of the storm is tight, solid, seamless. The storm will annihilate the coast that night. I am with Neal and my father that day, and Camille is south of Ship Island as we wake up. It had headed east the night before, toying with us, pretending it would skim past us and hit Florida. But it stalled, and it's now looking for a spot to come on shore.

The winds are at gale force when we wake up, and it's black as midnight. The front yard is already littered with green leaves and limbs and the rain is strong and steady in the streetlights. Our boats are anchored up the Jourdan River seven miles in from Bay Saint Louis and our storm windows are drawn tight. Mama and my baby sister went to Hattiesburg the day before and we're on our way. But first we have to go to Biloxi to help a cousin board up windows and move everything we can off the floor and onto tables and cabinets.

We leave Bay Saint Louis that morning before sunrise. Waves are crashing against the seawall and shooting foam and spray straight up. We use our low beams because the wind-driven rain throws the brights back into our eyes. The wipers beat as steady as a pulse. We follow the two yellows spots of light along the beach highway to Biloxi. The wind's already too strong for us to nail plywood over our cousin's windows. We have to settle for silver duct tape.

On the way out of Biloxi, we stop by Perinovich's house to see if he needs help. Cass is taking the *Miss Marie* up the Biloxi River to ride out the storm. The boat is new and uninsured and he has all his money tied up in it. Marie and Mike are going to the new civic center, two blocks in from Back Bay. Marie works for the city and knows that the specs for the new center are way above the minimum. The higher specs were put in at the insistence of the new public buildings director.

Mike is begging his father to let him go up the river to ride the storm out. I want to go too and whine to Daddy to let me. Cass tells Mike he's got to stay with his mama to make sure she's all right and doesn't get scared. Daddy tells me to quit talking crazy and to get back into the truck.

The scent of the hurricane quickens my pulse and clears my eyes. I hear the whoosh of the wind, I smell the pure warm air all the way from the Leeward Islands, the very smell of danger, of adventure. And even at that age I know. I know why people don't evacuate. Everybody knows the damn things are dangerous. But our Monday-through-Friday worlds of central air and supermarkets, of manicured lawns and retirement plans, have just bored us all to hell.

We leave the Perinovich house and drive back to the highway. The rain has lessened, but the winds are picking up. Ten o'clock in the morning and the streetlights are still on. Sand has blown across the road and smeared it with a dingy white coating. The flags at the city marina stand straight out, stiff as sheets of plywood except for the ruffling on their edges. Two big red squares with smaller black squares in their centers.

We stop at the Broadwater Beach Hotel, the only place still open, to get Cokes and coffee to go. The lighted marquee says Welcome Mississippi Florists and Nurserymen's Association. Daddy stops at the front desk to change a dollar. The woman behind the front desk is talking with the president of the association and his teenaged son. They've got to evacuate and cancel the convention.

A man comes running through the lobby, a suitcase in each hand. He throws a hundred dollar bill and his room key at the cashier and doesn't wait for any change. He runs out of the lobby, tosses the suitcases in the backseat of a white Mustang, and burns rubber out of the parking lot onto Highway 90. The car has Ohio license plates.

"That's some shot, isn't it," Weldon said. He had walked in behind me and stepped behind his desk. "The Hurricane Hunters took it just before sundown the day it hit."

"I would have rather been in that plane than down here."

"I rode it out," he said. "We lived in D'Iberville."

Everybody who lived on the coast when Camille hit says they rode it out. Makes me wonder who was driving that bumper-to-bumper line of cars that stretched all the way to Jackson.

"What can I do for you today, Mr. Delmas?"

"I need to know who was trying to buy Casper Perinovich's house."

He pinched his lower lip and studied the ceiling. "I guess it's not any secret that I offered to buy it. I don't know who else might have made an offer."

"Mr. Weldon, let me get to the point. You're trying to buy Mr. Perinovich's land and the land of several of his neighbors, but you don't want the land for yourself. You're trying to buy it for someone else, someone who wants to put a casino in the area."

"You're guessing."

"Guessed right, though, didn't I?"

"I don't have to answer any questions about this. What business is it of yours?"

"I've been hired to see if the explosion was an accident."

Billy's lips got tight and he breathed in loudly through his nose. "I don't appreciate being accused of a crime."

"I didn't accuse anybody of anything. I'm just checking out all the leads. Let me put it this way. I *know* you're trying to put together a block of land for a casino. I need to find out who's bankrolling you."

"What makes you think you know what I'm doing?"

"You told some people. Secrets don't last on Point Cadet."

He tapped his desk with the eraser end of a pencil. "What if I am? I don't have to tell you a thing. I can't. It would be unethical."

I pulled the sheet of paper from my back pocket, unfolded it, and laid it on his desk. "If you don't tell me, you can kiss the Perinovich property good-bye."

He snatched the paper and jammed on a set of reading glasses. The more he read the more he frowned.

"That's Sheila Zimarich's signature," I said. "You can call her if you like."

"I still can't tell you everything you want to know."

I pushed up in the chair and leaned forward to stand. He motioned me back down.

"Be reasonable," he said. "I can't tell you any more than I could tell Miss Zimarich."

"So tell me what you can."

"There is a casino that wants to develop that land. That's about it."

"Name?"

"Can't tell anybody yet."

I closed my eyes. I squeezed the bridge of my nose with my thumb and forefinger. Damn, I didn't want to have to wade through all this.

"Would you like some coffee, Mr. Delmas? How about some bottled water?" He picked up his phone and asked the receptionist to bring it in. "I'm afraid we got off on the wrong foot. I was just trying to protect my client. The same way I'll protect Miss Zimarich's interests if she decides to sell."

Not a bad shift of gears. He knew he needed me, and was ready to talk. Which was fine with me, since I was on a fishing trip.

"Why didn't Mr. Perinovich want to sell?" I asked.

"We had gotten to be pretty good friends. I really liked the old fellow. Deep down he really did want to sell, Mr. Delmas. It was just a fear of the unknown. You know that's what has held up more great projects than anything else in history. If they had listened to Leonardo da Vinci, we would have been flying three hundred years ago. But most people lack vision. Sometimes they can't even see things when you spell it out for them."

"Did you spell out this vision for Mr. Perinovich?"

"Oh, I tried. But, bless his heart, he just couldn't see it. I tried everything. I even took him brochures from that new high-rise condo they're building in Gulfport. Beautiful place, right on the water. I can't tell you the figure we were discussing for his property, but I can say that he could have bought a unit with a spectacular view of the Gulf and still had a substantial sum left over."

"I haven't heard about any high-rise condominium in Gulfport."

"They're going to start construction as soon as they get a lease. It's on the beach and that's state property, which you know the Secretary of State doesn't like to lease. But once they see the economic development potential, once they realize the taxes it will generate, they will. Mr. Delmas, the schoolchildren of Harrison County need that condominium. And there'll still be plenty of beach for everybody."

"The Secretary of State having a little trouble with the vision thing, too?"

"Not many people have it, Mr. Delmas."

"Maybe Mr. Perinovich didn't want to sell to some out-of-state corporation."

"I never said they were out-of-state. This is Biloxi money, or at least most of it is." Weldon stood and walked to the corner. An easel had been set up and held a stack of seven or eight posters, the top one being plain white. "Since you have Miss Zimarich's power of attorney, I feel safe in showing this to you." He lifted the plain poster like a magician pulling back a curtain and flipped it aside.

It made me gasp, much to Weldon's delight.

I grew up knowing well that stretch of beach in Biloxi called "The Strip." I've seen miniature golf courses where the last hole was in the lap of a Buddha fifteen feet tall. I've seen souvenir shops in the form of a Conestoga wagon. Strip joints, gambling dens, and arcades. Along the strip, hot pink and lime green are considered primary colors. But I had never seen anything as gaudy as the image on that poster board.

The casino was the enchanted castle from Cinderella. It had at least a dozen spires and a drawbridge. I imagined Tinkerbell flitting around it and changing its colors with a touch of a wand. The second poster showed limousines covered with the shell of a carriage straight from the prince's ball. The cocktail lounge was to feature pink drinks poured into a glass slipper. The name written above the castle, across the sky in electric blue, was Shazzam.

"Is this what you showed Perinovich?" I asked.

"Exactly. It'll be the biggest hit east of the Mississippi."

"Do you have any pumpkins or mice in all this?"

"That's in the second phase. We're going after the generation that grew up with all this. We're selling the dream."

"You checked with the boys down in Orlando about these plans?"

"We're working up a proposal," he said. But what you see has been modified from the Disney stuff. We're not copying it. If they want to get in on it we both make money. If not, we go with our version."

I stepped to the easel and examined the rest of the posters. I didn't see any black mouse with white gloves and oversized ears or any white duck in a sailor's suit. That must have been phase three. I swallowed hard and fought the urge to comment, and I studied each poster as carefully as if it held the cure for cellulite.

"Can't you just see that castle?" he said. "Imagine driving over the bridge from Ocean Springs and seeing it change colors every twenty seconds."

"And you say Perinovich couldn't see this?"

"He was a different generation. What can I say?"

I drew in a cleansing breath and blew it out and stepped back to my chair.

"It's really something, isn't it?" he said.

"Indeed it is. How much land would you need?"

"Thirty acres, and we've got options on eighteen so far."

"How many houses are on that eighteen?"

"Haven't counted that. Some of the land is empty, too marshy for houses. We'll have to fill that in."

"Mr. Weldon, are you sure the EPA will let you fill in that land? Those little bayous are where the shrimp hide while they're growing. You take away their hiding places and pretty soon there aren't any shrimp in the gulf."

Weldon scrunched his lips to one side like he was shaving. He sighed and started nodding his head. "We'll buy some swamp over in Louisiana and use it for mitigation. The shrimp industry is dying, Mr. Delmas. We live in a global economy nowadays and our boats just can't compete with the imports. Mr. Perinovich didn't want to admit that, but it's happening whether we like it or not."

"So if things get tight, we'll be left with crap tables and Mexico will have the fishing fleet?"

Weldon laughed. "That's a good one. But that won't happen. You need to read this book." He reached back to the credenza and held up a copy of *We Can ALL Be Rich!* "J. Morgan Miller calls that view 'depression obsession.' We've got to think outside the box. Get ahead of the curve. Push the envelope. If we keep it up at the pace we're going, the Mississippi coast will make people forget about Las Vegas."

He slid the book across the desk. In the lower corner it had a round blue sticker the size of a quarter that said "autographed copy." I picked it up and thumbed through it to give him time to cool down. A hundred years ago, Billy Weldon would have come into town on a horse-drawn wagon, banging a tin pan and hawking bottles of colored sugar water. No wonder Perinovich got that dog.

"So how close are you to getting the deal together?" I asked.

"We can do it, but if we don't get Miss Zimarich to come on board we may have to reconfigure the plat. I hope you'll talk with her. If she's left out of this project, her land won't be worth a fraction of what it can be."

"What has she told you?"

"I think she's warming up to the idea."

"Maybe you ought to wait her out."

Billy dropped the smile and put his elbows on the desk. He bit lightly on his upper lip. "I'll be frank with you, Mr. Delmas. Investors can't let money sit waiting on something to happen. The Gaming Commission can't hold off other investors who want a shot at the area. The Perinovich property is the last big piece to the puzzle. If we don't get that piece soon, the whole project will collapse. They won't extend the opening date on the permit unless substantial progress toward groundbreaking has been made."

"So unless it happens soon, there'll be no Shazzam?"

He cast his eyes downward as he nodded his head. "And once more Mississippi will lose out on a golden opportunity."

NINETEEN

I guess I could have gotten the name of the buyer out of Weldon if I had wanted to hang around a little longer. But he had told me it was Biloxi money and that there was a time limit the Gaming Commission had set. I could take it from there. I was already having to play games with Bayou Casualty, and I didn't feel like starting any new ones with Billy Weldon.

I was paying attention to the warnings this time, watching them closely. You get burned as many times as I have and you pick up on signals a lot sooner than you used to. If you don't watch for little shifts in the wind, the next thing you know you're miles from any safe harbor, reefing the sails and putting out the sea anchor. I still had time, but I couldn't wait much longer. Bayou Casualty, my main client, was on its way to becoming a pain in the butt. It was time to prepare for rough weather.

I had finished the work on the Point and had sent in the reports. But now they were nitpicking me about my expenses. It always starts with the damn bean counters. If the company had sent me to San Francisco or New York, they wouldn't bat an eye at a thirty-dollar plate of seaweed at some sushi bar. But you let me charge them seventeen bucks for a stuffed flounder at McElroy's Harbor House, something worth the money, and the damn green eye-shades and ledger sheets come out.

Neal always says if you have a dozen clients, you own the business; if you have only one, the client owns the business. It was time to get some more clients.

"It could have been a professional torch," Barron said. He reached to the booth behind him and stole the bottle of ketchup. "Not the best job I've seen, but good enough."

"So you're saying it was no accident," I said.

"Man, you are quick. That's exactly what I'm saying."

"And you think it might have been a pro?"

"Is there an echo in here? I already said that. I said it *could* have been a pro. But pro or not, it was definitely set. They filled the house up with gas and had a timing device to set it off."

Johnnie was gobbling my French fries as fast as he could pop them into his mouth. I was only halfway through with my ham po'boy and he had already polished off a Vancleave Special, that perfect balance of crabmeat, cheese, mayonnaise, and French bread that deserves more respect than to be called a mere po'boy. "Man, I was starving to death," he said.

"You find this out from the police report?" I asked.

"Don't ask me that question, man. Let's just say I've seen some things that let me know that it was set. And the damn explosion wasn't your fault."

Those were the words I had prayed to hear. My heart rose and it was all I could do to keep from jumping out of my seat.

Irene brought us the second round of Barq's root beer without a signal from me. She and her sidekick Vern started waiting tables at the Biloxi Schooner back when it was still called Rosetti's and they knew I always took a second round. Somebody had propped open the door to the kitchen. The smell of a gumbo roux floated through the room and there was a sharp clatter of silverware being dropped into a stainless steel sink.

"What kind of timing device are you talking about?" I asked.

"You do still call yourself an investigator, don't you? I mean anything that could set off the gas. The bell on some types of telephone, that'd work. They might have been counting on the thermostat to do the trick. That little blue spark when the air-conditioner kicks on in a dark room, that'll do it."

"Johnnie, I know that. You're talking Arson one-oh-one here. If it's that easy to figure, why do you think it might have been a professional?"

"Maybe the torch don't care if anybody knows it was set. Just long as he wasn't around when it went off."

"If it was an out-of-town pro, I'll never catch him. He's long gone."

"Forget about finding the torch," Johnnie said. "You need to find the guy who hired the torch. Besides, a job like this, maybe it wasn't out-of-town talent." He took a swig of root beer. "Jack, you're too close to this case. It's messing up your thinking. Know what I'm sayin'? You should have spotted this from your car."

"I don't follow you."

"When you drove up to the house, what did you see?"

"Two walls were blown out and the roof was sitting on top of what was left."

"And the condition of the roof?"

I leaned my head back and closed my eyes. How could I have missed that?

"Intact," I said. "Not a shingle out of place. And the side wall was blown out down low."

"Which means it wasn't a natural-gas explosion," he said. "You know that."

Yeah, I did know that. Natural gas is lighter than air. When a room filled with natural gas explodes, it goes straight up or out through the top portion of the walls. If the blast blows out the walls down at floor level, it was a heavier gas, like propane. Man, even Morgan should have spotted that.

"And those frames, they were nearly charcoal," he said. "And they were laying not six feet from the house. What does that tell you?"

"You're right. I should have spotted it right off."

"What does it tell you?"

"It tells me that the air-to-gas mixture was rich. That the explosion was more of a fireball than a blast."

"Just checking to make sure you ain't forgot everything," he said.

"But Perinovich didn't have propane. I've never seen any tank by his house."

"That's why I know it was a torch. I figured the guy who did it drilled a hole in the floor and ran a hose up into the house. So I crawled under and sure enough I found a fresh bored hole a foot in from the wall. He even sealed it up with a glob of Plastic Wood. Trouble was, he let all the gas run out of the tank and put too much propane in there. Then I'm thinking he went somewhere and dialed Perinovich's phone to set off the explosion."

"And there wasn't enough oxygen to set it off," I said. "Not until Mr. Cass opened the door and flipped on the light switch."

"They might have just wanted to blow up the house, Jack. Know what I'm sayin'? They might not have meant to kill him."

"Johnnie," I said, "they killed him. Do you really think I give a damn whether they *meant* to do it or not?"

TWENTY

I needed to tell Sheila what Johnnie Barron had found. Then it would be time for us to take it to the police, and I could start putting out feelers for some more clients. I wondered if the bean counters were going to say anything about me picking up Johnnie's tab at the Schooner.

I had Sheila's key, but I still knocked on the door. After all, I was sober this time. Joey, her son, answered the door.

"I met you the other night at Uncle Cass's funeral," he said.

"I'm Jack Delmas. Your mother and I are old friends."

"Yes, she told me. She's still asleep. Mama doesn't get up early unless she has to."

"I don't know anybody who does. I'll come back later. Please tell her I dropped by."

"Oh, no, please come in and have a seat. I'm sure she'd want to see you." He led me to the living room and I sat on the couch. "I'm afraid I can't stay very long, Mr. Delmas. I'm on my way to a job interview at the Gulf Coast Research Lab. Would you like some of this pizza?"

I thanked him and picked up a slice and dipped it in the plastic bowl of French dressing beside it.

"You must be from here on the coast. Mama taught me about the French dressing. She says the Mississippi coast is the only place they eat it on pizza."

"I was in college before I realized that," I said. "I learned how to eat it that way from your Uncle Cass. He taught me a lot of things."

Joey nodded. "He's the reason I studied marine biology. When I was twelve, Mama brought me here to stay with Uncle Cass for a few months. It was summertime. He taught me how to crew on his shrimp boat, and I got hooked. By the end of the summer, I could handle the boat. I could do everything but back it into the slip."

"Not many people can do that," I said. "Wooden shrimp boats with straight inboards aren't the easiest boats to maneuver in close quarters. Especially in reverse."

"But he let me try. I could back it in, but I'd bump the pilings. It hurt Uncle Cass each time I bumped into one of those creosoted posts. But he kept encouraging me to try."

Joey looked out at the gulf and that summer from ten years earlier replayed itself in his eyes. "When Mama came back I told her about my plans to become a shrimper."

"What did she say about that?"

"She said there was no way any son of hers was going to be a shrimper. But she was okay with me hanging around boats, as long as they were Chris-Crafts or Hatterases. Every summer I'd crew on some of the yachts in Miami Harbor. You'd be surprised, Mr. Delmas, how many of those people who own those big boats don't have the first clue as to how to handle them."

"Folks will pay a lot and do a lot to have things other people envy. It doesn't matter whether they know what to do with these things."

"From what Mama has told me, you don't have that problem."

"Everybody does to some extent. But she's right. I don't have any great need to spread my tail feathers. What does your mother think about you coming back to Biloxi?"

"Oh, it's fine with her. After all, she's coming back here herself."

He picked up on the surprise on my face.

"She hasn't told you? Mama is thinking about opening a hotel here in Biloxi. She says that with the casinos coming in, it's the fastest-growing resort in the nation. Maybe she wanted to come back all along and it's just a coincidence that her hometown has become a dream location for a new hotel."

"So she really was talking business with him," I said.

"I beg your pardon?"

"Oh, nothing."

Why did Sheila keep that from me?

"I mean it came as a surprise to me. Mama never wanted to come back here. I hate to say this, but she never even seemed to care much about seeing Uncle Cass. She brought me here from time to time, but she never stayed more than a day or two."

"Your Mama loved your uncle Cass."

Joey sipped his coffee, and walked toward the picture window and looked out at the gulf. "Mr. Delmas, you're a private detective, aren't you?"

"Yes, I am."

"Did Mama ever—"

"I thought I heard some people talking," Sheila said. She stood at the bedroom door in a terry cloth wrap with her hair turbaned in a towel. "I'm surprised you're still here, Joey. Don't be late for your interview, honey."

"I was just leaving." Joey drained his coffee. He kissed Sheila on the cheek and started for the door. "Good to see you, Mr. Delmas. I'll be back in a few hours, Mama."

Sheila stared at the door after he shut it behind him.

"You got a good kid," I said.

"He's the one consistent love of my life." She smiled, still looking toward the door. "Next to you, of course."

"I hope he gets the job."

She laughed. "Of course he'll get the job. For one thing, he's greatly qualified for it, and for another thing, I've taken steps to ensure that the job is his."

"Steps?"

"I've learned how the game is played. I've learned all about calling in favors. Of course, he doesn't know anything about it."

She could tell by my frown that I wasn't entirely pleased.

"Oh, don't look at me like that. For all he knows, he's going to get that job entirely on his own, and I'll never tell him anything different. I wish I'd have had some help somewhere along the line."

"You seem to have done all right for yourself. I'm sure Joey can, too."

"If there's one thing I understand, it's the male ego. No man ever wants to admit that he needs help. I know that you feel that way, and I love you for it. But I've got big plans for Joey."

"Are they his plans?"

"Not yet. And maybe he'll never want to be the biggest hotel owner in the South, but I'm going to give him that chance. Get another cup of coffee and I'll be right back."

She disappeared into the bedroom and her hair dryer clicked on. I stepped onto the balcony. In the parking lot Joey was getting into his car. I watched as he pulled into the street on his way to become a marine biologist or biggest hotel owner in the South or something. Was Peronivich looking down at him too?

It was like watching at a kid getting on a school bus that first time. I felt like I needed to go catch him and tell him about first jobs out of college, and careers, and working for other people, and following your own dream. But what would I tell him? The life I live isn't for everybody. Like Barron said, it could get a little crowded on that beach.

Sheila worked fast and was back before I finished my second cup of coffee. Her hair, makeup, and clothes were all perfect.

"So what will we do today?" she asked.

"Maybe we can do something later, but first I've got some work I've got to do. You hired me to find out something about your Uncle Cass, remember?"

"But I didn't put you under any time limits. Why don't you take the day off?"

"I found out that the explosion may have been deliberately set."

"Of course it was. I told you that at the beginning."

"How did you know?"

She raised her eyebrows. "I've got great intuition. Right now my intuition says there's something you're not telling me."

"Why didn't you tell me you were interested in coming back here and starting a hotel?"

Her voice got lower, with a twinge of irritation. "Joey told you that, didn't he? He's a dear boy, but he's not experienced in the ways of the world. I'll have to remind him to be a little more discreet."

"I don't see why you were keeping that from me."

"I wasn't keeping anything from you. I just didn't think it was important to your investigation."

"I don't know what's important to the investigation. That's why I've got to know the whole picture. You never know what might lead to something."

"Oh, all *right!* Yes, I'm looking into putting a hotel here. Every big-time hotel in the country is looking down here. Why should I be any different, especially since this is my hometown."

"Just where would this hotel go?"

She stared at me and the corners of her mouth tightened. "Jack, surely you don't think that Uncle Cass's property—"

"I don't see why not."

"Jack, dear boy, there's just not enough property here."

No, I thought, but Cass's lot was the last piece in somebody's puzzle.

"Sheila, you've never wanted to come back here."

She turned away and walked over to the window, where she held back the sheer and stared out at the gulf. "I've always wanted to come back, when I could come back with style. I'd like to say I don't care what everybody around here thinks of me, but Biloxi is the only place on earth where I do care. It's the only place I know well enough to know exactly what drives people. It's money and power, Jack, and the money comes first."

"But all cities are like that," I said.

"Of course they are. But I feel it more here because this is where I learned that lesson. I thought if I were a good person, if I treated other people well, that they'd respect me. Maybe they'd even like me. But right after Christmas when I was sixteen I found out different. Do you remember a girl named Lana Milam?"

"Was she the doctor's daughter? Lived down on the Beach?"

"We were in homeroom together and got to be friends. It was before I learned that rich people and poor people don't get to be friends. There's always a distance there. You may find one who'll hang around with you, but their group won't. When it comes to a choice between you and their rich friends, you'll lose every time.

"Looking back on it, it wasn't Lana's fault. It's just the way things are. Neither one of us could buck the system, although she may not have realized that. It's hard to realize you're the victim of a system when you're living in a mansion on the beach.

"What happened that Christmas?" I asked.

"Lana got a car. It was a red Mustang convertible with white leather seats. God, that was a beautiful car. Every night, Lana parked it in that circular drive right at their front door.

"Of course, Mama didn't have a car. Needless to say, I didn't either. We took the city bus or drove Uncle Cass's pickup truck. Mama was working the night shift at the Waffle House in Gulfport. I'd get home from school and Uncle Cass was usually out on his boat. After Aunt Marie and Mike died, he nearly lived on that boat. We hardly ever saw him.

"I'd drive Mama to the Waffle House. We'd take Pass Road on the way over, but on the way back I'd take the beach road. I'd go by the Milam mansion with those huge white columns, and when Lana wasn't riding with her friends, the Mustang would be there.

I wondered how it would feel to have a car like that, to live in a house like that. I'd dream about what the house looked like inside. I'd spin elaborate dreams about how they had servants and how every meal was formal. They'd all dress up and eat by candlelight. Isn't that silly? But I believed it.

"My Christmas present was a brand-new outfit from JC Penney, a plaid skirt with a matching blouse and sweater. And Mama was so proud to give it to me." Sheila paused and swallowed hard. She let the sheer drop and a tremor crept into her voice. "How many tables did Mama have to wait on to pay for that?" It was not a question directed to me.

"That outfit was so pretty and I was so proud of it and when we went back to school after New Year's, I wore it the first day. For some reason I didn't take the school bus. Uncle Cass gave me a ride. His old truck was in pretty bad shape. It needed a ring job, and it put out a lot of exhaust. It was cool that day and that made the truck smoke even worse than normal. He drove me to the front of the school where the parents put the kids out.

"Across the street in the parking lot, Lana was in her convertible with the top down. She was sitting there in the car with two other girls, the two biggest snobs in town. Janette Bowland, that haint, and that bitch Kathleen Mills. When Uncle Cass let me out, his truck was between the girls in the Mustang and me. I shut the door and he took off, and the truck put out a big cloud of smoke. I was standing there in the middle of this gray-blue cloud.

"I waved at Lana. She gave me a nervous smile and wiggled her fingers in sort of a half wave. Kathleen was in the backseat. She leaned up to Janette, who was in the passenger's seat, and whispered something to her. They both started laughing. Then they looked at me and started laughing again."

"What about Lana?" I asked. "Did she laugh?"

"No, she didn't. To tell you the truth, she looked as embarrassed as I was. She looked away, looked off down the street. She complimented me on my dress that day in homeroom and she was still friendly to me, but it was never the same. From that day on, I never tried to fit in with the beach crowd. I decided to beat them at their own game. I quit dating anybody but rich boys. Actually, rich men. And it was one of those rich young men who got me pregnant. But his family was having no part of any marriage, at least not to me, so I left town."

She turned toward me with fierce, defiant eyes, a little red, a little moist. "So, see, I've always planned to come back. But I made a vow to myself that when I did, I'd be able to buy and sell every one of those sons of bitches down on the beach."

"God, Sheila, I'm sorry."

"Oh, don't be sorry for me. I'm on the verge of being able to do it."

I stood and walked to her. I put my arms around her and she hugged me tight. I kissed her and held her and touched the side of her face. It was hot and she was crying.

Write it on the wall, Bubba. There ain't nothing in this world that'll make a man feel he's got to move heaven and earth any faster than hearing some woman cry. Doesn't matter if the woman is newborn or ninety-five years old. Doesn't matter whether it's your fault or not. You find some man who doesn't feel that way, he ain't worth a solid damn.

I wanted to stroke her as I would a small child, to rub her and hold her close and make the hurt go away. She took my face in her hands, kissed me again, and softly pushed away. She turned her back to me and wiped her eyes lightly with her finger.

"She never even invited me to ride in that car," Sheila said. "Not once."

I didn't say anything, nor did I move toward her. I couldn't come up with the right words. She sobbed for a minute or two, then she sniffled and rubbed her face with her plams. She took a deep breath and blew it out and rubbed the back of her neck.

Then she turned around. And that flashy smile was back, as fresh and natural as if she had never seen a bad minute in her life.

"Now," she said, "what were you going to tell me about this case?"

TWENTY-ONE

T he diesel-powered generator of the TV remote unit blew hot against my face as I walked by it on my way to the police station. One technician, his salt-and-pepper hair in a ponytail, was outside the truck setting up for a live remote interview. The beat reporter for the *Sun-Herald* was just ahead of me, walking toward the building. I called out to him and he held up and waited for me.

Mick O'Cain is from several places up North. I've never figured out which of them is his hometown. He's a hard-drinking Vietnam vet who still wears blue jeans. His hair hangs down below his collar, but is always a little slick, like he uses hair oil or mousse, and he always smells like a full ashtray. Mick's never told me why he left Cleveland and the city desk of the *Plain Dealer*. I suspect it was one too many weeks of not showing up for work. He ended up in Biloxi because twenty years earlier he did a two-year stint at Keesler Air Force Base and said he'd felt too many lake-effect snows. Mick is one of that sizable portion of Biloxi's population, the snowbirds.

"Why are they calling a press conference?" I asked.

"Bernie and the police chief are making some kind of announcement. You can bet it's something Bernie thinks he can use for reelection. Probably some kind of grant to buy new police cars, maybe a drug bust. Hell, I don't even try to find out anymore. I just sit there and let the games begin."

He pulled a notepad out of his back pocket and a pencil out of his shirt pocket. He stuck the pencil behind his ear. Mick has the hard-bitten look of one who has seen everything and heard everything. He's big city stuck in a small town, and we have the kind of rootless friendship you develop with such people. Mick O'Cain will go to his grave with nothing to show but a lot of war stories and a few yellowed clippings with his by-line. He's five or six more stops along the way from retiring, with neither family nor friends, to some trailer park in Florida.

A makeshift studio was set up in the foyer of the police station. A plywood backdrop, fresh cut by its smell, covered in royal blue burlap with a Biloxi tricentennial seal hanging in the middle. A full-size wooden podium with an American flag on one side and a Mississippi flag on the other.

The TV technician was setting up the Kleig light while the city public information director, a pretty blond girl fresh out of journalism school up at Southern Mississippi, tapped on the microphone, and said, "Testing, one, two, three, four," about eight times in a row with a soft girl voice and a southern accent even thicker than mine.

I walked around the plywood. The color monitor showed the map of the gulf and the Caribbean from back at the studio. The storm showed as a swirl of white, a pinwheel sending its curved blades north and west. It was so poorly defined that the weatherman had to point out the location of the center that would later harden into an eye. Still a depression, not yet a storm, with a name reserved but not yet earned. When the winds topped thirty-nine miles per hour it would become Tropical Storm Doreen. Perinovich once told me the wind knows when we name it. I had now met the storm, and it would be with me, with my thoughts, until it left the gulf.

Two dozen chairs had been brought in from the conference room and been placed in rows in front of the podium. A china doll with black braided hair twirled a portable microphone with the WLOX logo on its side. She was Chinese and Caucasian, probably an air force brat. A good number of the Keesler Air Force Base personnel had married Asian women during Pacific stints. This time it produced beautiful results. She wore the face and eye makeup of a TV reporter.

There were three other persons on the front row. Two young men I had never seen before, reporters probably, and a woman who wrote a weekly column for the *Seacoast Echo*, my hometown newspaper over in Bay Saint Louis. The two men laughed at a joke one of them told.

I was there to tell the BPD about the new evidence Barron had given me. I was about to walk past the podium and see if Louise could call Morgan for me when Morgan, Bernie, the police chief, and the fire chief walked in from a side door and took their places behind the podium, with Bernie at the microphone.

I sat on the back row to catch the news conference since it appeared that Morgan would be tied up until it was over anyway. The cameraman from WLOX flipped the light on and the two young reporters sat up and reached into their pockets for their pads. Bernie looked around and called for the policeman who was standing at the back door where I had come in.

The officer came up to the front, Bernie whispered something to him, and he disappeared through the door leading to the offices. Bernie fidgeted with the microphone, came out from behind the podium, and shook hands with the reporters on the front row, all except for Mick, who fended off the handshake with a frown and a glare. Soon the policeman returned to the room, five other policemen in tow, and they sat in the audience to beef up the crowd a little.

Bernie resumed his position behind the microphone and began to read a statement. "Ladies and gentlemen, two weeks ago, the city of Biloxi was shocked as one of our longtime citizens died in an explosion. On my orders, Biloxi Fire Department began an investigation to see if the explosion was an accident or a deliberate act. Today, we are here to announce that based on the investigation that I ordered, we have arrested a suspect and charged him with the crime of capital murder by arson."

Barron must have told Morgan what he found. I was miffed that he had not give me time to talk with Morgan first, but maybe he figured the kid needed the heads-up to come from somebody other than me, somebody he would trust. And Johnnie never promised he would keep quiet about it. But I was still put out that he had not called me to tell me they had a suspect.

"The suspect is a fifteen-year-old juvenile," Bernie said. "State law prohibits us from giving his name. I can only say that the investigation is ongoing and we expect additional arrests. The citizens of Biloxi can rest assured that under this administration the police will vigorously investigate all criminal wrongdoing. I now turn the mike over to Officer Morgan, head of the arson unit, for any questions you may have concerning the case."

Morgan stepped to the podium. Barron slipped into the room and sat beside me. Morgan stepped to the mike, cleared his throat, and spotted Johnnie and me just before he spoke. He held his gaze on us a little longer than he should, then he reached for a glass of water and took a big sip.

"I'm ready to entertain any questions." He looked straight at Johnnie.

"Is the juvenile from Biloxi?" Mick asked.

"Yes," Morgan said.

"Why won't you give us his name? The name can be released in a capital case."

Morgan stammered and cut his eyes toward Johnnie and me, then to Bernie, who in turn signaled for the city attorney.

"We'll have to consult our attorney on this one," Bernie said.

"Any further questions?" Morgan asked.

"I got a call from Louise," Barron whispered to me. "Said I needed to get down here for this. You remember what I told you about the explosion?"

"You said it was a professional-looking job. You never told me they had a suspect."

"They don't. I ain't never seen no fifteen-year-old pro, know what I'm sayin'? This is gonna blow up in their face big-time."

"The city attorney has advised me that even though the crime is capital murder, no indictment has been returned," Bernie said. "We will at this time decline to release the name of the suspect."

"Is the suspect a member of a gang?"

Morgan nodded yes before he caught himself. A quick glance over to Bernie let him know that he had screwed up, and he stopped abruptly.

"Any one of those gang members would have blown themselves into the Gulf trying to fool around with a propane tank," Barron muttered.

"Is the suspect a member of a gang?"

"A grand jury has already been impaneled and is sitting as we speak," Bernie said. "I anticipate the district attorney will take this case to them within the next four or five days."

"Will we get the name of the suspect at that time?"

"If there is an indictment for a capital crime." Bernie looked over at the city attorney, who nodded in agreement. "That is my understanding."

There were a few more questions, but they couldn't get anything more out of Bernie and the news conference quickly ended and everybody stood.

"Morgan still don't know about that hole in the floor," Barron said. "I don't know what the hell they've got."

"Maybe they found the hole."

"Morgan woulda called me. We got us an agreement."

"You don't know who they arrested?"

"Hell, no."

I chased after Mick. One night, when we were both midway through our third Old Charters, Mick said he was losing his edge in Biloxi. "They're so damn *nice*," he said, shaking his head. "They'd rather tell you some graveyard secret than hurt your feelings by telling you no." I told him to lay off, said if he kept taking advantage of the good nature of Biloxi cops and burned them a few times they'd grow as jaded as the ones in Cleveland. He looked as if I had just asked a cat to quit chasing mice, and killed the rest of his drink.

"Who did they arrest?" I asked.

"Some gang banger. They found his baseball cap near the house."

"And?"

"That's it. That and some phoned-in tip. It's pretty weak."

"You think the election coming up might have had something to do with this?"

"The sun gonna rise over Ocean Springs tomorrow morning?" He bolted toward the door to catch Bernie and Morgan, who were leaving the chamber.

"You got it figured out, Jack," Barron had walked up behind me. "Morgan told Bernie there wasn't a chance of catching a pro, so Bernie decided to pick out the easiest target. They'll try to hang this kid. And that won't be hard, considering how 'most everybody down there feels about them Vietnamese gangs."

"You don't think he did it?"

"You continue to amaze me. You're a natural at this detective business. If it's some Vietnamese, it ain't one of this bunch around here. The Dragons, they don't fart without clearing it through Los Angeles. If they decide to use a torch, it'll be some imported talent. It shore as hell ain't no fifteen-year-old sittin' on the hood of a car on Third Street."

On the streets of Biloxi that evening there were two separate attacks on Vietnamese. Three white guys in jeans and T-shirts, two of them wearing caps, cruised the Point in a blue Ford Ranger pickup hunting for young Vietnamese men walking alone. They found two, both walking alone on the sidewalk along Howard Avenue. They hopped out of the truck and punched them out, no more than six or eight blows, most to the abdomen. Neither of the victims had to go to the hospital.

The young men who were assaulted couldn't give a good description of their attackers. Thought they were older than teenagers, and the biggest one wore his cap backward. Couldn't see their faces too well in the streetlight. But they both remembered the pickup truck with the decal on the rear window. It showed a cartoon character taking a whiz on a Chevrolet logo.

TWENTY-TWO

W hy did they call me?" Neal said. "I don't even live in Biloxi, and I don't do all that much criminal work."

"Who're you trying to kid? You're one of the best criminal defense men on the coast," I said. "Nguyen probably heard Perinovich bragging on you and remembered it. He needs some help. They'll hang his grandson for this."

"But it's a capital case. I'm running for senate."

"Are you telling me you won't take this case because it might hurt you politically? Have you sunk—"

"Oh, for pity's sake," Neal said, "who are *you* trying to kid? Spare me the sermon. You've made it clear you weren't cut out to be a banker or a lawyer. I'd suggest you add preacher to that list. I'm saying that a case this serious needs undivided attention. I can't be trying to save some kid's life in between political rallies."

"But this case is a slam dunk," I said. "They got Hank's baseball cap and a phone tip and that's it."

"There's never been an easy capital murder case. Hank's in a gang that's been throwing beer bottles at an old man who went to mass every Sunday and lit two candles for his dead wife and son. Hell, half of Biloxi thinks that alone is enough to send him to Parchman for life. Plus, the cops have announced that they got their man. You can forget about presumption of innocence. The way to get a murder defendant off is to make the jury think somebody else did it. If you don't get them thinking that some other guy did it, they figure your guy must have."

"The cops said that they were probably going to make other arrests," I said.

"Yeah. You can bet it'll be other Dragons. All that's going to do is make them all look guilty. That's all I need, to be standing beside my client in the courtroom when they haul in a bunch of street thugs who look just like him and they all have a history of hanging out with each other. Oh, yeah, this is a slam dunk."

"He's not a Dragon," I said. "At least not yet."

"They got some kind of membership card or something? Look, I'd like to help out, but there's no way I can take this case."

I have to go through this little dance with Neal a few times a year. I browbeat him into taking some case he'd probably take anyway, but I give him the satisfaction of telling me how he's losing his shirt doing good deeds and that the public defender's office was established for such things and that he can't cure the ills of the world.

"Okay," I said. "Forget it. I'll find another lawyer. I'm sure Gerald Garner will take it."

"Garner? This isn't a damn DUI."

"I'll find somebody. It's okay. But the least you can do is help me out with Sheila's investigation." I shifted in the side chair. My butt had grown numb from pressing on the wooden seat. I pushed back and rested my feet on his desk. I laid my head back to get into the draft of air sent down by the ceiling fan and stretched out nearly parallel to the floor.

"Sheila's not my client," he said.

"Who's got enough money to be backing a casino on the Point?"

"Roy Enberg," he said. "Donald Trump. Circus Circus. Bill Gates. You want some more names?"

"How about Stash Moran?"

Neal tented his fingers and rubbed his fingernails against the afternoon stubble on the bottom of his chin. "Stash Moran doesn't have enough money to even buy the parking garage of the Beau Rivage. We're talking a hundred million at the least to get into the casino game."

"Somebody emptied a propane tank into Mr. Cass's house through a hole in the floor. I need to know who was the money behind that casino Weldon's been lining up."

"Propane?"

"Comes in a white or silver tank. You see it out in the country a lot."

"I know what it is. Did Mr. Cass use—"

"I'll explain it some other time. Who had the money to be backing a casino on the Point?"

"That won't help you much. Probably not at all."

"I'm betting it will."

He stood up and stepped toward the minifridge below the sink by the door. "There might not be any big money involved. At least, not yet. I'd bet Weldon is a flipper. He's lining up options on some land and getting zoning and environmental permits lined up. If he's lucky, he gets the Gaming Commission to grant him a permit to open a casino. The permit is good for ninety days at most. That gives him time to sell the deal to somebody in Las Vegas and take his cut. No way Weldon or even Stash can get the financing to build a casino on their own."

The jukebox in the Low Tide Lounge had been modified to play CDs and two big Peary speakers had been added. It was in the far corner of the room, past the two pool tables and the electronic pinball machines. The neon greens, yellows, pinks, and blues from the jukebox bathed that end of the room with a pastel glow and hid the years of grime on the cinder-block walls. "Fats," all three hundred pounds of him, hung off both sides of the stool at the far end of the bar, a bottle of Crown Royal in a purple felt bag in front of him. The aroma of his cigar overwhelmed the room. Bobby, the bartender, kept the fat man's glass fresh with ice. I sat near the door and sipped a cream soda and waited for the right time to approach him. If there had been a professional torch in Biloxi in the past month, Fats ought to know it.

He was having a slow day. In July the only action is on baseball games and horse races and neither has a great following on the coast. The bettors were trying to look inconspicuous, which naturally drew attention to them. One at a time they approached him to pay or collect on earlier bets. Protocol demands that very little be said, that eye contact be kept to a minimum, and that you don't flash the cash. Fats keeps the bets in his head, far from the reach of any subpoena. Nothing in writing, nothing over the phone. That's also how he trades information.

The last of the bettors walked away, a young man in a muscle shirt who thumbed through the short stack of bills as he walked back to the pool table. Fats frowned at him and made a note in his head to be careful about dealing with so flagrant a customer in the future. I reached into my pocket and wrapped my fingers around a roll of five twenties. I could have gotten by with less, probably sixty, since it was his slow season. But he had been good to me in the past.

He stared at the ESPN channel on the TV behind the bar as I approached. He knew I was coming. It was said he had eyes in the back of his head.

"Jackie D," he said. "I thought maybe ya got run outta town or something. Haven't seen ya in a while."

"I've been around. I just haven't been around here."

"Got a special for ya, Jackie. The Giants are in Houston, three-game series. The money's been heavy on the Astros, but Lance Berkman was seen loadin' his bags into the Astros' limo right after the Zephyrs' game night before last."

"So Bagwell's shoulder is bothering him again?"

"They don't give a triple A first baseman a limo ride to the big dance unless they plan to put him into the game. Nickel'll get ya a dime if ya lay some on the Giants right now."

"Sounds good, Fats," I said, "but I don't put money on any game where two inches either way on a ninety-mile-an-hour fast-ball can be the difference between a grand slam and a ground out. I was there for a while."

"Yeh. I often wondered, Jackie, why didn't ya go into the minors? You hit for good average up at Ole Miss."

"I went to a tryout camp. The right-handed pitching was about the same as it was in college. But a leftie can start in the Southeastern Conference throwing eighty miles an hour. You get to the pros and it's ninety. Couldn't handle the lefties."

"Yeh," he said, "that was my problem, too."

Bobby set a fresh glass of ice in front of Fats. I waved away the offer of a second cream soda.

"The explosion that killed Cass Perinovich," I said. "I've got some information that it was a pro."

"Now, Jackie, ya know it's mighty tough to catch a torch. They're just like hit men, except they don't talk as much."

"I'm not so much after the torch, I'm after the guy who hired the torch. And the guys who hire, sometimes they do talk."

Fats nodded. "Yeh, sometimes they do. But the information is hard to come by, if ya know what I mean."

I folded the twenties and slipped them onto the bar. I set the Crown Royal bottle on top of them. "Here's a little start-up money. I'll go up to five hundred on this one." That raised his eyebrows. I was normally good for three hundred. A quarter dropped into the slot of the pool table behind us and there was a clatter of wood knocking on wood as the rack of balls fell.

"Yeh," Fats said, "somebody must want this guy pretty bad."

"Real bad."

He slid the money into his front pocket. He poured some

Crown Royal into the glass before him and swished it around. "I'll keep my eyes open."

I swiveled on my stool and noticed that one of the guys playing pool was staring at me. He held the pool cue with one hand and a Budweiser tallboy with the other. He still had on the polka-dot cap turned backward, still grinned at me the way he did that day at Belter's.

"Fats," I said, "what do you know about a character called Eight Ball?"

"Why you want to know?"

"Got a feeling I might run into him from time to time."

"Yeh. Eight Ball's a bad dude. Claims to be a welder. Does mechanic work over at Fat Johnny's Ford, mainly radiators and water pumps. Gets into fights when he's drunk. Shoots a mean game of eight ball until the beers kick in. You talking about that guy behind us, ain't ya?"

"We've been talking the whole time, and you haven't turned around yet," I said. "How'd you know he was in here?"

"You ain't heard? I've got eyes in the back of my head." He sipped the Crown Royal. "And them eyes are tellin' me you better not mess with the sum'bitch in the polka-dot cap shootin' pool behind us. Specially when he's been drinkin'."

TWENTY-THREE

Y ou sniff real hard and you can still smell the Hai Karate cologne. Stash Moran's El Matador Steak House has not changed one bit since Gerald Ford was president. Leisure suits are common and the bar still has B-girls. Julie is the best one of all. She pulls down good money, partly because she is gorgeous, but mainly because she likes to talk to people, especially men. Any good-looking girl can get a man to talk when he's drinking doubles and she's drinking pink soda water. But Julie has a steel-trap mind for any details she hears and an instinct for knowing what is valuable. She's also got enough sense to know when she can repeat what she hears.

The El Matador is on Pass Road, the main east-west corridor on Biloxi's north side, a busy four-lane street that parallels the beach two miles inland and runs halfway through Gulfport. It is the road where Biloxi shops for groceries and fills up its gas tank and buys its towels and underwear and socks. No casinos, no souvenir shops, no high-rise hotels.

Stash's steak house is a blond-brick building, one story, with lots of arches in what passes for Spanish architecture. The restrooms are designated Señors and Señoritas, and posters showing bullfights festoon the walls along with sombreros and serapes. The lighting is low, the tables and chairs are made of heavy dark wood, and the booths are upholstered in red Naugahyde. The food is surprisingly good. The bar is well stocked and well run and features the best margarita on the coast.

The regulars tend to favor bright shirts and pinky rings. In the piano bar is a wall with thirty pictures of Stash Moran and various sports figures and politicians. One shows Stash and Brother Dave Gardner, a comedian who got his start in the Biloxi night clubs forty years ago. Also in the picture are three men in dark suits. One of them resembles Carlos Marcello, the New Orleans mob boss, but his face is at an angle where it is impossible to make a positive ID. When asked whether it is Marcello, Stash shrugs and smiles and says he has friends everywhere. I don't think it's Marcello, but it makes a good chapter in Stash's legend.

Julie's long blond hair glowed from the green lighting behind the bar. She showed a long stretch of leg from the slit up the side of her blue cocktail dress. Business was slow, it was still early, and she was looking over the movie listings in the *Sun-Herald*. I walked up unnoticed and sat on the stool beside her.

"Jack, baby! How in the world you doing!"

"Why don't you buy me the drink for a change and I'll tell you all about it."

"I don't know how to buy one, darling. Never had to."

I held up my hand to order a round and Julie told the bartender to make it a real one. Five years earlier I tracked down her ex-husband, who had taken a job as a pipefitter at Ingall's Shipyard and helped her get the two years' of back child support for their six-year-old daughter. Afterward, he came after me one night in the Castaway Lounge in Pascagoula and I threw him through the front door. That solidified my friendship with Julie.

"Where you been so long?" she asked.

"Round and about. Mainly New Orleans."

"Well, I'm glad you stopped by." She looked over my shoulder to a man in a business suit who had settled in at the other end of the bar. "Is there something I can do for you? It looks like that poor man is having to drink alone. You know how I hate that."

I laid a fifty-dollar bill on the bar. "Why don't you stay and talk? That guy can drink alone for a while."

"So he can," she said. "He'll probably feel more like having company after a drink or two anyway."

In an invisible move she slid the bill off the surface of the bar. Julie knows that once the money is showing there's no up side in letting it sit. I explained what I was looking for and offered her the same five-hundred-buck deal I had offered to Fats. I didn't put a time limit on it, but I let her know that Fats was looking too. While we were talking, she reached out and squeezed my hand.

"Hold up," she said, "somebody's headed this way."

One of them was young with coal black hair, slicked back and shining. He had a smooth face, a little red at the cheeks, but with the hard eyes of the aspiring mobster. He was heavyset and his shoulders strained against his coat. The top button of his shirt was open to allow room for his stumpy neck. The second man was the same size but softer from an additional twenty years. Salt-and-pepper hair and the flattened nose of a boxer. The younger guy stepped in so close he filled the space between Julie and me.

"Mr. Moran says he wants to see ya," he said in a high-pitched voice.

"I'll be glad to meet with him during regular business hours," I said.

"Maybe ya don't hear so good."

"Before we were interrupted, I was carrying on a conversation with this young lady."

"Get lost, Julie." He punctuated his order with a jerk of his head.

Julie looked at him with anger and amusement in her eyes. She was one of Stash's favorites, and wasn't about to take orders from this guy.

"You need to learn some manners," I said.

"You think ya can teach me some?"

I pushed away from the bar, far enough to where I wasn't likely to get pinned against it. Julie slid off her stool and slipped away with the practice of one who has seen many a barroom brawl get out of hand. The young guy opened his coat. Surely, I thought, this guy is not enough of a rookie to be pulling off his coat after challenging me. I watched for the exact moment when both hands were behind him and both arms in the sleeves. Twenty years earlier I would have considered it a point of pride to let him remove the coat and not take advantage of that one moment when he was in a self-imposed straitjacket. That was before I learned that in a barroom fight a sense of honor will get you killed. Besides, I hadn't started this.

He hitched one shoulder of the coat down. His older companion stepped forward, grabbed the lapel, and slid the coat back up into place. He tapped the young man lightly on the cheek and turned a palm to him in a silent command to stay put.

"You'll have to excuse the exuberance of my young friend," he said. "He didn't express himself so good. What he meant to say was that Mr. Moran would be honored if you'd visit with him." He smiled and gave me a slight bow with his head.

That's one problem about growing up in the South. You're an absolute sucker for good manners, even if you know they don't mean it.

Stash sat behind an oversized desk, turned and facing away from us, and held up the back of his hand when he heard us walk in. He clicked the mouse and ran through the short pile of turn cards three times looking for the red queen before giving up and hitting the deal-again button. He turned and flashed a big smile. Then he walked around the desk and shook my hand, pumping it furiously as if I were an old lost friend.

"Jack Delmas. Welcome to El Matador. It's good to have ya here today." He stepped back around the desk and gestured for me to have a seat. The two men who brought me stood behind me at the door.

"I'll stand until my two friends back there join us," I said. "I'd hate to be accused of bad manners."

Stash kept his smile and gestured with an index finger for the two escorts to take their seats at the desk on either side of me. Once they sat, I picked my chair up and scooted it back far enough so that neither one of them was behind me. I learned in the army MPs that getting yourself into proper position is nine-tenths of a fight. I also learned that when you're outnumbered in a closed room, the best defense is a clear path to an unlocked door.

Stash, still smiling, clicked the computer off. "Now. Is everybody comfortable? Can I offuh ya anything?"

"I'm fine."

"Was everything all right downstairs?"

"It was the best, Stash. Everybody knows you run the best place on the coast."

He leaned back in his chair, propped his elbows on the arms, and touched his hands together. He rested his chin on the tips of his fingers and the smile eroded. "I do run the best place on the coast. I'd like to keep it dat way. I understand ya been doing something that may damage the reputation of the El Matador."

"Would you like to tell me what that is?"

"Solicitation for criminal activity. I hear ya been askin' where ya can find someone to blow up a building."

"You got your signals a little crossed."

"I assume it's in connection with the death of my old friend Casper Perinovich."

I eyed the two men flanking me. They appeared to be relaxed, but the young one glanced at me from time to time, sizing me up. "I'm on a job, Stash. I can't talk about it."

"You can't talk with me about the explosion that killed an old friend, but ya can ask lowlifes at the Low Tide Lounge about it? You tryin' to insult me or what?"

"Come on, Stash."

The young guy, sensing that the conversation was taking a confrontational tone, tensed and sat forward in his chair. This guy was hell-bent to get a piece of me.

"I'm a private investigator and I'm asking about an unexplained explosion. Why do you take this as a threat?"

Stash leaned back and smiled. He picked up a blue rubber ball and began squeezing it. "I don't take it as a threat. In fact, I'll help any way I can."

"Then tell me who else may have been interested in Perinovich's property."

"Who else? You say dat like I was after it. I guess we've all heard the rumors about some big casino operation looking to develop the Point. But I'm not a big operatuh. I'm a restaurant owner. Dat's all I wanna be."

"Cut the crap, Stash. You've been trying to get in on this casino boom for the past three years."

I felt the men beside me stiffen as they looked to Stash. Stash's face reddened and he clenched the rubber ball until it bulged at both ends of his fist.

"You think I'd come in here and ask around for a torch if I suspected you were behind the explosion?" I said. "You think I'd come up here with these two? If I thought you were even remotely involved with Mr. Cass's death, I'd come straight after you, believe me."

"Watch it, mister," the young guy said.

"Listen, De Niro," I said. "I've had about enough of your tough-guy act. I'm talking to Stash. I don't know who you are or why the hell you're in here."

He pushed up on the arms to rise from his chair. I shifted my weight so I could spring toward him.

"Please!" Stash said. "Jack has a point. He doesn't know either of you two." Stash dropped the ball into a desk drawer and began cracking his knuckles. "Go outside and let us talk in peace." He dismissed them both with a wave of his hand. They stood in unison and headed for the door, the younger one glaring as he walked past me.

"What's with the gangster act, Stash?"

He laughed. "I guess it did look like a scene from some movie. But ya got to understand my concerns. I've had my run-ins with the feds before. I can't have this place gettin' a reputation for being a hangout for criminal types."

"Well, maybe you could start by taking down the picture of Carlos Marcello."

"I'm insulted ya thought you'd find a torch in here. I hear ya looking for the guy who did Perinovich's house."

"Damn, Stash, you're good. It's not like I've been taking out ads in the paper."

"It pays to keep ya ears open."

"Well, maybe you can tell me who's trying to open the casino on the Point?"

He shrugged and laced his fingers behind his head.

"Are you and Sheila involved in it?"

"She's your client. Ask her."

"Sheila's always telling me she's talking business with you. I'm just asking what kind of business."

He smiled and shook his head. "Go downstairs and have yourself a steak on the house. But look for the criminal types in one of those dives over by the air force base. Oh, and I'd suggest ya not antagonize Arthur."

"Arthur?"

"The young man with the big neck who was in here earlier. He's sometimes a little overprotective."

"I appreciate the offer of the dinner," I said, "but I'll have to take you up on it later."

"I want to get us clear on one thing. I don't have nothing to do with that casino they're talkin' about putting in on the Point. I wouldn't turn down a good investment opportunity, but so far nobody's come to me with one. At least not one on Point Cadet. Whoever that is, I hear they're running out of time with the Gaming Commission."

"Is that a problem?" I asked. "The commission's never turned down a license for a casino."

"But some of these out-of-town investors don't know that. They see a time limit, it makes them edgy." He pushed the chair back and stood. "A lot of people stood to gain with Perinovich out of the way. I'm not one of those people. I wasn't in on a casino deal on the Point and I'm still not. Why would I solicit a bombing, a capital crime, to make someone else rich? Especially if it was an old friend that got whacked."

The tone of Stash's voice surprised me. It wasn't anger, which I would have expected. It was hurt. To be suspected of causing the death of Perinovich hurt his feelings.

"You've read a lot into a little bit, Stash. I'm not even sure it was set. I'm shaking the tree a little to see what falls out."

"Well, don't shake dis tree no more."

I gave him a nod and turned to the door. Stash called out to me just as I got there. "Let me walk ya to the car. If ya won't take a free steak, the least I can do is to see ya out."

"That's not necessary," I said.

"I insist."

At the first table sat Billy Graves, the Toyota dealer, and his wife.

"Welcome to El Matador," Stash said. "Y'know my old friend Jack Delmas, don't ya?"

I smiled and nodded, but before I could say a word, Stash eased me toward the next table. He introduced me to a Dr. Easley, a chiropractor who had opened a new clinic in Gulfport. Again, all I could say was hello before we moved to yet a third table where

Colley Denkman, a plumbing contractor was seated with some red-headed woman who spoke with a piney woods twang. We didn't hang around long enough to talk.

"Why the introductions, Stash?"

"I speak to everybody in my restaurant. It's only polite to introduce ya since we're together. It's rude to talk to people without making sure everybody in the conversation knows each other."

He made sure that two other people saw me alive and well before I went out the door. There were no lights in the parking lot, but there was a bright moon and plenty of spillover from passing traffic and the street lights on Pass Road. As I slipped my key into the ignition, I saw Arthur standing in the shadow of the long canopy covering the sidewalk to the front door, his white shirt emitting a blue luster. He leaned his back against the brick wall and flicked a butane lighter. His face glowed in the yellow illumination of the tall flame as he touched it to the tip of his cigar.

TWENTY-FOUR

The only thing I had learned for sure from Stash was that the word of my reward was out on the street. I almost believed him, almost believed that he wasn't in on the new casino, despite every instinct that told me different. I just couldn't see Stash teamed up with Billy Weldon.

I was ready to get home and get started typing my wrap-up report for Bayou Casualty on the Point Cadet fires, so I turned off Pass Road onto Cowan and headed up to the Interstate. Casino traffic makes driving down the beach at night a bumper to bumper affair, and the Interstate was the quicker route. I was going to recommend that the company refuse to pay off and let the lawsuits come. Even if I never got a ruling of arson out of Bernie's police force, there's no way those policy holders wanted to get under cross examination. Once I sent the report off, I could forget the Bayou Casualty cases, put out a few more feelers for the torch, and see if Sheila would spring for a bigger reward. A big, anonymous reward paid in cash is usually the fastest and cheapest way to crack a case.

It felt good to have my truck back. The Sable had been nice, but I never broke it in. My gas guage was reading near empty, probably enough to make it to Bay St. Louis, but the needle sometimes sticks, and it didn't move even after I tapped it a few times.

I pulled off at the next ramp and headed for the Conoco up Palmetto Road.

The stars twinkled and there was no moon. Trees crowded the road and fireflies sparkled in the woods. There was a strong smell of honeysuckle and the chirping of crickets, and the road was dark and empty. Behind me a dark sedan came off the same ramp. Its left headlight was bright and blue, but the right one had yellowed and pulsed as if about to go out. A bank of trees in a curve a quarter mile ahead hid the gas station, but its lights glowed around them.

I eased to the pump. The sedan pulled in and went around to the back of the store. After I filled up and got back on the road, I rounded the curve and met a fast-moving log truck. The blast of wind he kicked up jostled my pickup. I merged onto the interstate and had gone no farther than a mile when I spotted headlights some two hundred yards behind me, the right one dim and flickering.

He came at me fast and made up the ground between us in fifteen seconds at most. There were no other cars in our lane, but he rode my bumper and flashed on his brights. I held my hand over my rearview to signal him to dim. He jerked into the passing lane. His engine whooshed into overdrive and he came up fast. He pulled even with my rear bumper. In my side mirror, I caught a glance of the shotgun pointing out the passenger window. I hit the brakes and wheeled to the shoulder.

The blast made my ears ring. Pellets cracked the right side of my windshield and shattered the window on the passenger side. My heart started racing. My right tires sank in the rain-softened dirt, tugging me hard off the road. My left tires were still on the shoulder, kicking up gravel which clattered against my floorboard. I resisted the urge to yank the wheel back to the left, and I kept my eyes on the sedan.

His brake lights flashed and he slowed. The guy on the passenger side moved his upper body out the window to get an angle for a head-on shot at me. But a group of cars was coming from behind so the driver showered down on the gas and took off in a cloud of blue exhaust.

My right rear tire hit the rough pavement of the shoulder and chirped as it caught. It threw me toward the left lane and the car coming up from behind lay down on his horn as he zipped by, almost grazing me.

I flashed on my brights and scanned the sides of the road to see if the sedan was waiting for me. It was tough to see through the shattered glass. I needed to stay behind him. Without any moonlight I couldn't see anything outside the beams of my headlights. I slowed each time I encountered a thicket of trees beside the road.

I checked my rearview to make sure I hadn't missed him. I didn't see the bright blue/dim yellow combination of headlights coming up behind me. Traffic picked up and it got harder to look both ahead and behind for the sedan so I exited onto a lonely road, the back way to Woolmarket. I whipped down an old gravel road I knew well from hunting trips. I could take back roads all the way to Bay Saint Louis. I pulled my .45 from under the seat, flipped the safety off, and laid it beside me.

My heartbeat slowed back down, and I mulled over calling the sheriff. I decided against it. The only description I could give was mismatched headlights. The car was dark, but was it black, blue, or green? And the sheriff would have me retrace my steps. It was sure to come out that I had been asking about a professional torch. That would make the *Sun-Herald* and the last thing I needed was a front-page story telling the world who I am, what I do, and why I was there.

TWENTY-FIVE

The kitchen was at one end of the church's auditorium, separated from the cavernous basketball court by a waist-high serving counter. Neal dipped the brush into the bowl of melted butter and spread a coating across the sheet of biscuits. I smelled an earlier batch baking in the big stainless steel oven.

"So you don't believe Stash?" Neal asked. "You think he might have been involved with the explosion?"

"It's too early to believe anybody's story. But it's a heck of a coincidence. I'm in the El Matador asking around about a crime Stash may have committed, and thirty minutes later some cowboy tries to unload a twelve-gauge into my face."

"Who else would have reason to take a shot at you?"

"I've asked myself that question a couple of hundred times. I thought maybe you'd remember somebody I might've overlooked."

I was taking Barron's advice this time. If Johnnie thought I was too close to be objective about the Perinovich investigation, I can just hear what he'd say about me investigating a case where I was the one who was shot at. And then there's the fact that the sonofabitch put a few holes in my truck. You mess with a man's pickup and it clouds his thinking.

"Let me think," I said. "A reason to shoot me. If you mean within the past month, I'd say anybody who might not want me poking around into the Perinovich explosion. If you mean ever, I'd have to write out a list."

"You need to go to the police."

"A fat lot of good that would do me. The only thing that would get me is a report on file."

"Oh, silly me. I always thought the investigative unit did just that—investigate. Of course, I'm not a trained private eye like you."

"They'd do a great investigation if that load of number-four buckshot had hit me instead of the windshield. It'd suit half the force just fine if that shotgun scared me off the case entirely."

Neal grabbed a potholder and put the tray of biscuits in the oven. "You think this'll be enough biscuits?"

"You'd better fix another batch. This group can eat a lot."

The retractable basketball goals were both drawn up toward the vaulted ceiling. The clang of metal chairs filled the room as the Men's Prayer Breakfast Committee set up for the sunrise meeting. I had brought cheese grits, one of my specialties. The meeting was interdenominational, more Rotary Club than prayer group, but I was counting it as church. If you've got to listen to a sermon, you might as well get a meal out of it. The smell of coffee, fresh biscuits, and frying bacon filled the room and the group began shuffling in.

"I suppose you want to hear about my latest case," Neal said. He dropped a stick of butter into a stainless steel bowl and set it over a low flame.

"I'm glad you changed your mind. We owe it to Perinovich to help Nguyen's grandson."

"We?"

"I'll help."

"Let me say this just once. I'm going to handle this case only through the preliminary hearing. Shouldn't be fooling with it at all. I've got a campaign to run."

"Then why are you doing it?"

"Aren't you the same guy who got on me for not wanting to take the case because of politics? I looked into it and I don't think the kid is guilty."

"Told you it was a slam dunk."

"I didn't say that. If the public defender handles it and it gets mixed in with a thousand other cases, it could get out of hand real fast. Your friend Johnnie Barron has already called me. He's going to make Bernie and the rest of the Biloxi Police Department a laughing stock if they don't back off the case."

"Well, what's wrong with that?"

"Maybe nothing," Neal said, "unless that makes Bernie decide to dig in his heels and make the case a top priority after the election."

The central air-conditioning unit kicked in with its distinctive sound that always reminds me of an eighteen-wheeler gearing down on a steep grade. I first noticed it when Sandy and I would come here on Sunday mornings after dropping off Peyton at the nursery. Besides saving us the effort of making Sunday morning breakfast, it was free, and in those days that counted for a lot. Peyton had been a shepherd in a Christmas pageant on the stage at the far end of the room. She was barely old enough to walk. She wore a blue sheet with a white sash and a hand towel tied around her head. I have a videotape of it, and sometimes when I'm by myself I play the tape.

"So," Neal said, "you still haven't told me what you plan to do about somebody taking a shot at you."

"I plan to check my rearview mirror a lot. In fact, I plan to check it every ten seconds tomorrow on my way to Jackson."

"You're going to Jackson?"

"I thought I'd go to the Gaming Commission to see if anybody's applied for any licenses lately. If the rumors about a new casino are true, somebody ought to be making sure nobody else beats them to the punch."

"Rumors? Is that what you think all this casino talk is?"

"All I've seen is some cartoon drawings at Weldon's office and a lot of talk. Strong talk, I admit, but nothing official."

"I am impressed," Neal said. "Checking out facts. That almost sounds like a lawyer thinking."

"Don't forget, I spent almost a full year in law school before coming to my senses."

"It *almost* sounds like lawyer thinking. Stop by the office tomorrow before you get out of town and I may be able to save you a trip." He started buttering another tray of biscuits. "Besides, you do plan to have that windshield fixed before you go driving up to Jackson, don't you?"

"I've got a rental. But I'm real proud of you. Normally that windshield would have been your cue to harass me about buying a new car."

"Between dents that don't get fixed and holes from shotgun blasts, it would be a real waste for you to have a new car." He rinsed the melted butter off of the brush. "If I was going to harrass you about anything, it'd be getting yourself this deep in a case where people have started shooting at you with shotguns. You've wrapped up the Bayou Casualty jobs. I suggest you give Sheila a final report on her Uncle Cass's house and start that sail to Key West you're always saying you're going to take."

TWENTY-SIX

When I finished washing dishes after the prayer breakfast, I drove to the youth detention center to see Hank. Maybe a few days in there was enough to get him to talk about the explosion.

Harrison County has taken in a lot of casino taxes, but few dollars have made their way to the youth detention center. It was built in 1965 when the county had maybe half as many people as it does now. But the building is solid and well kept and I've seen a lot worse. At least it's clean and is, of course, air-conditioned, which draws the predictable number of letters to the editor. They usually start with the premise that an air-conditioner makes the jail so nice that kids are dying to get in there.

Fully one-half of the crime on the coast and anywhere else is committed by kids under twenty-one. And a kid can get put in jail for things that aren't even crimes. They can get put in for being "incorrigible." Try putting an adult behind bars for that one and see how fast the ACLU can move. Despite the numbers, there are a dozen times as many beds in the adult system as there are in the juvenile centers.

That's the reason I want Neal to win his senate race. Not that he would or could change anything. I'd just like to get a closer look at the thinking behind some of this stuff.

When I reached the detention center, the sun was at the top of the sky and the heat had squeezed the oxygen out of the air. Clumps of gray-bottomed clouds were mounting in the west, the first dark sign of Tropical Storm Doreen. She had crossed the Yucatan and was off and running in the gulf. The coming rain-clouds would break the heat in a couple of hours; New Orleans got an inch and a half in less than an hour earlier that morning. A street drain in Kenner got backed up and it put six inches of nasty, brown water into a shopping center.

As I stepped toward the sidewalk, a car pulled into the parking lot behind me. The stereo was turned up so loud that I felt it. It was a Cadillac, a black Fleetwood trimmed out in gold with gold hubcaps. The windows were tinted, too dark for me to see who was in it. It pulled into one of the four handicapped slots outlined in blue paint. The California plate on the front bumper caught my eye, and I stopped to see who got out of the car.

The passenger door opened and a young man stepped out, a Vietnamese. His hair was gelled, black and glistening. His navy blue pants were tight with sharp creases. His loafers were soft and expensive and his pale yellow shirt was silk. Attached at his belt was a pager. He caught me looking at him and stuck his head back in the car and said something to the driver. He then walked to the front of the car and leaned against it. He slipped on a pair of blue-lensed sunglasses, crossed his arms, and smiled at me.

Sammy stepped out from the driver's side. He kept his eyes trained on me as he walked to the front of the car. He didn't lean against the hood. He wasn't smiling.

"Sammy!" I shouted. "The only handicap you've got is between your ears! You get that pimp wagon out of that parking space right now!"

A fat man and a bleached-blond woman in front of me, both in shorts and T-shirts, turned to see if a fight was brewing. Sammy leaned back against the car. His companion laid his sunglasses on the hood and took two steps toward me. He stood with a wide stance, on the balls of his feet, his hands at his side.

"Don't tell me," I said as I stepped toward them, "this greaser is your muscle. Knows a little karate, and he's ready to take me on, right?" I stopped four steps from them and pointed straight at the yellow silk shirt. "You stay put. I'm in no mood for any crap out of either one of you two, and if you try anything, I'm going to mess that shirt up real good."

His jaw muscles started working as he looked me up and down, moving only his eyes. Sammy pushed away from the car and stood beside him.

"You're here to see Hank," I said, "and that's a real bad idea."

"Hey!" Sammy said. "We got as much right to be here as you do, man."

"You want to talk about rights, go to law school. I'm telling you it's time to take that pimpmobile and hit the road."

Sammy tried to speak but his companion stopped him with a glance and a frown. This other guy must have been further up the ladder with the Dragons. He held a stare at me for a second before giving Sammy a hand signal and they got back into the car. I wondered what the shine of those headlights would look like at night.

Sammy put it in reverse and stomped it. The tires squealed and left a black streak as the Cadillac lurched back. The smell of burning rubber drifted to me. Before the car came to a stop, Sammy slammed it into drive and it jerked forward and raced across the parking lot.

The orange jump suit was a couple of sizes too large, making Hank look even smaller and even more frail. He sat behind the Plexiglas across from me. Fear had entered his eyes, replacing the surliness and defiance.

"Hank, I know Sammy's been here. Who's the guy with him?"

"I don't know," he said in a quiet and low voice. "I never saw him before."

The room was stuffy, almost hot. It smelled like burned bread, or maybe pizza.

"You don't need to be talking to them," I said. "They're the reason you're in here."

"Well, what am I supposed to do?"

"For one thing, you don't have to come out here and when they stop by. I'll ask Judge Ward if he'll keep them out of here. They're trouble, Hank."

Hank nodded and lowered his eyes. His chin trembled as he fought back tears.

"Hey," I said, "look up at me, okay?"

His eyes were misted, and he licked his bottom lip.

"Sammy won't mess with me," I said. "You let me know if he comes back and I'll take care of him." I winked at him and he smiled, just a little. "Have you seen your grandfather?"

"Yes, sir, he was here earlier this morning."

"Yes, sir," I said. "That sounds a lot better. My brother is handling your case right now. Have you talked to him?"

Hank nodded.

"He's a good lawyer, but he can't work miracles. You've got to tell him everything you know. Were you there when they rigged Mr. Perinovich's house to blow up?"

His mouth dropped open and he shook his head no. "They didn't do it. I promise you, the Dragons didn't do it."

"Quit protecting them. They're setting you up to take the fall for them. They called in the tip that got you arrested. The only way you can get out of here is to tell the truth."

"I *am* telling the truth. Why won't anybody believe me?"

"Maybe it's because they saw you and the rest of them out on the street that night. Maybe it's because they found your cap at the scene. Maybe it's because y'all had been harassing Mr. Perinovich for months."

Hank swallowed hard and wiped his nose with the back of his

hand. The room darkened as clouds moved over the detention center. A few fat drops of rain splatted against the barred windows up near the ceiling.

"When you talk to Neal don't be afraid to tell him everything. He's your lawyer. He can't tell anybody else what you say. I bet Sammy has told there's no way they can convict somebody your age of capital murder. That's not right, Hank. They can. It happens all the time. Sammy would be happy to let you take a fall for him. Do you know what the term 'turning state's evidence' means?"

"Yes, sir. That means ratting somebody out."

"That's gang talk. Are you in that gang?"

"No, sir. I'm not a Dragon."

"But you're hanging around with them. You're running errands for them. That's where you got those shoes isn't it?"

Hank nodded.

"Do you want to become a Dragon? Is that what you want?"

"No, sir! Not anymore. I just can't rat them out. They'd kill me. They told me they would!"

"There's nothing to rat out if they didn't do it."

"They didn't blow that house up. But there might be some other things." He bit his upper lip as if forcing himself to say no more. "I didn't go to Mr. Perinovich's house. I'd never go in the yard with that dog."

"The Dragons hire the best lawyers to get their members out of jail. Have they hired a lawyer to talk to you?"

A look of realization came across his fifteen-year-old eyes. His focus shifted downward like a car on a country road at night clicking down to low beams.

"They'll go to bat for a Dragon but they won't go to bat for you. They've used you up and now you'll do the prison time and they'll just laugh about it. Is all of that worth a pair of shoes?"

Hank put his face in his hands. He dropped his head. He started sobbing and his skinny shoulders shook.

TWENTY-SEVEN

W hen will Speedy be back in?" I asked.

"Depends on how the shrimp are running," she said. "He says if it's good, he'll stay out all night."

"That storm's gusting up to sixty-five miles per hour and it's moving pretty fast."

"He's got a radio."

I had seen her a few times before at the marina, and she was wearing the same T-shirt each time. "Don't piss me off," the slogan read, "I'm running out of places to hide the bodies." I took it as advice. She was probably younger than I am, but she had run up a lot of mileage. A big woman, big hands and forearms, with short cropped brunette hair. Wouldn't know any more about putting makeup on her face than I would.

"Is he really thinking about staying out tonight?"

"The storm's headed for Luziana," she said. "He's got a radio."

"You heard anything about him wanting to sell the boat?"

She shook her head and reached to the breast pocket of her T-shirt for a fresh Winston. "Last I heard, he was talkin' about quittin' his job at the concrete plant and shrimping full-time. That don't sound like he's looking to sell."

"You think he'll have enough sense to come back in if the storm turns?"

"I got two kids and my ex is three months behind on child support. I got to track down twenty boat owners and tell 'em to come tie down their damn boats so they don't smash up my piers if that hurricane decides to make a run over here. I got enough to worry about without adding Speedy Cline to the list."

The sky was a soupy gray and the sun was a spot of dim, fuzzy radiance. Belter's boat, the *Side Pocket*, was out. It looked like a good time to ask the daughter-in-law if her memory had gotten any better. Maybe she'd at least remember Hank. That is, if she wasn't making it all up anyway.

The dogs in the chicken-wire pen in the far corner of the yard began howling and barking. There must have been ten in there and one looked like you could put a saddle on it; its back was higher than my waist. The front yard was sand, packed hard where cars had driven over it. The few green spots were patches of weeds. One side of the yard was shaded by two gray-bearded live oaks and one big pecan tree, and under the overcast sky it was as dark as twilight. Limbs and pecan husks, some crushed by truck tires, were scattered across the yard and rotting from having been there so long. Dampness and decay hung in the air and a green coating of mildew had spread across that shaded side wall.

She stepped out to the front porch, summoned by the sound of my truck and the baying of the dogs. She leaned against the wall with her arms crossed like a man's. Her blond hair was stringy and she wore faded jeans and a man's shirt, the ends tied together at her waist.

She could have been pretty if she wasn't so mad all the time. But I could see why she'd be mad. I wondered what she would look like in a nice dress on a shopping trip at the mall. What she'd look like having lunch with friends at a café in the Riverwalk in New Orleans. I'll bet she wondered that too.

"Good morning," I said. As I neared the house, I caught a whiff of hot grease and from inside the house a radio played rock music. She blew a pink bubble until it popped. "Is this a good time for us to talk?"

"Lennis ain't here, if that's what you mean. He's gone shrimpin'. Won't come back in until tomorrow, unless that storm turns."

The wind was steady and cool and it fluttered the leaves, so heavy and green that they flapped rather than rustled. These were Doreen's messenger winds. I rested my right foot on the first wooden step and tilted my sunglasses onto my head.

"I see that Lennis likes dogs."

She glared at the pen where the barking had quieted down except for the ten-pounder that danced on his toes and yapped with his head pointed straight up. There's always one who wants to keep some trouble stirred up. The bigger dogs figured they had done their job and retreated to the dark coolness under the tin roof in the rear corner of the pen.

"He don't like dogs," she said, "he loves 'em. God, I wisht he'd spend as much money on food for them young'uns as he does on that damn dog food."

"How many has he got?"

"Depends on how many he brung home with him last night. You hear all this stuff about dogs being able to spot a good person? That's bull. You could take a pit bull with a toothache and Lennis could make friends with it. Shows you what dogs know."

"Have you given any more thought to what we talked about?" I asked.

"Some."

Charging ahead didn't feel like the best strategy. "That sign out there by the road, the one written in Vietnamese. What does it say?"

"It says, 'Warning, slant eyes! These dogs will eat you before you can eat them.' " She laughed. "Them gooks, they was the ones who was out on the street that night. They blew up that house. I couldn't sleep that night so I was out here rocking in the swing. I seen that big black car drive over up, and they was a bunch of 'em sittin' on cars out by the road. They sit out there all night and smoke dope and drink them quart bottles of beer. That cheap shit. I could hear 'em. You can hear 'em when they start talking that Vietnamese."

"You said a big black car?"

"It was that big long one they been ridin' around in here lately. Probably stole from somewhere. That Sammy was driving it."

"You could tell it was Sammy? At night and him in a car?"

"I reckon I know what I seen."

"Where were these kids when the house exploded?"

"They run to where the noise come from. I s'pose they wanted to see what they done."

"Did you tell the cops about this?"

"They never asked me nothin'."

"Did they ask Lennis anything?"

"Lennis don't know nothin' about none of this and if he says he does he's lying. He warn't even here that night. Him and Eight Ball stayed out all night."

"This Eight Ball, do you know what he drives?"

"What do you think? A damn pickup like everybody else around this place. I'm sick of pickups. I got a good mind to trade Elvis's in on a Camaro while he's in jail."

"Eight Ball ever drive a dark sedan?"

"He might. He does mechanic work sometimes. Takes the cars to his house to fix 'em. I don't keep up with what he drives."

"And Eight Ball and Lennis were out together that night the house blew up?"

"What difference does that make? Look, Lennis ain't gettin' no reward money. If he says he knows jack shit he's lying. He was gone out all night, him and Eight Ball. I'm the one that knows what happened, not him. And I'm telling you it was that Dragon bunch."

I've got an old army MP buddy on the New Orleans police force, a thoroughbred Cajun who has become, of all things, a computer nerd. He swears that the Internet is going to put private investigators out of business.

Maybe that's my problem with computers, I must be scared of them. If I ever run into a psychiatrist who doesn't look like he's the one who ought to be on the couch, I'll ask him. Maybe he could tell me why I don't own a car phone, why I don't have a computer in my house. It's probably Mama's fault. But I'm sure she meant well.

Neal's desktop was visible, so it had to be Monday. On Monday he takes every scrap of paper and piles them on the right-hand edge of his desk. He then calls in Gladys, who retired three years ago from thirty years of opening new accounts for the Hancock Bank. He works down through the stack and Gladys decides what needs to be done. Neal flicked the report toward me and it slid across the desktop. I caught it as it fell off the edge.

"No charge," he said. "Gladys had some free time and decided to do your work for you."

It was articles of incorporation faxed from the Secretary of State's office. The company was NuCoast Enterprises, a Mississippi corporation headquartered in Biloxi.

"You're a regular sweetheart," I said. "You're not charging me for something I didn't order and have no idea what it's good for. You'd better watch out, they might bring you up on charges before the Bar Association. Not billing for something like this sets a bad precedent."

"Read on, big brother."

"By the way, I dropped by to let you know that the Dragons didn't have anything to do with the explosion."

"You've got proof?" he asked.

"Lennis Belter's daughter-in-law said the night it happened a bunch of the Dragons were sitting on cars on the street in front of Lennis's house. When the explosion occurred, they all ran toward it."

He tapped his fingertips against each other and nodded. "And?"

"And what?"

"What does that prove?"

"Neal, when somebody sets a fire, other than a pyromaniac who gets his jollies that way, they get the hell out of there. It's a natural reaction for people to go see a fire. When you see somebody running the other way, they become automatic suspects."

He sighed and shook his head. "Very interesting, professor. But I'm afraid I can't get the walking-the-right-direction defense admitted into evidence. I'll let you know when I need help with Huang's defense. Read that report."

Some people just won't listen to experts.

"So who's this NuCoast Enterprises?" I asked.

"That's the group that's puting together the deal down on the Point, the deal that includes Perinovich's land."

"How do you know that?"

"You've got your sources, I've got mine." We never ask each other about our sources. Makes it easier if either of us is ever put under oath. "Trust me and take a look at the incorporators."

Two names were listed instead of the usual three. I recognized Billy Weldon. He was president. The secretary-treasurer was Matilda Bethea. No address given.

"You're welcome," Neal said.

"So what do I have here?"

"I figured you'd want to find out who was trying to put that casino in. The places you hang around, it was unlikely that you were going to bump into anybody who could rub two quarters together, much less put together a multimillion-dollar casino deal. I called up to Jackson and got them to fax the incorporation papers down and save you a trip. Your driving record is a little spotty these days what with people shooting your windows out and all."

"Weldon's no surprise," I said, "but who is this Matilda Bethea?"

"Gee, I don't know. Maybe you ought to hire a good private investigator and find out. Look at the next page."

The next document was on Gaming Commission letterhead. It was an application for a casino license from NuCoast Enterprises with an X in the box marked "Application Granted." Under general terms and conditions, right after the part about no criminal records allowed, was typed in the phrase: "Application granted on condition that applicant provide to the commission no later than close of business day August 15 proof of sufficient capitalization as evidenced by letters of credit and/or sufficient sureties in the amount of not less than $250,000,000. Further, applicant shall, no later than close of business day August 15, secure situs for proposed casino and hotel as evidenced by deeds, leases in excess of thirty (30) years, and/or options to purchase those properties described in Exhibit C attached hereto."

"Where's Exhibit C?" I asked.

"I've ordered the plat. They couldn't fax it. It's the property around Cass's place."

"So Weldon really does have a deadline. No wonder he was pestering the hell out of Mr. Cass and everybody else down there."

Neal stood up and stepped to the window. He raised the blinds and a big shaft of sunlight streamed in and hit the floor. "There aren't that many sites available. With Mr. Cass out of the way Sheila is holding the last piece in a puzzle for one of the choice sites on the Point."

"With Mr. Cass out of the way?"

Neal drew in a deep breath and let it out slowly. That's a sure sign that he is weighing his words before speaking. "I'm not accusing anybody of anything, Jack. All I'm saying is that you've got to be careful not to let your libido blind you to all the possibilities.

NuCoast has everything in place except for this one big property right in the middle of their proposed casino site. With Cass's death, Sheila owns it. And with an August deadline, the price is going up every day. She knows what she's doing. She could get five times the price Perinovich would have ever gotten."

"Tell me something I don't know."

"Sheila and Stash have both filled out questionnaires at the Gaming Commission."

"What kind of questionnaire?"

"Background checks. They're for people who want to buy or establish a casino."

That was something I wish he had kept to himself.

TWENTY-EIGHT

I'm afraid you'll have to fill out the form, anyway," he said. "We can't let just anybody go into these safety deposit boxes. There's a liability factor, you understand."

"Kenny," I said, "I'd appreciate it if you didn't refer to me as 'just anybody.' I've known you for the last thirty-five years. And this power of attorney gives me just as much right to go into the box as anybody in the family."

Kenny had jowled and he had a lot more gray than the last time I saw him. He was breathing hard just sitting at his desk. This guy was a tailback in high school, two classes ahead of me. How could he have let himself go like this?

His office was dark and cool with the sleep-inducing drone of air-conditioning softly whistling through the ceiling vent. Kenny sagged into the leather chair, which had contoured to fit his broad seat. Light from a table lamp struck his face at an angle that accented the droops and shadows. He had crossed the line, the line I push against every day, the one I try to keep ahead of me, the one I try to keep from crossing.

"Do you have your driver's license?"

"Driver's license? My gosh, Kenny."

"Procedures."

His voice told me that procedures grated on him too. But Kenny isn't like me; he's responsible. That means he takes whatever the company dishes out and fritters his days away behind a desk looking for that retirement the actuaries know won't hit before the cholesterol does.

When Sandy and I first married, I worked in her father's bank in Memphis. This bean counter kept harassing me for not turning in weekly reports and sent me a memo about it with a chickenshit carbon copy to the division manager. I answered with what I was told later the "impolitic" move of storming to the dweeb's desk and giving him the choice of eating the damn memo or having it inserted into his only other orifice big enough to hold it. I resigned the next day after telling Sandy my next career move was to the Gulf Coast to get back to boat repair and shrimping. She was delighted at first. It wore off two years later.

"These procedures," I asked, "they apply even to the president of the bank?"

"I'm only president of this branch."

Kenny wrote the number of my license in the appropriate space and signed the form with a flourish, a big signature with a lot of loops. I wondered if the bank had thought of having his handwriting analyzed. I wondered if they had thought about having him take a whiz into a jar. I made a note to speak to Neal about such things when he became senator.

"We'll have to go out to the island sometimes," he said, "maybe when the redfish go into the honey hole this fall."

"Sure, Kenny. That sounds fun."

I had just guessed that there was a safe deposit box. Big Jim Brannan, the man who brought me into the investigation business, checked for one in every case. Sheila had never told me about it. I don't think she even knew, judging by what was still in it. And the log book didn't show anyone checking the box out over the past two months.

I set the drawer on a table in the middle of the vault. I piled up all the papers and began using Neal's system of taking each paper off the top and examining it. The third sheet was from a composition book, its tattered edge like broken mill work. The writing was in blue ink.

> I, Casper Perinovich, leave to my niece, Sheila Perinovich all of my money and property. Except for my boat, which goes to Sheila's son Joey. It is my wish that Sheila takes care of my sister if she is still alive when this will is read. If she has to sell the house to do it, so be it. It is also my wish that she give a nice gift to my church. And not just money, but a gift.
> Signed, Casper Perinovich.

The next item was a clipping from *Newsweek* about illegal waste dumping and how the Vietnamese in New Jersey were getting into it. There was also a form letter from the city clerk stating that under the Mississippi Public Records Act, the attached information was being forwarded along with a fifty-cent bill for photocopying. The attached information was a listing of bids on the hazardous waste removal contract let by the city. NuCoast Enterprises was the next-to-lowest bidder. The lowest was a group that listed its president as Dan Lu.

A letter to the circuit clerk requested a copy of Bernie's marriage license. I noted the book and page number.

Another letter from the Secretary of State's office in Jackson certified that NuCoast Enterprises is a Mississippi Corporation and listed as officers Billy Weldon and Matilda Bethea. Perinovich had circled the names.

A clipping reported on a city contract to clean up an abandoned creosote plant on Back Bay. The cleanup had been ordered by the Environmental Protection Agency. The job was awarded to NuCoast. A protest had been lodged by Perinovich that NuCoast was not the lowest bidder. The mayor was quoted as saying that it was not the lowest, but it was the best.

I unfolded a sheet of newspaper, only a little yellowed despite the dateline of July 2 fifteen years earlier. It was a Life and Leisure section of the Sunday *Sun-Herald*. Bernie Pettus had one foot on the pontoon of a seaplane and the other on the stoop of the cockpit door. Looked like Lindbergh boarding *The Spirit of St. Louis*. The headline read "High Office: Councilman to Patrol Holiday Skies." Bernie was pulling duty for the Civil Air Patrol that Fourth of July, flying his Cessna 185 seaplane over the islands looking for boats in distress. Perinovich had circled Bernie's face with a black marker.

I caught myself staring not at Bernie's face but at the circle drawn around it. Had Perinovich become irrational? This was more than the usual antigovernment tirades you can catch on any call-in radio show. This was personal. It was like Mr. Cass was planning to shoot him. I got the hollow feeling that I was looking at the personal effects of a stalker.

Why was he so damn angry with Bernie Pettus?

TWENTY-NINE

I'm glad you're here," Daddy said. "We need you to settle an argument."

Just what I wanted to hear.

I needed to ask Daddy some questions about Perinovich, but I sure didn't feel like getting into the middle of a fight. I have arbitrated arguments between Neal and him for years. I learned at the age of fourteen that arguing with your parents is futile. But Neal, the smart one, has never figured this out. It's amazing, but Neal can present a case that will dazzle the Supreme Court and couldn't win an argument with Daddy even on a point of contract law.

"I'm not here for that," I said. "I've got to get ready for a hurricane." I sat in an armchair in front of Neal's desk. "I never settle any of your arguments. All that happens is that both of you get mad."

"It's not an argument," Neal said.

"You always say that," Daddy said.

"Daddy, it's just a discussion. Can't we have a simple discussion without it elevating into some type of a conflict?"

"All right, Jack, this simple discussion is about your brother going back on his promise to keep factories and casinos and stuff out of the bay."

"I never made any such promise."

"It sure sounded like it to me."

"What I said was I would make sure the bay was not polluted and that any development would need EPA approval."

"Big deal," Daddy said. "They have to do that now. Pretty soon you can drive across the bridge and look at the shoreline of the bay and all you'll see are oil refineries and casinos."

"That's ridiculous," Neal said. "No casino would locate next to an oil refinery. Besides, you've got to balance things. I think more people around here would want jobs and—"

"Everybody I know who wants to work around this place has already got work."

"Daddy, it's what people want. My political consultant did a poll and that's what they're saying."

"A *poll*?" Daddy shouted. "Hell, it was a public opinion poll that picked Barabbas over Jesus!"

"What part of the bay is Neal going to put this oil refinery on?" I asked.

"Don't you start too," Neal said.

"You mean they let state senators put factories anywhere they want? Wow, no wonder you wanted to run for the senate."

"The legislature can't tell a refinery where to go," Daddy said, "but they can sure stop one from going somewhere."

"All I said was, I'd have to take a look at the individual situation."

"You better not be talking about letting any smokestacks or neon signs or anything else go up there," Daddy said. "I got to go. I told Dave Harmon I'd help him tie down his boat. Now that I don't have a boat anymore, I got time to help out those who do."

He turned toward the door.

"Glad I could help," I said.

Daddy muttered something as he walked out the door. I turned to Neal. "You're a smart guy, Neal. When are you going to learn?"

Neal threw up his hands and rolled his eyes toward the ceiling.

"Believe me, I tried my best on this one. He came in here looking for a fight."

"You get that shrimp boat back and get him back out on the gulf, and I'll bet he mellows out some."

"Speedy's being unreasonable. Every time I make an offer, he counters with a higher offer."

"I'm telling you, he thinks you're rich."

Neal sighed and looked down at the floor. "Do you think you could talk to him?" His voice was small.

I bit my upper lip to hold down the smile. "I'll see what I can do. Of course, I may have to hire somebody to be the negotiator, since even old Speedy, slow as he may be, will figure that you're bankrolling me."

Neal frowned as he braced for yet another dressing-down. But I couldn't do it. He usually goes light on me, like he did that time I got myself set up on a murder rap in New Orleans. That was almost as stupid as arguing with Daddy.

"I'll see what I can do," I said. "Now, tell me what you know about hazardous waste disposal."

"Oh, my gosh, I just got the environmental lecture. Why didn't you and Daddy just double team me so we could save time?"

"I haven't talked to Daddy about any of this," I said. "Tell him you won't let anybody touch the bay and hope nothing comes up in the next four years. I've got a more immediate concern. What do you know about hazardous waste dumping?"

"Why?"

"Perinovich seemed concerned about it."

"Are you asking about dumping or disposal?"

"Is there a difference?"

"Disposal is when they do it the right way. All of the chemical by-products of industry have to go somewhere. In the old days, they'd just dump it into the water. But that was before the stuff was as toxic as it is now and there wasn't nearly as much of it. Today they have to take it to approved sites, usually a landfill that has a nonporous base to it so it won't seep into the groundwater. It's not cheap. It's probably a hundred dollars a barrel."

"A hundred bucks a barrel?"

"Give or take a few dollars," he said.

"That much money can draw some interest from a lot of people."

"It has. Some companies handle their own disposal. Small amounts can be incinerated right on the spot. Some can be land farmed, which is nothing more than plowing it into the soil and letting the sunlight break it down. The big companies have their own disposal sites or have their own trucks to carry it. If you only produce a barrel or two, it's not worth it to have your own trucks, so you pay somebody to haul it off."

"And that's where the bad guys come in," I said.

"In some places the mafia has gotten into it, which comes as no surprise. They load up liquid waste and just spray it on the highway. Or they can do like your old buddy Lennis and load it on a boat and dump it overboard a few miles out. A lot more of that goes on than we'll ever know until a few years from now when the barrels rust through and the redfish and mackerel and shrimp start dying and floating up on the beach."

I pictured that scene, and I kept seeing the profile of Lennis on that damned leaky boat of his. I leaned forward and gripped the arms of the chair to push up. "I guess I better go help Daddy board up his windows."

"I need some help, too."

"You've got storm shutters. All you need to do is close them."

"That's not the kind of help I was talking about," he said. "Do you think you can go see Speedy Cline in the next few days?"

THIRTY

Daddy banged each nail nine steady times to drive it through the plywood into the window frame. The ping of the hammer on the nailhead echoed against the garage, forty feet away. The storm had turned our way the night before.

In front of my cabin, the tempo of the splashing of the waves on the beach had picked up overnight even though the sky was still clear. A lot more seagulls and albatrosses than normal were flying and floating near the shore. And they were constantly feeding, as if there would be no food tomorrow. They knew a hurricane was in the gulf.

I felt it, a sense of exhilaration and foreboding in my gut, a visceral and instinctive response to this change in the rhythm of the sea, this warning signal as old as time. Three hundred years ago, the Biloxi and Pascagoula Indians knew the feeling, knew what it meant, and prepared for the blow. Today we call such feelings anxiety and take a Valium.

"So you don't think Perinovich was spending way too much time complaining about Bernie Pettus?" I asked.

"Sure he was," Daddy said. "So what? He hated Pettus. I don't have a whole lot for the sorry scoundrel myself."

"He kept photographs of Pettus in a safe deposit box. He ordered copies of Pettus's marriage certificate from the circuit clerk.

He wrote a letter a week to the editor all but cussing Bernie out."

"It wasn't just Bernie he wrote about," Daddy said.

"It was most of the time. What I'm saying is that it doesn't seem normal. Do you think Mr. Cass had gotten a little off-balance?"

"He wasn't crazy if that's what you mean."

"I didn't say crazy. I mean obsessed."

"Hand me some more nails," he said. "I don't know what all these fancy words mean."

"What fancy words?"

"Abcessed. You make it sound like he had a bad tooth or something."

"No, Daddy. I said *ob*sessed. I mean Mr. Cass was always thinking about ways to get Bernie Pettus. That's how he spent most of his time."

Daddy dropped a nail and it bounced off the windowsill into the grass. "He had his reasons. I just wish he'd lived long enough to send Bernie to the pen where he belongs."

"What reasons did Mr. Cass have to hate Bernie Pettus the way he did?"

Daddy stepped up the pace of his hammering. He was holding two nails between his lips and rolled them around with his tongue. He shook his head slowly from side to side and looked as if he was talking to himself.

"Mr. Cass is gone," I said. "I'm trying to find out what happened. If you know some secret he was keeping, I need to know what it is."

He spit the nails into his hand and drove one in with only six blows of the hammer. The next one he hit twice and bent it.

"You got me all distracted," he said.

"Why did Mr. Cass hate Bernie Pettus?"

Daddy wiped the sweat off his forehead with the back of his hand. "Let's stop for a minute. I need some of that tea."

We stepped around to the shade of the front porch and poured glasses of sweet tea from the pitcher Mama had set out a few minutes earlier.

"You check on Trish?" Daddy asked. "She'll need to board up."

"I've already done it."

He sat on the swing, and I sat across from him on a wicker chair. The ice had melted to where it was squishy.

"What do you think so far?" he asked. "You think Bernie Pettus had anything to do with Cass's death?"

"Why are you asking a question like that?"

He took a sip of tea and laid his arm across the back of the swing. "I'm asking because Bernie Pettus was the one who killed Marie and Mike."

THIRTY-ONE

Daddy pushed the swing by shifting pressure from his heel to his toe and back. He squeezed the lemon wedge and its scent drifted to me. He studied the high wispy clouds that the leading winds of the storm were spreading across the sky.

"Are you going to tell me what happened," I said, "or are you going to make me pull it out word by word?"

"It's a long story."

"I've got time."

He finished the rest of his tea without moving the glass from his lips. "There's a storm coming."

"We're almost through. Go ahead and tell me what happened."

He handed me the empty glass and I filled it back up. The ice had melted, but it was cool and wet and that was good enough.

"You remember that day Camille hit?" he asked.

"Of course I do."

"The storm had been sitting out in the gulf for days," he said. "Like it wanted to build up as much punch as it could before going ashore. They say we didn't take it serious, but that's wrong. We knew it was a bad one.

"Perinovich called Wade Guice. You remember him, used to be Civil Defense director? Well, Wade says this is a bad one. The Hurricane Hunters say it's wrapped up tight, more like a tornado than a hurricane. Cass, he knows Wade Guice'll shoot straight with him, won't try to scare him. But nobody knew where it was headed. We sat and watched it for a week. It'd go toward Mexico. Then it'd stop and go right back at Florida. I'm talking about a hundred and eighty on a straight line. The thing was pacing back and forth across the gulf like it was angry at something.

"That Saturday, the day before it hit, I just couldn't wait any longer. So I sent Mama and your little sister off to Hattiesburg to get us a place to stay."

That image is as clear to me as the day it happened. Mama kissed us good-bye and looked at us like we were being invaded and she was leaving us to face the enemy. She made Daddy promise to get on the road the minute we got everything boarded up, and, if the thing turned north, to drop everything and get out of there, boarded up or not.

That night there was a copper sunset and warm winds and the smell of the Yucatan. It was pure and rich like mountain air, only warm. And we slept well in this air, because it appeared we would be spared. Before we went to bed, Daddy and Neal and I prayed for the people in Florida where the monster was headed.

The storm stalled that night and turned its eye to the north. We made hurried final preparations before sunrise and drove to Biloxi in a stinging rain to aid a cousin who lived away from the water and planned to ride it out. On the way out of town, we stopped by Perinovich's house.

"You and Mike wanted to go with Cass up the river," Daddy said. "He had to take his boat up there."

"But why did he have to stay with the boat? Why was it that important to him?"

"Cass had every penny to his name tied up in that boat. And you can't get insurance on a wooden boat, least you can't pay for insurance on one. He couldn't just tie it off at the dock and leave.

"Marie was working for the city back then, and her boss was no one other than young Bernie Pettus. Cass wanted her and Mike to leave with us and go to Hattiesburg. But Marie said no, they'd go to the new civic center. They had built it good and strong.

"Bernie had gone to the site every day and personally inspected the work. He told them they had to use three-quarter-inch bolts where three-eighths would have done fine, stuff like that. It ran the costs way up, but Bernie said we get too many big winds down here to cut corners. So, see, that's why Marie wanted to take Mike there. Even Camille wouldn't be able to knock that place down.

"So Perinovich sent them to the center and took the *Miss Marie* up the Biloxi River to ride it out. He found a place about where the I-10 bridge is now, course there wasn't any interstate back then. He set the anchor out with plenty of scope, maybe a hundred and fifty feet. It was a big Danforth and he found some sand bottom and backed it down until it set. Then he turned on his VHF and set the other radio on WWL for the weather reports.

"The winds had been gusting pretty good all day, but when it started getting darker, they picked up speed. And the rain got heavy. Hell, it rained over a foot and a half in just that one day, people forget that. Way before the storm was at its height, Cass said the rain was blowing in at him so hard it looked like somebody was spraying a garden hose full blast on the windshield. He couldn't see a thing.

"The storm sent out a surge ahead of it. It was really a tidal wave. Nobody knows how high it was. I've heard twenty feet, some say twenty-five. But it was at night and black as tar and nobody could see it. Cass said he could tell when the surge got up the river to where he was because the water rose so fast it felt like the boat was going up on a hydraulic lift. Rose so fast it almost made his stomach flip.

"He kept the motor running all night and tried to keep pointed into the wind. Keeping the wheel straight was like tightening lug nuts by hand. He said after the storm his hands shook for a day from keeping up the pressure so long. He got to worrying about another boat or a log slamming into him. He said an empty skiff sailed by him and it was moving so fast it was like it had an outboard pushing it. That wind would knock a man down. Or worse, pick him up like so much newspaper. It was roaring so loud you couldn't have heard a gunshot in the next room.

"Cass said the worst part was wondering if Marie and Mike were okay. He couldn't get anything on the radio because the lightning was nonstop so the static knocked out any sound. Every once in a while he'd get somebody on the VHF, but it was mainly May Day calls.

A high gust of wind rustled the top leaves of the pecan tree out by the road. Daddy set his glass beside him on the swing and pinched the middle button of his shirt. He flapped it back and forth to let some air in.

"The storm passed through around midnight," he said. "Camille was such a tight storm that it had clear edges to it. When it passed, the winds and rain dropped off fast. The front edge had come from the southwest and pushed the water in and it was slow going back out. As soon as the winds died down to a reasonable speed, forty miles an hour or so, Cass headed in. He was so tired he sat in the pilot's chair and laid on the top of the wheel. He was steering it with his chest.

"By this time, he was getting radio reports. And they were scaring him sick. You remember them. They were the same ones we were hearing that next day."

I did indeed remember that morning. When we pulled out of Hattiesburg, the radio was reporting 100 percent destruction in Bay Saint Louis and Waveland. Long Beach, Pass Christian, Gulfport—all gone. We were sure nothing would be standing. Daddy led the way in his pickup, we followed in the station wagon. We stopped twice to hook a chain to pine trees across the highway and drag them to the side.

We topped off the tanks in Wiggins because we wouldn't have any gas for a while down on the coast. There was no power, wouldn't be for three weeks. The man at the Esso station opened up the panel at the front of the pump. He took the blade off of a Yazoo lawn mower. Then he rigged a fan belt between the pulley of the gas pump and the blade axle of the mower. He cranked the mower and the fan belt spun the pulley and pumped the gas up from the underground tank.

"The ride back down the river was slow," Daddy said. "Hundreds of loggerheads, some of them whole trees ripped out by their roots. A house trailer was floating in the bay, nothing showing but the roof. Cass rounded the bend and there was their house, pretty as you please. The water had risen up to the top step and was still in the yard, but that was it. He docked and took a quick look. The steps to the house were slimy and he slipped and tore the knee of his pants and drew blood. He went into the house and took a quick look around. Then he started running as fast as he could to the civic center.

"It took an hour to get there because he had to dodge water moccasins and downed power lines. You couldn't even see the street, it was covered waist-deep with pieces of busted-up houses and cars flipped over. And you remember how hot it was. There were people climbing over piles of lumber looking for their houses.

"When Cass saw Dukate School and got his bearings he knew he had trouble. The civic center was behind it and he couldn't see anything there. Sure enough, the closer he got, the more he knew it was gone. There wasn't much more than a slab left standing.

"Cass just went crazy. He started throwing boards around trying to get to the bottom of every pile of lumber on the Point, the whole time shouting their names. The National Guard had moved in and they told him he'd have to leave, but he said they'd have to shoot him to get him out of there. They could tell he meant business so they left him alone. Once they got some tents set up, a couple of them helped him search. By this time Cass was running on nothing but nerves.

"When sundown came, folks who had gone inland were coming back to see what was standing and they were crawling over the debris like so many ants. The only light came from flashlights. Dogs were barking and people were throwing boards around trying to get to whatever they had left. Lot of yelling going on, people calling out for lost folks. Cass said he remembers cutting his hand pretty bad on some broken glass. He sat down to wrap a strip of his T-shirt around it to stop the bleeding. He didn't remember anything after that."

Daddy's eyes disengaged. The past thirty years melted away and it was once again the day after Camille hit. He rocked back and forth and laid both arms across the top of the swing. The winds were picking up and I smelled the moisture in them. I poured him the last of the pitcher of tea.

"They woke him up the next morning," Daddy whispered. "He was on a cot under a Red Cross tent. The kid said, 'Mr. Perinovich, I'm afraid we found your wife and son.' The kid didn't look all that much older than Mike, just some young guardsman they sent to break the news to him. Cass said he just laid there on his back and blubbered like a baby, didn't even have enough strength left to wipe his eyes."

Daddy drew in a deep breath and his Adam's apple worked as he chewed on his bottom lip. He turned his head and looked toward the garage. The light creak of the swing kept a steady pace and the leaves in the live oak swished in a gust of breeze.

"But what does this have to do with Bernie Pettus?" I asked. "Was it Bernie's fault that the center collapsed? Sounds like he tried to build it right."

He stopped the swing and leaned forward and rested his elbows on his thighs. He stared at the floor of the porch as he talked. "Cass made it through the funerals better than I thought he would. Looking back on it, he was holding up as a show of respect until we at least got them into the ground, or maybe he was on tranquilizers. But he started drinking that very night. Didn't stop for two years.

"A week after the funerals, he got some pink plastic flowers and went back to the slab of the civic center. The bulldozers had moved in and they were pushing pieces of houses, trees, wrecked boats, anything that wasn't claimed by that time into big piles in the street. I can remember the smell of all that smoke when they set those piles on fire. There were front-end loaders filling up dump trucks and they were hauling it off to salvage what they could and dump the rest. The National Guard was sifting through some of it for bodies. After a week of sun, it was getting easier to find the bodies underneath all the junk. They could smell them even through the smoke. The guard had to use gas masks to keep from throwing up.

"Cass put the flowers into a hole in the stump of one of the concrete columns and said the Hail Mary for Marie and Mike. The column was broken off three feet above the ground. He stood back to look at the flowers and noticed a reinforcing rod sticking up and inch or two out of the concrete. He felt the top of it and realized that it was no bigger around than the tip of his little finger. He knew that wasn't right. He took his knife and scraped around and could only find four steel rods in the column, little skinny rods. There should have been eight big ones. He spotted a piece of the sheet metal wall stuck in a low limb of a tree. You know those three-quarter-inch bolts Bernie had been bragging about and the city had been paying extra for?"

"They turned out to be three-eighths?" I said.

"Exactly. That place wasn't built to no super specifications. The city only got charged like it was. And that damn crook Bernie was pocketing the difference.

"Perinovich, he just went ballistic. He went down to the police station to file a complaint, went to find the district attorney, he went to the general in charge of the National Guard." He shook his head and chuckled. "I'm telling you, that Cass, he was a handful."

"So what happened? Why didn't they arrest Bernie or fire him or something?"

"You got to remember the times, son. It was right after the worst storm in history. The National Guard was having a hard time just getting food to people. The cops had their hands full looking for looters and price gougers. Plus, the cops lived in Biloxi themselves. A lot of them had their own disasters to fight with. Not to mention, there was a hell of a problem with snakes, there wasn't any place to take a bath, bodies were starting to rot in the heat. It was hot as hell and the chain saws were running full-time clearing away the trees and limbs, and I mean full-time. The place sounded like a herd of souped-up locusts had invaded. It wasn't the best time to launch any investigation.

"Another thing, Perinovich was doing all this hell-raising on foot. His truck, they never did find out what happened to it, and a tree smashed Marie's station wagon. It took him three days to get to the offices he was going to. By the time he got some assistant DA to listen to him, they went back to the civic center and everything was gone. There wasn't one shred of evidence of anything he had been saying. In fact, it was amazing how the public works department crew went out of their way to haul off each and every piece of the place. So there wasn't anything anybody could do. That civic center is probably right now an artificial snapper bank out in the gulf."

Mike's funeral had been the first time I thought about my own death. Mr. Cass sat on the front pew with his mother and father. His father looked just like Mr. Cass was going to look a few years later. Mr. Cass's sister, who was Sheila's mother, sat behind him and kept Sheila on her lap the whole time. Even Sheila's father showed up. Mr. Cass had a full head of black hair back then and was firm muscled and straight as a flounder gig. Daddy might be right about the tranquilizers.

Everybody around Mr. Cass was crying; I was too. Poor little Sheila looked like she was three years old curled up in her mama's lap. The doors of the church were propped open. It was dark inside and dust motes drifted in the shaft of sunlight coming through the front door. Everyone was waving cardboard fans from the funeral home. I tried to think what it would be like not to see Mike again, but I wasn't old enough to project such thoughts past the next week.

"So Cass dove headfirst into a bottle and didn't come up for air for two years," Daddy said. "When he did, he wrote letters to everybody from the governor on down. He'd write a letter to the editor every week. And he'd call names, he didn't give a damn. But there was no evidence and pretty soon folks started passing it off. Just some poor ol' drunk who needed somebody to blame 'cause his wife and kid died. Truth is, Cass died in Camille, too. It just took him thirty years to stop breathing.

"But I believed him. When he finally realized the civic center thing was impossible, he started watching everything Bernie and his bunch did. He figured they'd slip up somewhere down the line. Cass wasn't crazy, not by a long shot. You young people think that old guys like Cass and me and that Nguyen fellow don't have good sense, that we're helpless. We're not."

A surge of wind blew a few soft, green leaves onto the porch. Daddy stretched his legs and reached behind him and massaged the small of his back and pulled himself up using the chain that held the swing. "You ready to finish up?"

It grew darker as a line of clouds crossed the sun. The air had cooled and picked up some weight. The hurricane color of the low western sky caught his eye and he paused and studied it.

"Son, I want you to keep your ears open. See if anybody's got a shrimp boat they might want to sell."

THIRTY-TWO

Daddy's story about Bernie and the Civic Center cleared up my doubts about Mr. Cass's sanity, but it didn't get me one bit closer to finding out who set up the explosion. Somebody planted Hank's cap at the scene. Johnnie Barron said the Dragons would set up kids on weak criminal charges and then step in like a white knight to save them and make the kid a true believer. It sure sounded like that was what happened to Hank. I decided to go to Nguyen's store and make another run at him. Now that Hank had been arrested, he may be more willing to talk.

A layer of fresh brown shrimp covered the beds of crushed ice and gave off a strong saltwater smell. The foot traffic in the store was steady. The women who came in were small, none of them topped five two, and some of the older ones wore the flat, conical straw hats they grew up with in Vietnam. I caught only a few phrases in English. But even in Vietnamese, in any language, I knew they were haggling about price. The pitch rises and the talk speeds up. I've heard the same speech patterns in Germany when I was in the MPs. I also heard it at the sidewalk markets in Nuevo Laredo on one memorable road trip, of which I have little memory, after exams my sophomore year at Ole Miss.

I sat on a stool inside the door to the back room and sipped Nguyen's dark iced tea. Like Biloxi. Very cold. Much sugar. The noon news on the little TV said Doreen was aiming at Vermillion

Bay, two hundred miles to the west in southwest Louisiana. The last customer walked out complaining in a singsong. Must have been the price.

"Sorry to have you wait," Nguyen said. "Busy day. We are selling many batteries and much water in bottles."

"I need to know about the Dragons." I said. "My brother can only do so much unless he knows what he's up against."

"The Dragons are bad, they steal money."

"And is Huang one of them?"

The two-toned bell chimed, someone had come in the front door. The store was close-packed, with narrow aisles. The sun that came in through the front windows filtered through hand-painted signs announcing products and prices, and shafts of light reflected through a white haze of dust. The store smelled of cantaloupes and liver cheese and the air was chilled and weighty. Nguyen slid off his stool and walked up front.

The walls of the back room were plastered with posters advertising hair dressings and shampoos and showing smiling, light-skinned Vietnamese models whose only Asian features were their eyes. Other posters displayed delicate hands with exquisite red nails.

"You like more tea?"

I shook my head. "Huang is in trouble. I need to know who else is in this Dragons gang. You give me some names and I'll take it from there."

Nguyen sat and stared at his feet. He flexed his fingers, stiff with arthritis. I leaned against the concrete block wall and scratched my back by moving up and down. The drip into the stainless steel sink beside the back door grew louder.

"I'm your friend, Nguyen. I'm not a cop."

The light from the front accented the deep creases around his mouth and at the edges of his eyes. The eyes were milky, probably cataracts, and his skin was like crumpled paper. He stared at a point just past my shoulder.

"I was clerk for American army when they leave Saigon. From different class than Dragon boys. I knew how to leave, I got on cargo plane. The end of war was coming, I knew that. My son, Huang's father, was in ARVN. Da Nang. His mother died with flu two years before."

"Did you take Huang with you?"

He nodded yes. "I take Huang and his sister. Cousins live in Biloxi. They work on boats to get shrimp. We sleep on floor of cousin's house and save money for store."

"How long ago was that?"

"Huang was five when I buy this store. He worked here when he was very little. His sister is in Jackson at college to be a doctor."

"Is Huang a Dragon?"

Nguyen lifted his feet and propped them on a blue plastic milk crate. He leaned against the wall and rubbed his side right above the waist. "Huang is a good boy. He studies his lessons. Fifteen is a hard year for boys."

"Nguyen, I can't talk in riddles all day. I need to know the names of some of Huang's friends, some of the younger ones. I'm pretty sure Huang and his friends didn't have anything to do with the explosion, but I've got to find somebody who was around when it happened. If you don't know, I'll ask Hank."

"Huang will not talk about things like that."

"Is he that scared of them?"

The doorbell rang and Nguyen slid off the stool and reached both hands to his stiff lower back and rubbed with the tips of his fingers. He shuffled through the doorway to wait on his customer. Nguyen was probably right; his grandson wouldn't talk about such things. I can usually outlisten anybody I encounter in an investigation, but I had never gone up against a Vietnamese man who grew up in a lifelong war around the spies and sadists who passed for police in Saigon, a man who had seen more rubber hose interrogations than I had seen football games. Asking Nguyen for information about his grandson and possible criminal activity was like asking him to stop a twitch in his eyelid. I sipped the tea and tried to plan my line of questions to get as much information as I could without making Nguyen commit to something he couldn't weasel out of later. It would be up to me to decode the oracle when he came back.

"No! Go out!" Nguyen shouted. I jumped off the stool and dashed through the open door. One of the two kids on the other side of the counter barely came up to my armpits. But the other one had a goatee and a cigarette dangling from his lips and stood a good four inches taller than Nguyen. They glared at the old man and the bigger kid crossed his arms in the posture of a demand. He held a vinyl bank bag, pinched between his fingers.

"Get out!" Nguyen held a two-foot-long stick and the veins on the back of his hand stood out like strands of blue yarn.

"What's the problem here?" I said.

The smaller kid took a step back, but the bigger and older one didn't move.

"No more money!" Nguyen shouted. "Get out!"

The older kid said something in Vietnamese and Nguyen shouted back at him in the language and venomous tone of Saigon during the war years.

"You boys need something?" I asked. "Maybe I can help you."

"They want money. No more money! Get out!"

"Is that right?" I asked. "Are you here for money?"

The younger kid got his courage back and stepped back to his place beside the older one. The older one took a step forward and slapped the bag down in front of Nguyen. Then he swept it across the countertop, knocking the cigarette and aspirin displays to the floor. "Come on, old man—"

I jumped around the counter and grabbed the kid at the nape of his neck. The adrenaline of anger kicked in, anger for his disrespect to Nguyen and for his in-your-face attitude toward me. I jammed his face through the bed of shrimp and into the crushed ice. The little kid dashed out the front door like a big-tailed cat with a snarling dog on his ass.

"You don't say 'old man,' asshole!" I pulled his head out of the ice. "You hear me?" I shoved it back down and ground his face into the ice and shrimp like I was grinding out a cigarette. I grabbed the back of his collar and yanked him off the ground. He sucked in a lungful of air with a loud gasp. He wiped the shrimp juice off his face with his forearm as I dangled him on his tiptoes.

"You don't come in here and pull shit like that!" I shouted. "We straight on that?"

He nodded four times in rapid order and cleared the crushed ice away from his eyes with his fingers. His eyes were as round as plates and he was panting like a sled dog.

"What does this punk want?"

"He want money. They say I pay money or they break my store into pieces." Nguyen shook so hard the stick was wobbling.

"How much does this shrimp sell for?"

Nguyen and the gang-banger I was suspending from the floor both looked at me as if they were sizing me up for a straitjacket.

"How much?" I shoved the boy down the aisle and pointed a finger at him to tell him to stay put. He pulled his T-shirt up and wiped his eyes.

"Four dollar a pound," Nguyen said.

I scooped three handfuls of shrimp and ice into the tin pan below the scale hanging from the roof by the fish counter.

"Three pounds of shrimp," I said. I picked up the bank bag off the floor, it held a stack of twenty-dollar bills laid in sideways. I stuffed the shrimp into the sack. Then I opened a bottle of Tiger Sauce and poured it over them. I zipped it shut, walked to the kid, and slapped it against his chest. "Take this back to Sammy and tell him he got twelve dollars this trip. And tell that son of a bitch that this is the last payment."

THIRTY-THREE

T he tropical storm grew up that night. Sustained winds of seventy-eight, ninety in gusts, and poorly defined edges, but it had the name now. Hurricane Doreen. Its peripheral clouds covered the northwest gulf. The eye sat two hundred miles off the Texas coast and was moving about as fast as your average jogger, but the usual pattern in the northern gulf is a swing to the northeast. And that could set it down in our laps.

The sky was a dome of gray as seamless and smooth as if some dingy mortar had been spread across it. The raindrops were tiny, like liquid sand, and fell soft and steady, as they had since early morning. These harbinger rains softened the ground and soaked the trees and grass and muffled every sound except for the swish of the tires along the slick asphalt.

I parked in the lot of an abandoned 7-Eleven, a hundred yards from the front gate, checking out the NuCoast crew through my Bushnells. The main problem I was having was keeping the windshield of the truck clear enough for me to see through the binoculars. When it wasn't raining, the heat inside the truck fogged the windows.

Perinovich thought something wasn't right about the contract the city awarded to NuCoast. I had to find out what that was, and I figured scoping out the job site was a good place to start.

The chain-link gate was ten feet high with concertina wire

swirled along the top. I had a clear look at the trucks being loaded with fifty-gallon drums and following them when they left would be child's play. NuCoast Enterprises had put the DOT numbers on the side of the green truck in a good contrasting white, easy to read with my field glasses when I could get a clear line of sight.

The site was an abandoned truck repair garage the city bought twenty years after it had closed, and ten years before the EPA determined the place had such residual contamination that the top ten inches of soil had to be removed and the underground tanks drained and the city had to pay for it. It was slow work. Everybody wore rubberized suits, gloves, masks, and goggles, and the Biloxi heat, even with the misting rain, made them stop every ten minutes for water or to take off the head gear.

I got tired of listening to the radio and reading the sports pages and working crossword puzzles, and every half hour or so I drove down in front of the plant to gauge the progress of the job. The truck waiting for a load was a short flatbed. After three hours, the driver stepped out of the Quonset hut. An EPA technician in full protective gear shut the truck's tailgate and walked to the driver and held up a clipboard and gave the driver a pen.

The NuCoast truck drifted past the opened traffic arm at the gate. I fell in behind it, staying back several car lengths. My wiper blade had a gap in it and left a swath of mist and road film right at eye level so that I spent half the time straining up to look over it or crouching down to look under it. The yellow lights atop the cab made the truck easy to follow, and the rain gave me good cover in case the driver was cautious. That didn't mean much in the city, but might mean a great deal if we got into the countryside. The sky was darkening, as if a giant dimmer switch was being turned down. The day was ending and the sun could not be seen except for a stain of lightness to the west.

We headed west until we got to Cowan Road, the feeder road to Interstate 10, which is four miles north of the beach and runs parallel. Through their truck's wide rear windshield, I tried to size up the two men in the cab. But it was tough seeing through the rain and the road spray and it was getting dark. They were of average size and both were wearing caps.

The rain picked up and the red glow of their taillights fanned out through the raindrops on my windshield. On the flatbed, tied together with yellow fiberglass rope, stood six drums of liquefied sludge, three hundred gallons of low toxic ooze that might be headed for the gulf.

Hundreds of these drums can do some damage to the food chain. But these six drums, by themselves, would do little damage if taken far enough out to sea, no more than the natural seepage from the Gulf of Mexico's oil-rich water bottom. It's a crime with no identifiable victim and no immediate deadly effects. In other words, a lot of money for little risk of big jail time. A natural draw for every criminal above the purse-snatching level.

The coast doesn't travel inland very far, maybe five miles from the shoreline. There is no tapering off into the piney woods. As soon as you lose the salt smell, as soon as marsh gives way to red clay, T-shirts and shorts change to jeans and cowboy boots and men who would be shrimpers if they lived five miles south are hauling pulpwood and raising Herefords.

It is an area thick with pine trees interspersed with veins of hardwoods along the creeks that flow to the bays and estuaries of the gulf. The serpentine creeks are clear because the water is filtered through the carpet of pine needles on the floor of the woods. Sugar white sandbars fill out the S-curves of the creeks. There is a network of logging roads, usually nothing more than two ruts formed by overloaded trucks hauling poles and pulpwood to the main road. These roads can wash out in an hour's worth of heavy rain and they are graded only when they become absolutely impassable.

The truck turned onto one of these roads and into a bank of

pines. I drove a hundred feet past the entrance and pulled onto the shoulder. I twisted around and looked through my back windshield and caught glimpses of the taillights through the trees until the truck rounded a curve and got too deep into the woods for me to see anything. I backed up and followed them.

They couldn't lose me on a logging road, not a wet one. I hung back out of the range of their rearview and followed the fresh tracks. They couldn't go far, the Biloxi River was somewhere close by and in the direction the little road was headed. The road was better than most and I heard the gentle scrape of my oil pan against the soft clay only twice. The pine trees were an impenetrable wall and blocked out the dying, grayish glow of the late afternoon sky.

It was too dark to see the road, so I used my headlights to watch for the holes. Some can bury a car to its axle. The rain was hard now and loud against my roof. I turned my wipers up a notch and kept an eye out ahead for their taillights. A quarter mile farther into the woods, their tracks turned at a tiny lane, so narrow that some of the tips of bushes on both sides were freshly broken where the truck squeezed through. I shone my flashlight up the trail. It crested and disappeared over a rise a hundred feet away. The road had twisted through the woods and there was no sun, so my bearings were less than sure, but I sensed that the marsh where the river emptied into Back Bay would be on the other side.

Thirty yards beyond the little trail the truck had taken the road widened out. The rain had let up and the ground looked firm, with a cover of grass and no standing water, so I drove past the trail and parked on the side.

As I walked back to the little trail, I tucked my camera under my parka to keep it dry. In the clearing between the trees, the sky was still a white-gray, but the light couldn't reach down to me. The rain had soaked the pine needles on the ground and had weighted down the limbs of the trees and the drops falling from the limbs were heavy, much heavier than the steady light drizzle from the sky. The wet earth and the soaked blanket of pine needles provided a good sound cover, no way anyone could hear me. But the fat drops off the trees pelted the rubber parka like drumbeats so I couldn't hear them either.

Footing on the little road was tricky, with a lot of holes, and I almost turned my ankle, so I started planting my front foot before putting weight on it and this made walking very slow. The smells of wet earth and wet pine blended with the honeysuckle and wisteria that wrapped around some of the trees. The fireflies twinkled in the leaves and the branches.

On the far side of the rise, the slope led down to the banks of a bayou. A broad, beige savannah spread out before me and to the south lay that portion of Back Bay called Big Lake, wide and gray. Along the far shore of the bay, some three miles away, the lights of Biloxi were coming on.

To the right was a bait shop, a wooden shack with peeling paint and a corrugated tin roof. It almost looked abandoned, but in a window facing the water was a glowing neon Budweiser sign. Beside the bait shop was what looked like a huge boathouse, unusual in its width and in that it had a chain-link gate across the open end. The bottom edge of the gate almost touching the water.

I put the zoom lens on the gate. Behind it was a single-engine seaplane facing out. The bayou was long and unusually straight, a natural seaplane runway. On the right side of the bayou, maybe two football fields away, was a grouping of cypress trees festooned with Spanish moss and beyond the clump of trees, at the Point the bayou spilled out into the Biloxi River, was a derelict steel trawler. The boat was resting on the marsh, no doubt deposited by the high waters and wind of some long-ago hurricane, and canted slightly toward the bayou. It appeared to be a pile of rust, but its steel rigging was still intact and the twenty-foot pipe, which at one time had held a VHF antenna, stuck out like a tilted flagpole.

The NuCoast truck was directly below me, parallel to the bayou beside a Biloxi lugger, a thirty-five-footer. The yellow glow from the truck's running lights let me make out the shapes of the boat and of the truck, but there was no way to take any pictures. The water rippled as the wind picked up from the south and east, the outside cusp of the backside swirl of the distant hurricane's counterclockwise pattern.

The boat had good lines with a high bow and the cabin set to the stern in the traditional Biloxi style. The sides were low and the rub rail extra thick. I spotted a plywood patch on the side and recognized the boat as the *Side Pocket*.

The cabin light came on and even through the rain I knew Lennis Belter's sharp profile. There was another man with him in the cabin.

The two guys from the truck were up on the bed rolling a barrel toward the Tommy-Lift platform at the rear. One of them was Eight Ball, still in that same cap. By the time they got the last of the drums down to the ground, the sky had deepened from charcoal gray to black. Lennis flipped on the white light at the front of the boat and Eight Ball and his partner rolled the dolly up the ramp with the first of the six barrels.

Lennis and the guy in the raincoat sat inside, dry and warm. The guys from the truck struggled with the barrels with no help from the two inside the cabin, like they were in different unions and that was written in the contract. They pushed the first barrel up the ramp and over the side and walked it across the deck to the area above the ice hole in front of the pick-out box. They laid it on its side.

I had seen enough by the time they loaded the third barrel, and I wanted to get to the main road ahead of Eight Ball and his partner to position myself to follow them. Although I got no pictures, maybe I could get the sheriff to intercept the boat and maybe they could trace the barrels back to NuCoast.

The back side of the rise was muddy and slippery and I had to grab little saplings to get a handhold to scale its slippery face. On the other side of the crest, I fell and smeared mud on my parka.

I cut my hands from grabbing the rough-barked pines and my shin ached from where I banged it on a stump. The parka didn't breathe and I was sweating and it stung my eyes but my hands were too muddy to wipe them.

I turned my truck's ignition key. There was no sound. None of the lights were on, not even the dome light, and I cursed myself for leaving on whatever I had left on to run the battery down. But I had not been gone long enough to run it down that dead, no matter what I left on. I got out and popped the hood latch and shone the flashlight on the battery. The cable fitting had been pulled off the battery terminal and lay dangling against the side of the wheel well.

An alarm went off in my head. I wheeled around to run into the woods. I took one big stride and a beam of light hit me square in the face. It was a lantern flashlight, too bright for me to see behind it.

"Hold it!" a gravel voice shouted. "Get those hands up!"

THIRTY-FOUR

I held up both hands. Twenty yards up into the woods along the logging road, a pair of headlights flashed on and came toward us, moving up and down as the car hit big holes in the road. It stopped and the driver opened the door and flipped the headlights to bright. I squinted against the glare.

"What'd he see?"

"I guess he saw ever'thing," the gravel-voiced man said. "Whaddaya think we oughta do with him?"

"Well, we sure can't take him with us."

"Why don't we just tie him up here? It'll take him all night to get loose. If he don't, a logging crew'll see him tomorrow."

"It's a felony, dammit! What he saw can put us both away for the next ten years. And that's just for the barrels. The cops start looking into this, they'll find out about everything else."

The rain blunted the tiny gradations in timbre and pitch and resonance that allows us to recognize a particular voice. I had never heard that ragged voice, but the cadence or maybe the choice of words of the other guy, the guy who had been driving the car, sparked some recognition. It was too faint to call up, but it was there. A Point Cadet accent, no doubt about that. I tried to search my mind for it, but my mind already had plenty to handle.

"Turn around."

A rush of hollow fear ran up my chest. Was it going to end like this? My hands were already tingling because I had held them up so long. The left one started shaking. I could no more control it than I could stop a hiccup. The image of the hole at the end of his gun barrel popped into my mind, and a spot on my back just above my kidney began throbbing as I pictured a red hot bullet ripping into me right there. It was all I could do to keep from bolting toward the woods.

"Get moving."

Lightning raced across the sky and lit up the path in front of me. They ordered me back up the little trail, back up the incline. I thought about diving to the ground and turning on them. I decided against it. If I could keep from getting shot in the back, I'd get my chance. I always had before.

We were halfway to the bayou when a big searchlight from the boat hit and froze us where we stood. It was one of those blinding, ten-thousand-candlepower jobs and we couldn't see far enough to take our next steps.

"Don't come no closer!" a voice shouted from the boat.

"It's okay, Belter!" the guy behind me growled. "It's us!"

Belter stepped to the side of the searchlight. Half his face was in light, half in shadow, like a child making a scary face at a camp-out by holding a flashlight below his chin. He held a rifle by its barrel with the stock resting on his foot. The gun slipped out of his hand and thumped against the deck.

"He's drunk," the gravel-voiced man said.

"You surprised?"

The NuCoast truck had already cranked up. The diesel made a low, pulsing hum and I smelled its exhaust. The yellow lights on top of the cab shone soft through the rain. When we got to the clearing at the edge of the bayou, the truck geared down and chugged up the rise and took a long time before shifting out of first gear.

The guy behind me pushed me at the small of my back and I stumbled ahead and fell to one knee. When my chance came, the son of a bitch would pay for that. I sensed that there was now only one man behind me, the one with the rough voice. The second one was lagging behind. Lennis stepped full into the spotlight.

"Whaddaya bring him for?"

"Didn't bring him, fool. He was already here. He was watching y'all from up on that hill."

"Well, whaddaya gonna do with him?"

"Ain't decided yet. Bring some rope over here and tie his hands. I'm tired of holding this gun."

The second guy on the *Side Pocket* was still behind the spotlight, but he took the rifle from Lennis and held it with the stock resting against his hip, the barrel pointed high over his head. I thought about grabbing Lennis if he got close enough. But with one gun behind me and another one on the boat, there was no way to position Lennis as a shield. And I wasn't real sure it would keep them from shooting anyway. I'd get a better chance.

"You snooped around a little too much, didn't you, college boy?" Lennis used a length of half-inch nylon, softened from wear. He yanked the knot tight on my wrist. With my hands behind me the rain mixed with the sweat on my face and head and burned my eyes.

Off to the side where the truck had been, the second man, the one who had lagged behind, came walking toward us holding an umbrella. Lennis's partner on the boat killed all the lights. There was no moon and everything went black. The smell of the tropics was in the wind. I knew the smell, it was hurricane air, Perinovich's bad wind.

"Sit down," the gravel-voiced man behind me said.

The wet mud seeped through the seat of my jeans and the rope chafed my wrist. Good thing it was nylon and not fiberglass or it would be drawing blood by now.

"Well, we can't just let him go."

"Let him go, hell!" Lennis said. "They done got my boy, Elvis, in the jail for one crummy barrel. They'd throw my ass *under* the jail for six."

"What are y'all doing out there?" It was the man inside the cabin on the boat. "Y'all hurry up."

"Keep your shirt on!" Lennis yelled.

"Ain't that Billy Weldon?" the gravel-voiced man asked. "What the hell's he doin' here?"

"Boss sent him," Lennis said. "I don't like it no more'n you do. But I can't handle them barrels by myself, and this ain't exactly a job you can advertise in the paper for."

"Yeah, but he could screw this whole thing up."

"He ain't got to do nothing but roll some barrels overboard," Lennis said. "We didn't bring him out here for his brain."

"I bet this is the first time anybody ever brought Weldon to supply the muscles."

They both laughed.

"Y'all hurry up," Weldon said.

"Shut up and turn that light back on!" Lennis shouted. "I cain't see shit out here." The hard steel of the pistol barrel tapped against my shoulder. "Get up, college boy. Get up and get to the boat. Nothing funny, you understand?"

I stood and walked toward the light, nudged along from time to time by the point of the gun. There was a gangplank consisting of two long poles crossed with three-foot-long two-by-sixes. It was crude but I had seen it hold a grown man and a full fifty-gallon drum.

"What are we going to do with him?" Weldon asked.

"Shut up, Billy."

"Maybe we ought to just leave him here."

"He's seen too much."

"What have I seen?" I said. "All I've seen is some oil drums on a boat. I don't have any idea what's being done with them or what's in them. I haven't seen anything."

"Shut up!" Lennis turned to the man who had lagged behind. "What do you think, boss?"

"Delmas is right," Billy said. "He hasn't seen anything. Let's don't let this get out of hand, boys."

"It's awready out of hand," the unseen voice of the boss said.

"No, it's not!" Billy shouted. "It's not out of hand yet!"

"Shut up," the boss said. "This guy's a private eye. Ya can bet he knows too much, or he wouldn't be out here in a rainstorm at night."

"But he's right," Billy said. "He ain't seen anything yet. And you're gonna keep quiet, right?"

I nodded vigorously.

"We don't need to let this get—"

"Calm down," the boss said. "We're gonna think of something. Just take it easy."

"Look," I said, "you guys don't need to do anything stupid here. I haven't seen anything I can testify to. Besides that, it's no skin off my nose, anyway."

"Come over here, Lennis," the boss said.

The boss remained in the shadow the whole time, I never saw him. The gravel-voiced guy must have gone back up in the woods to the car. The rain had began falling harder, and I still couldn't quite place the cadence of the boss's voice.

"Take him up front, Weldon," Lennis said as he walked back into the light of the boat.

Billy grasped my arm at the elbow and eased me toward the bow to a spot between the pick-out box and the anchor chute.

"Billy, y'all better think about this," I said. "If you let me go, by the time I get to the cops, the evidence would be long gone and it would be my word against everybody here."

"You better just sit here."

"Think about it."

"I am thinking about it. Sit down, please."

I sat cross-legged. He lifted up a leg of the pick-out box a foot off the ground. "Now," he said, "slide your hands under that table leg."

"Right now we're talking misdemeanor at worst and no proof. If you take me out in this boat, it's going to be kidnapping. That's a federal offense, Billy."

Weldon had quit talking. He took a four-foot length of hemp and slipped it through the nylon rope that Lennis had tied around my wrists. Billy's hands shook as he looped it around a leg and a cross brace of the pick-out box about three times in figure eight fashion. A true landlubber, he thought the more loops, the stronger the knot. My chance might have come.

"You better talk to him, Billy."

He walked toward the gangplank and searched the edges of the darkness to see where the boss and Lennis had gone. The rain had started coming down in hard drops, and the wind had kicked in as well. The rain splattering my face made it impossible for me to make out anything but vague shapes on land. Two figures came from the dark perimeter into the light cast by the boat. One held an open umbrella and even in the rain I knew the other was the lanky frame of Lennis Belter.

"So what are we going to do?" Billy said. "I think we ought to just leave him here. He hasn't seen anything, there's nothing he can testify to."

"You let us do the thinking," Lennis said. "Did you tie him down?"

"Yeah, I put a good knot in it."

"In what?"

"I tied him to the pick-out box," Billy said. "He's not going anywhere."

"You check for a gun like I told you to?"

"I know what I'm doing, Lennis."

Lennis laughed.

"Aw, shut up Lennis."

Lennis and Weldon stepped into the cabin. I could see them

clearly, at least as clearly as I could see anything with rainwater in my eyes. Lennis said something that sent Weldon into a session of arm waving and pacing. Lennis stepped out of the cabin and weaved toward me. He held a brown glass quart of Red Dog beer and turned it up and took a swig before stepping out from under the cabin's extended roof into the rain.

"Shit! I had me somebody who can tie a knot, I wouldn't be screwing around in a friggin' hurricane."

My chance just slipped away. Lennis knew his knots. He held the leg of the pick-out box to steady himself and knelt beside me. He stuck his head under the box and set the bottle under it out of the rain and fumbled with the ropes at my wrists.

"You bring me that money your old man owes me, college boy?"

"Kiss my ass, Lennis."

"You know how to swim, Delmas?"

He felt around to determine if Weldon's knot was worth a damn, which even in my position I could tell it was not. But it was dark and he was drunk and a lightning bolt struck like a bomb blast in the woods right beside us, close enough to where the thunder was instantaneous and ear-splitting. It startled us and Lennis jerked his head straight up and banged it against the bottom of the pick-out box.

"Damn!" He pulled himself up by grasping the side of the boat. "Screw this! You ain't goin' nowhere anyhow." He staggered back to the cabin.

The wind gusted and the rain stung. It was cold and I shivered in the dark. The millions of windblown raindrops, coming down at a forty-five-degree angle, reflected in the lights of the rigging overhead.

Weldon's figure eight knot holding me to the pick-out box was loose, but Belter's knot holding my wrists together was a good one. I shoved back against the box. It was freestanding, not nailed to the deck. Under it were three quarts of Havoline 10-W-40 and a coil of yellow fiberglass rope. Cradled in the coil of rope was the quart bottle of Red Dog Lennis had forgotten.

The talk in the cabin was heating up. Even through the Plexiglas, I could hear shouting, but I couldn't make out any words. The cabin door swung open and banged against the outer wall.

"I didn't sign on for anything like this!" shouted Weldon.

"You in it whether ya like it or not," the boss said from the shore.

Lennis was laughing. It was a drunken and deriding laugh aimed at Weldon. Nobody had said anything funny.

"If we just put him out somewhere, it'll take two days for him to get back to town," Weldon said. "He can't prove anything anyway. It would be his word against ours."

"If you done it like I told ya, none of this'd be happening," the boss said. "If you hadn't tried to cut corners, and went ahead and got some out-of-town talent, we wouldn't have any private eye on our ass."

"I didn't hire this drunk fool to *kill* anybody," Weldon said. "That was his fault."

Lennis laughed.

"You in as deep as ya can get," the boss said. "Don't think you can save yaself by letting him go."

"Well, if Lennis had done what I told him to do—"

"I done just what you told me," Lennis said. "You was the one who was supposed to make sure everything was clear." Someone sloshed around in an ice chest, and then tapped his finger on the top of a can. "You told me to set it so nobody could find out it had been set, and that's what I done."

"How many of those beers you had, Malloy?" The boss asked.

"We'd better just let him go," Weldon said.

"Yeah, well, I gotta go," the boss said. "Y'all do what I said. Don't screw this up."

The outline of the boss and his umbrella faded and then disappeared as he walked into the dark night toward the car.

"I didn't sign on for this!" Weldon shouted after him. "It's stupid!"

"Get back in the damn cabin, Billy!" he shouted from the dark. "You screw this up and ya go to the pen anyway."

"We can't do this!"

The diesel fired up and Lennis goosed it and the engine roared. "Drop that plank," Lennis said. "Just push it over the side and let it drop on the bank."

"I'm not going. I'm getting off."

"Naw, you ain't. After you cast off, you gettin' your ass back in this cabin and countin' this money. You done been paid in advance. They ain't interested in gettin' no refund."

"But I didn't agree to this," Weldon whined.

"We didn't know that college boy was gonna follow the damn truck out here. Just like I didn't know that old fool Perinovich was gonna come back too early and flip on that light switch. It was their doin's, not yours. Neither one of 'em got nobody to blame but their own selves. Now get in here and shut that door before I catch the pneumonia."

The door shut and the voices became nothing more than a murmur under the cover of walls, rain, the diesel engine, and an increasing wind. The storm was easing in from the south with that combination of temperature and dropping pressure that triggers our atavistic warning bells. But the storm was far away and moving slowly and headed away from us. It was aiming toward southwest Louisiana and it wouldn't hit that night, certainly wouldn't hit us for another day even if it turned and put Biloxi in its gunsights. It was just sending out its warnings, its messages to get everything in and tied down and get ready for the days of trees blocking the roads and ruined roofs and no water and no electricity. The *Side Pocket* would go out and be back into port long before Doreen hit.

But where would I be?

THIRTY-FIVE

The wind was rising and the thermometer dropping, and the ride down the straight little bayou to the Biloxi River was rough. I worked against the nylon rope binding my wrists, but succeeded only in rubbing the wet skin raw, and the rainwater running down my arms stung where I rubbed a blister. The deck, rough from sand Lennis mixed into the paint to keep it from getting slick, was scraping my ass raw.

There was a chop on Biloxi Bay, but the boat was heavy and the little whitecaps didn't move it much. They broke against the topsides and the spray blew in over the side. The spray was on the salty end of the brackish scale, and that wasn't helping my chafed ass one bit.

The barrels at my feet smelled of kerosene. One of them was leaking around a cap that wasn't screwed down tight, a pale green ooze. It mixed with the water on the deck, and the lights inside the cabin gave the film it created a rainbow sheen.

The lights of a cabin cruiser came into view. Belter cut the cabin lights and steered wide of the approaching boat, not that there was a chance the other boat would see a man tied to a pick-out box. I tried to think of some way to signal, but it was too windy and still too dark since we weren't far enough down the bay to pick up much light from onshore. The cruiser passed two hundred yards to port, its red port running light twinkling in the rain.

I worked my fingers into Weldon's series of loops that passed for a knot. I pulled and stretched the loops, six inches at most, but that was enough to let me explore the deck with my fingers to see what I could reach. The box was freestanding and I pushed it back and felt the end of the coiled rope stored underneath it. I pulled the rope to me an inch at a time by pinching it and pulling as far as my tied hands could. The coil stayed intact enough for me to pull Lennis's quart of Red Dog to me.

We passed below the Highway 90 bridge to Ocean Springs. The tires of the cars and freight trucks sang as they crossed the wet steel-grid center span. Once in the open water of the Mississippi Sound, the wind became a gale and the chop grew to waves, four-footers. The *Side Pocket* began rising and falling with them and the oil drums clanged against each other.

I gripped the neck of the beer bottle and slammed it on the deck. The two guys in the cabin didn't notice the thump. Either that or they figured it was the barrels bumping around. The rope around my wrist kept me from raising the bottle any higher than two feet. I bounced it off the deck three times. I would need to smash it on something harder than wood.

Lennis Belter is a piece of cow dung, but he is one hell of a boat handler. He could have set our course on a speed and at an angle to minimize the pounding. But he pounded the waves, jarring me against the leg of the pick-out box and slamming the barrels against the sides of the boat. I'm sure the intent was to even further scare the hell out of Billy Weldon. Lennis is the kind of chip-on-the-shoulder redneck who delights in the few chances he gets to humiliate anybody.

Three miles past the bridge we cleared the eastern tip of Deer Island. Lennis turned due south and pushed the throttle up yet another notch. It had to be close to redlining. We bucked through the waves, and I wondered how far out Lennis was planning to go before dumping the barrels and me over the side.

The wind and rain hid me from their sight. The one sharp, hard edge anywhere around me was the rim of one of the steel drums. They had turned the cabin light on. They were taking turns at swigging from a fifth of Kentucky Tavern. Neither held the wheel. It moved back and forth on its own; it was on autopilot.

I shoved the pick-out box toward the nearest barrel. I twisted and got my best angle and slammed the beer bottle against its rim. The bottle shattered like I had christened a destroyer at Ingall's Shipyard. I sat on what was left of the neck of the broken bottle to stabilize it. I lowered my hands and ran the rope at my wrists up and down a three-inch edge of sharp glass, slicing my hands up pretty good.

I eyeballed Weldon as I sawed at the rope. He scratched his ear with a playing card. Must have drunk enough whiskey to forget about me and felony convictions, and started a game of gin with Lennis.

The lights of the channel glowed faint and fuzzy in the blowing rain. A sheet of lightning revealed the silhouette of a mountain plowing toward us from behind and to starboard at the five o'clock position, inexorable, unstoppable, raising my childhood nightmare of deep water on a dark night and something being out there. It was a raft of barges, three abreast and four deep, running full speed, high and empty, fleeing the storm toward Mobile or out to deeper water where the waves would be spread farther apart. The barges had rounded tops towering forty feet above the water and hiding the tug. The only light at the front of the barges was a single white bulb on the middle one, no brighter than a porch light, and a set of red and green running lights, mere colored smudges in the driving rain.

Lennis, like a fool or a drunk or both, had been weaving in and out of the channel, but we usually stayed outside. The card game was still going on, but the radar overhead was turning, so Lennis could see on the screen the approaching boat with its load big enough to cover a football field. If he bothered to look at the screen.

I was cutting my hands more and more, and time was running out unless we were going way past the barrier islands, which was doubtful. The only other boats were small ones hightailing it in to port or big ones headed to deep water to ride it out, and, since there was little chance of being spotted, it was safe to dump the barrels at any time. I couldn't imagine Lennis was having such a good time with his new buddy that he'd want to go farther out than he had to.

Two hundred yards away, to the starboard, another trawler, dark except for the running lights, ran toward us at high speed. It pounded the waves in a seesaw rhythm sending ten-foot walls of spray to both sides of its bow. It was on a course and at a speed to cross our bow in another half mile, a hell of a dangerous course any time, but foolhardy in a tropical gale and with a raft of barges coming up behind us.

A sharp ping echoed above me, the distinct ring of a bullet ricocheting off metal. I dropped and a second bullet pinballed around the rigging. Weldon ducked out of sight. Lennis's bony hand reached up and doused the dome light. The running lights went out, and it got so dark I couldn't see my feet.

The trawler was gaining. Yellow bursts flashed from a rifle barrel. The rat-a-tat of the semiautomatic sounded like soft pops in the roaring wind. The bullets danced overhead around the steel rigging and sounded like wind chimes. I ducked, hoping the heavy wet sides of the boat would protect me from the hot rounds. The cabin window shattered and glass flew all over the deck.

I bore down on the rope and forgot about the gashes I was making on my hands and wrists. If one of those rounds hit the drums at my feet I was fried. The broken bottle crunched through the tough fibers of the rope. Felt like cutting a stalk of celery. I yanked on the rope and it cut into my wrists. Ached like somebody was going at them with a hacksaw. The rope was still too strong.

I sliced away even harder and held my breath as I yanked again. Pain shot up my arms as if I had plunged my bleeding wrists into a bucket of alcohol. The rope finally popped in two.

I scurried behind the big winch, a steel cover from the bullets. The lights of the other boat framed the guy shooting at us. He was holding a side stay to steady himself and had an automatic rifle slung over his shoulder.

The cabin door flew open and slammed against the outer cabin wall. Heavy running footsteps trailed off behind me. From the stern, Lennis fired back with a rapid set of shots. Our attackers closed the gap to fifty yards. A brilliant flash of lightning lit up the gulf. The water was gray, their boat red, and their port light was pink. And clear as the world, there was Sammy at the bow, jamming in a fresh banana clip.

I guess if you want to eliminate your waste-dumping competitors, the gulf during a tropical storm and at night is as good a place as any. There would sure be a lot less chance of having witnesses. Their boat, the *China Sea*, was a steel, high-sided Florida rig, a hell of a lot better suited to ride out a storm than the *Side Pocket*.

Another three shots rang out from our stern and Sammy ducked to the deck. The wheel in our cabin was still moving on autopilot. Weldon was keeping out of sight. From the aft deck, Lennis kept firing. The sparks of one of his rounds glanced off the steel cabin of the *China Sea*. I scooted to leeward, away from Sammy and his damned rifle. If he hit me in this storm, it would be pure luck, but he could sure hit one of those drums full of kerosene or jet fuel or whatever the hell it was. Our cabin door was still open. Weldon was sprawled out on the floor, a dark red circle pooling beneath him.

I knelt beside Weldon. He was warm and was breathing, but each breath was a raspy struggle. I turned him over on his back and slipped a life jacket under his head. He had taken a hit in the chest. He tried to talk, but I couldn't make out the words. Another burst of gunfire shattered the windshield and blue sparks cascaded through the cabin as the VHF mounted on the ceiling exploded. Weldon raised his hand with slow, painful effort as if the hand was ascending not by a conscious and deliberate attempt but was being lifted by an unseen string. His hand fell back across his body and he went limp. His eyes stayed wide open and reflected the glow of the running lights.

I checked him for a gun, but he didn't have one. Lennis was occupied with Sammy, but I still didn't need to get into his gun sights. I flipped on the searchlight and trained it on the *China Sea*. Lennis zeroed in on the target and let fly with a new round. I left the searchlight on and stepped outside into a roaring wind and a stinging, blinding rain. I stayed near the open door and looked through the cabin at the *China Sea*. It had pulled even and was headed for our side, closing in fast. Sammy was so close I could see the anger in his eyes. He popped back up and took aim, not at Lennis but at the barrels up front. Before he got off a shot, another round from Lennis rang out and Sammy again hit the deck.

The *China Sea* banged into us, a glancing hit that shuddered the deck and nearly knocked me overboard. She turned away and circled and headed for us again, this time aiming her steel bow straight at us. I slipped on the wet deck but caught the railing and broke my fall. Lennis recovered and started firing away at the *China Sea's* pilot house, but the waves were bouncing both boats around and his shots were wild.

Lennis staggered to the cabin and stumbled to the wheel. I ducked and huddled outside the door, ready to jump over the side. Lennis spun the wheel to angle the *Side Pocket* to avoid another direct hit. He had sobered up some. His maneuver not only avoided a direct hit, it moved the barrels out of range of Sammy's rifle.

The wind blew the tops off the waves between the boats. The rain was pounding us, coming in nearly parallel to the water. We plowed through the five-foot waves at top speed and a salty scud sprayed over the decks. If my guess was right, Sammy was down on the foredeck loading some tracer rounds into his rifle. There were too many targets on the deck and he was too close to miss much longer. If I was going to end up in the water anyway, it was better to jump into it than to get blasted into it.

Lennis kept the boat turning away from the *China Sea*. The circling along with the waves made me dizzy. I stepped to the rear deck, knowing that even if I jumped, I could get ground up by a prop with the boats circling each other. I grabbed a handhold to steady myself. The beam of our searchlight bounced around as the *Side Pocket* tossed about. It swept beyond the *China Sea* and lit up a brown mountain range headed toward us from behind.

If those barges had been casting a shadow, the *China Sea* and the *Side Pocket* would have both been in it. The horns of the tug blew deep and loud. Five short blasts, the danger whistle. The barges, two stories tall and wide as a city block, pushed up a seven-foot wall of water, frothing and roaring and close enough to hear even through the wind and the rain. The horn sounded five more short blasts.

It would take miles for the tug to stop, a mile for it to even slow down. Throwing it into reverse and gunning it would only break the fastenings holding the barges. They were as unstoppable as an avalanche.

Sammy lifted himself to the cap rail of the *China Sea* and steadied the rifle against a cleat, oblivious to the warning horns of the tug. The barges looming over us, their rain-slicked sides shining from our lights, gave me the sensation of looking up, frozen in fear, at a skyscraper as it was toppling over on top of me.

A halo ringed each streetlight along the beach in Ocean Springs. They were close enough for me to swim to them with flotation. Lennis stumbled out of the cabin, still holding the rifle. His eyes looked as if he were ready to shoot the whole damn world in this last surge of a lifetime of rage. He glanced my way. He paused as if he had forgotten me. He grinned as he turned toward me and raised the rifle.

I plunged off the stern and went deep. The water shut out the gunshots, the roaring wind, the thunder, the frantic blasts of the horn by the enormous tugboat, all noise except the underwater buzz of the engines and the propellers and the bubbling of my escaping breath. I swam to the left in case Lennis shot where he thought I would come up. My lungs were about to burst. I broke the surface and I sucked in a gallon of air.

A shot sang across the water. I turned toward the sound. A second shot flashed, aimed fifty yards behind me. Was this son of a bitch crazy enough to try to shoot me when he was about to be either blown out of the water by Sammy, or smashed into splinters by a million pounds of steel skimming across the gulf? A third shot at where he thought I should be told me he was every bit that crazy.

I swam as fast and as far as I could on a single breath, praying that the suction wouldn't pull me down. I stopped and looked back. Lennis was in the spotlight of the *China Sea*, tottering and jamming a clip into his rifle. A burst streaked out from Sammy's rifle. Lennis jerked around and fired back as fast as he could squeeze the trigger. Sammy returned the barrage. The hot rounds sparked on both boats and the ricochets off the steel chimed across the water.

Maybe they didn't know the barges were on top of them. But I believe they did. I believe both of them knew they were about to be ground into driftwood.

I bobbed like a plastic bottle in the rough seas. From that level, the mammoth barges hid the entire western sky. Sammy fired off one last burst. It hit home, exploding one of the barrels on the foredeck of the *Side Pocket*. The explosion was deafening and the fireball lit up the *China Sea* and the barges and a hundred-yard radius all around. The white sheets of rain twinkled in the brilliant orange glow.

The fire at the bow of the *Side Pocket* raced along the stream of fuel that had leaked out of one of the barrels and run down the side deck toward the stern. Lennis stumbled away from this racing flame, barely ahead of it. He dropped his rifle to the deck. The flames caught him and ran up his pants leg. Lennis kept running and jumped off the stern just as the barges smashed the *Side Pocket*.

The wooden frames of the little boat cracked as the steel giant slammed into them. The impact flipped it over and it made a huge hiss as the flames hit the water. The *China Sea* had turned, but too late, and its stern slammed against the side of a barge. There was a screech of metal and a shower of sparks. The red steel trawler spun around like it was a bathtub toy and the suction drew it up against the moving wall of the barge. The entire stern was knocked out, and the *China Sea* started sinking like a split beer can.

I treaded water and rose and fell with the waves until all twelve barges and the three-decker tugboat passed by. They had flipped on all the lights and the tug was lit up like an old Natchez stern-wheeler, with lights ringing all three decks. The twin diesels, a thousand horsepower each, rose in pitch as the captain slipped them into neutral. He cut back on the throttle and let the barges drift to lose some momentum before even attempting to back the tug up. Another half mile and he reversed it and showered down and the tremendous roar of the engines rang across the gulf.

I swam toward the wreckage to find something to hang on to. I was a hundred yards away, but the swim felt like it was a mile. The winds calmed and the waves flattened out some. The rain remained steady, but lighter. There was a smell of kerosene and raw diesel and there were patches of burning fuel floating in the wake of the tug. I spotted what looked like a raft and I side-stroked to it. It was the pick-out box from the *Side Pocket*, upside down with its legs sticking up. The box didn't have enough bouyancy for me to use it like a boat, but it did float my upper body. So I laid my shoulders and chest on it as if it were a child's paddleboard and turned it toward Ocean Springs.

The searchlight from the tug came on and scanned its wake. Once they flashed the light wide and shined it on me, but I ducked into the water. I didn't want to be rescued just yet. The *Side Pocket* had been broken in half, the stern upside down and sticking out of the water, the brass propeller glinting in the spotlight. Two of the steel drums were bobbing around it. Ice chests and orange net floats and plastic milk jugs for marking crab traps all floated along with shards of wood, some charred from the explosion. The *China Sea* was on its side, its immense underbelly showing red beneath the spotlight. Basketball-sized bubbles of escaping air broke all around it like water in a rolling boil. I was too low to see much, but I couldn't see any sign of Sammy, Lennis, or the pilot of the *China Sea*. Weldon had probably gone down with the front half of the *Side Pocket*.

The wind and waves were in my favor. I paddle-kicked for a while and rode the tide for a while. The wind slowed and the rains lessened and soon died. The cuts on my fingers and wrists began to bother me now that I had time to be aware of them.

I was a mile from shore when the flashing blue lights of the sheriff's patrol pulled out of Fort Bayou into Biloxi Bay and started gliding along the surface of the water toward the scene of the wreckage. Bright little lights of coast guard helicopters out of Gulfport showed to the west and soon the bubbling of their blades sounded over the now calm waters. Searchlights from the water or the air covered every inch around the wreckage and the helicopter blades made ruffled circles below. I never saw them pull anybody out of the water.

I touched the bottom with my feet three hundred yards out from the shore. I stood and it was chest deep, so I waded in from there. I trudged across the sand and plopped down on the concrete railing along the boulevard, in the dark spot between two streetlights. I leaned forward and rested my elbows on my knees, too tired to care that I was soaking wet and scraped up. I watched the helicopters weave their lights over the water. Reminded me of the pattern of a sky beam when they open a new tire store or Wal-Mart. I kept looking for two hours, until the big tug fired up its diesel and revved it up. The boat strained, churning up a ten-foot wake but barely nudging the barges, trying to rebuild the momentum to continue the trip to Mobile.

THIRTY-SIX

Wat did you do to your hand?" Neal asked.

"I cut it on a piece of glass."

The sunlight bounced off his desktop. The hurricane had turned North and hit the Texas-Louisiana line. The winds I had fought the night before had been its eastern edge. The clouds had cleared out and the temperature rose into the nineties. Neal punched on the window unit air-conditioner. The oversize Fedders roared and pumped out a rush of cold air.

"You hear anything about that collision out on the gulf last night?" Neal asked.

"I haven't seen the paper."

"It was the strangest thing. A big tug pushing barges out from Biloxi plowed into two shrimp boats. One of the shrimp boats exploded from the impact. You ever heard of anything like that before?"

I shook my head no. A radio station was reporting that a man in Ocean Springs was on his screened-in front porch and saw a fireball around the area of impact. But the weather was bad and few people were out and there was a heavy rain at the time. The police were withholding comment until they talked to the coast Guard divers.

"One boat belonged to those Belters over in Biloxi. The other one was Vietnamese."

"Anybody get killed?"

"They haven't found anybody dead or alive from what I hear. The Coast Guard's still out there searching."

Trish Bullard was letting me stay with her for a few days. The boss thought I was dead, and I needed to keep it that way. If he thought my bones were being picked clean by the blue crabs, he'd let down his guard and I could find out who he was. I had strained my brain to place his voice the whole time I was paddling ashore and all morning as well and still couldn't find it. It was bugging me real bad by this time.

Finding the boss would be extra tricky, since I couldn't let anybody know I was still alive. I've worked a lot of undercover cases, but this was the first time I had to play the role of a dead man. The good thing was that I didn't have to search for a living human being. All I had to do was find some papers. If I found out who was making money off of NuCoast Enterprises, chances are I'd find the boss.

"Anything new on Mr. Cass's case?" Neal asked.

I shook my head.

"How's Hank's case going?" I asked.

"It's pretty much over. The DA remanded it to the files. Insufficient evidence."

"Insufficient meaning none?"

Neal nodded. "That really pissed me off. We've had ten years of peace since the shrimping wars, and then they go and stir up every peckerwood from here to Bayou La Batre by arresting some Vietnamese kid they knew didn't have anything to do with it."

"I guess they didn't really know if he did or not."

"They knew they didn't have a case. We're just lucky those guys in that pickup truck didn't kill one of those Vietnamese that they jumped on. Can you imagine what *The New York Times* would do with that one? They can cram five thousand Asian immigrants into garment district sweatshops and nobody'll say pea turkey. But you let some redneck beat the hell out of a Vietnamese down here they'll have the damn Branch Davidian S.W.A.T. team in on us. I blame the Biloxi police for even arresting Huang in the first place. That was nothing but an election year stunt by Bernie Pettus."

"Elections draw out the lowest type of scum," I said. "How's yours going?"

"About the same. He's started telling people I'm soft on crime because I'm getting gang members out of jail. I'm beginning to wish I'd never signed qualifying papers."

"So where is this gang member you turned loose to rape and pillage?"

"He's here in Bay Saint Louis. His grandfather enrolled him in Saint Stanislaus and we moved him into the dorm yesterday. Nguyen's too old to keep up with a fifteen-year-old. Besides, the kid needs to get away from the Dragons."

"Did you talk with his grandfather?"

Neal chuckled as he shook his head. "I'll tell you, that is one tough little dude. The Dragons tried to start the old protection racket. Nguyen got all the Vietnamese store owners together and they agreed to tell the gangs to stuff it. The Dragons sent this team of junior high thugs to collect the payments and Nguyen and some other guy stuck a bunch of shrimp and cocktail sauce and God knows what else into their money sack."

"What did the Dragons do?"

"Nothing so far."

I sipped my coffee and rubbed the scab on the back of my hand. It was sore and red along the edges, but it was too big to cover with Band-Aids, so I was pouring Dr. Tichenor's antiseptic on it every hour or so. That stuff burns like a white-hot poker, but it'll kill any germ that's ever been born.

"I guess you haven't gone to the doctor about that cut," Neal said.

"You guessed right." I've got the worst case of white coat fever in the world. "If Dr. Tichenor's won't cure it, I'll try some salt water."

"Salt water. That reminds me," he said, "Speedy Cline wants to sell the boat back to me."

"How much he hold you up for?"

"Nothing. I can get it for the same price I charged him."

"Let me guess. He sank it."

"Close," he said. "Speedy got caught in the storm last night and grounded it on a sandbar off Cat Island. Nearly scared him to death. And of course, he's spent every penny of that shrimp money and he doesn't have enough to get it hauled off. It'll cost two grand at least. He called the house so early this morning he woke me up. I said I'd give him his money back and not a penny more."

"God, you run a hard bargain. So you'll be out two thousand and whatever repairs it needs?"

He blew out a loud breath. "A bargain if there ever was one."

The relief at getting out with only a two-thousand-dollar bath shone in his eyes, so I let my normal smart-ass remark slide. Throwing cold water on such a happy time would be like choosing Christmas Eve to tell a child about Santa Claus. I threw a wadded-up sheet of paper at his head and stood to leave.

"Did you turn up anything on NuCoast?" I asked. "The last time we talked you said you were going to check with some contacts in Jackson."

"That incorporator we didn't know, that Matilda Bethea, lives on the other side of Mobile."

"Did you get an address?"

"Of course I did. When I do your work I do a good job."

"Hey, I could've gotten her address."

"Do you want the gas purchase option?"

"No, thank you," I said.

"Do you want extra coverage?"

"No, thank you."

"Do you want to upgrade? It's only ten dollars."

"No, thank . . . Upgrade to what?"

"A Lincoln Town Car."

I was charging the rental to Sheila, so I felt guilty about doing it. But the Lincoln would make my cover more convincing. I was going to Daphne, on the other side of Mobile Bay, to call on Matilda Bethea. I was using my favorite cover, John Doggett of Taylor, Brock, & Johnson, P.A. I had on my good suit, a white starched shirt, paisley tie, black wingtips, and, God forgive me, a briefcase. Neal says the only time I wear a suit is special Sundays and when I go undercover. He says it like there's something wrong with that.

It was a good thing the Lincoln was part of the disguise, because my truck was nowhere to be found. My old friend Roger Partridge gave me a lift, and he and I returned to the woods the night before to search for it. Roger is the acting sheriff back home in Hancock County. I figured even though we were out of his jurisdiction, his uniform might come in handy. I made up a story about how I happened to lose my truck a mile up a logging road. He's been my friend too long to believe a word of it. But if he had any suspicions about why my truck would be there, he kept them to himself. He's also been my friend too long to ask questions.

The ruts were still there where I had parked it. A fresh set of tracks showed where a dually rigged had backed up to it. Roger said he'd help me fill out the stolen vehicle report, but I told him I'd do it later. He reminded me that I'd have to fill out the report, or I wouldn't be able to file a claim on my insurance.

The main drag through Daphne is Highway 98, a north-south road that leads to the high-rise condominiums and seafood restaurants on the beach at Gulf Shores. I searched for the street number while trying to avoid being rear-ended by the vans out of Montgomery and Jackson and Hattiesburg headed to a few days of cold beer and seafood platters and Lanacaine.

After my third pass, I stopped at a convenience store to look at the telephone book. Nobody named Bethea. The only thing I saw in what should have been the 700 block was what looked to be a nursing home. I pulled into Bayside Realty. No, they had never heard of Matilda Bethea. The same for the law office and the orthodontist's office next to it.

I pulled into another convenience store and called Neal and asked him to double-check the number. It was the same one I had. Rather than give up, I decided to try the nursing home. Who knows? Maybe Matilda Bethea was the administrator or something.

Bayside Care Residences was fairly new. The floors were polished and the place was well lighted, and there was no smell of soiled bed linens. An attractive and well-groomed black woman in her sixties sat behind the round receptionist's desk. She had an eager smile.

"I'd like to see Matilda Bethea, please."

"Yes, sir. Mrs. Bethea is in room one-oh-four." She pointed to a hall where a team of orderlies was pushing a cart filled with dinner trays. "Please sign in."

"Ma'am," I said as I signed the sheet of paper, "I'm not here to visit one of the residents."

"You did say Matilda Bethea, didn't you?"

"Yes, ma'am."

She gave me a puzzled look.

"Sir, do you know Mrs. Bethea?"

"No, I'm here on business."

She gave me a once-over, paying special attention to the brief-case, before she reached for the sign-in sheet. "Mr. Doggett, what is the nature of the business?"

"I'm afraid I can't give the specific nature. I'm here to talk to her about some of her business holdings."

"Business holdings?"

From down the hall I heard an old female voice yelling some incoherent babble. An ancient man wearing a VFW cap wheeled toward me. A television set blared from the big open room to my right. The phone at the desk rang and the receptionist put it to her ear and pointed down the hall.

There was no answer when I tapped on the door. I eased it open and called her name. Still no answer. I stepped inside. On the bed, propped up on three pillows, was a tiny woman shrunken with age, her wispy white hair in disarray. She looked with uncomprehending eyes at a television set suspended from the ceiling.

"Mrs. Bethea, I'd like to talk with you about NuCoast."

She had bruises on her arms, some gone to scabs, and paper-thin skin showing the blue veins and sores of the long-term bed-ridden. I walked to the side of her bed. Aside from raspy breathing through her open mouth and a few blinks of her eyes, there was no indication that she was alive. The monitor showed a heartbeat and the bag of clear liquid suspended from the stainless steel scaffold dripped a drop every three seconds. I slid the band around her narrow wrist to read the name.

"May I help you?" The voice behind me was female, authoritative, and peremptory. She wore the traditional nurse's cap. A top sergeant type with a no-nonsense look.

"Yes, I'm John Doggett. I'm here to see Mrs. Bethea on some business."

"Are you sure you have the right person?"

"Not entirely," I said. "Has she been here long?"

"Mrs. Bethea was one of our first patients when we opened two years ago. She's been just like you see her the whole time. I've never known her to conduct any business."

Matilda choked and coughed and the nurse stepped to the bedside. She wiped her mouth with a swab from the jar on the bedside stand and aligned her head straight on the thin foam pillow.

"Is it possible that I'm looking for her daughter? Perhaps some other family member named Matilda Bethea?"

"Mrs. Bethea only has one daughter. She lives in Biloxi, and her name is not Matilda." She checked the readings on the monitor and pushed a few buttons.

"Could I get in contact with her daughter?"

"I'm sorry, sir," she said, "we can't give out information without our patient's consent."

"Mrs. Bethea doesn't look like she'll be giving consent. Can you give me the name of somebody in the family?"

"I'm sorry," she said.

THIRTY-SEVEN

I had slept under the ceiling fan with the French doors open to the screen porch. It was a rainy morning, and the patter of the rain on the screen made it hard to wake up. I needed a secret place to crash for a few days, and sleeping on Trish's couch was normally no problem, but Sandy's engagement ring complicated things between Trish and me.

Trish didn't say she knew about the ring, but I figured Kathy had told her. Trish got burned so bad by her ex that she may never want any man hanging around more than a day at a time. Which is fine, at least it *was* fine, because I had really been thinking all along that Sandy was coming back. But now I was wondering if Trish was thinking that since Sandy got engaged I might be thinking that we ought to get more serious. And if Trish thought that was what I wanted, it'd piss her off because a change in my relationship with Sandy didn't have diddly squat to do with how shitty her ex-husband treated her, and it would be presumptuous, make that egotistical, of me to assume that now that I was free, she should suddenly be interested in me.

To tell the truth, I didn't know how I was feeling about the whole thing myself now that it didn't look like Sandy and I would be getting back together. And since Sandy went and got herself engaged, I didn't know if I wanted to get back together with her even if she wanted to.

But, hell, I had no idea if Trish was thinking any of this or not. I didn't even know if she knew, or, for that matter, gave a rat's ass, if I was unattached or not.

Damn! Sandy and I have been divorced almost six years and she's four hundred miles away, and she's still screwing with my mind.

While Trish got herself ready for work, I drank some Luzianne, black with no sugar, and read the *Sun-Herald*. They recovered four bodies from the collision, and made positive ID on three of them. Sammy was found a mile from the wreckage. First reports showed the cause of death as drowning, but the coroner had ordered autopsies on all of them. Weldon was found by divers in the submerged front half of the *Side Pocket*. Lennis had been plowed over by the barges. He was torn up pretty good by the impact of the collision and the scouring effect of the barnacles. The fourth man, Vietnamese, got tangled in the ropes of the *China Sea* and was dragged down with it. No positive ID had been made.

"Got to run," Trish said. She wore her sun-streaked hair up, off her neck and shoulders. "If you're not going to be here when I get back, leave me a note and let me know when you'll be back, okay?"

"I'll move out as soon as I can, Trish."

"I've got company coming this weekend," she said, "but you could sleep on the couch if you still need a place to—"

"I'll be out by then."

The papers Neal had given me listed two directors for NuCoast Enterprises, Billy Weldon and Matilda Bethea, and neither was in a position to operate any business. Neal had arranged the papers in chronological order. I unfolded a blue-backed document from the Forrest County circuit clerk's office. It was twenty-four years old. It had a gold seal at the lower right-hand corner. Marriage certificate. It showed that in Forrest County, Mississippi, Bernie Pettus of Biloxi had been married to a girl from Hattiesburg, Janice Clarissa Bethea.

THIRTY-EIGHT

W e got one pothole's been dere so long I'm catchin' crawfish in it."

Two other residents were in line to express similar complaints to the TV camera set up in the hall outside the city council chamber. There were at least fifty citizens already in there, grim-faced and ready for a fight. The old water main the city had promised to fix for twenty years had broken again and washed out Bayou Fourche Road.

Besides the folks on Bayou Fourche Road, there were a lot of people in suits. The word was out that the Point Cadet casino project was going to be announced that night, and the usual chamber of commerce and Tourism Board types were all there. Now that Billy Weldon was dead, I supposed someone other than NuCoast Enterprises would be making the announcement.

I didn't care about any water main. Didn't care too much about any casino. I was there to see the boss.

I sneaked up the outside staircase to the third floor and hid out in the Public Affairs office as the hall filled up. Didn't want to be seen early. I waited until five minutes after starting time before going back down to wait outside the rear door of the chamber room.

A TV camera aimed at the podium. There wasn't an empty seat. I looked through the round windows of the double doors and saw Stash Moran inside the railing up front. His legs were crossed and he kept examining his fingernails. Sheila sat beside him, looking like a movie star in her trademark red business suit. Her coal black hair glowed almost blue. The dress accented her red lips and her porcelain skin. Yeah, they made a handsome couple, damn it all. I didn't know the man with them. I don't know much about suits and their cuts, but this guy didn't buy his off the rack at McRae's like I do.

Neal's suspicions must have been right. Stash and Sheila were the ones all along who were planning the damn casino. I should have known. I was a little pissed that Sheila hadn't been straight with me, but I guess that's business. And maybe I hadn't been all that easy to find the past few days. Maybe she would have told me.

Bernie was up front shaking hands with the council members as they took their seats behind the extended desk set five feet out from the back wall. He didn't look his usual radiant self. In front of them, down on the floor and to the left, was a podium like they use for pulpits in country churches. A table supporting a video projector sat in the middle of the room, and the video screen had been pulled down.

The people of the pothole faction had seldom attended official meetings and didn't know the protocol and figured silence was the safest option. The councilmen scanned the crowd and waved at familiar faces, it being election year and all. The president of the council brought the gavel down three times and the sharp report echoed through the room. Bernie assumed his seat in the center of the arc of the council's desk. He made opening remarks which I couldn't hear through the door.

The television crew got busy. The cameraman with a shoulder-mounted camera scanned the council and the crowd for background shots. Several people in the audience held up signs saying Fix the Leak!

The council president said something into the microphone at

his seat and a local Baptist minister stood and people bowed their heads. Since it was Biloxi, a good number of the people in the audience made the sign of the cross. After the prayer, Bernie stood. He gave the cameraman time to set up before making any remarks. Sheila gave a sign to a young man in a suit seated just beyond the railing, and he started passing out printed flyers to everyone in the audience. There was a murmur in the crowd as they started reviewing the pictures.

I slipped into the room and sat in the back row behind two large women with big hair. I hid behind them and watched through the opening between them. The TV cameraman flipped the light on, and Sheila radiated in the glow and the anticipation of the upcoming announcement. A few people flipped through the packets, but most of them looked up front.

The president of the city council announced Stash, who stood and waved to the audience and drew applause, much to his delight. He announced Sheila, and she stood and waved. The man in the good suit was head of Premier Entertainment out of Las Vegas. Also on hand was the chairman of the Gaming Commission down from Jackson and the head of the Gulf Coast Hospitality Coalition, a flighty, middle-aged woman with coifed, streaked hair and a perpetual smile who had been a Hollywood gossip columnist in a former life. She stood and waved at everyone and threw the councilmen a kiss. You'd have to know this woman.

Stash walked over to the pulpit and adjusted the microphone. "Ladies and gentlemen," Stash said, "it's my pleasure to announce what'll be a destination for tourists throughout the world, the Bienville Royale!"

I stood and walked down the center aisle, keeping my eyes on Bernie. He was reading the brochure as was everybody else in the room. I was halfway to the front when he looked up.

Bernie's eyes met mine, and all the color drained from his face. It removed my last doubts about him being the boss. He dropped the brochure and stood and hooked his finger inside his shirt collar and pulled it away from his neck. He bent down and said something to the councilman beside him.

The video began with a timpani drum roll and a voice-over telling about the next triumph of American culture, the Bienville Royale. Bernie stood and said something to the councilman beside him. The guy from Las Vegas stood and scowled and gestured to a young man in the back of the room to douse the lights. Just before they went out, Sheila spotted me and smiled and gave me a little wave.

I closed my eyes to adjust to the sudden darkness. There was still some light bleeding into the room from the windows of the main doors and the reading lights along the council table. I caught Bernie's silhouette walking to the back door. He stopped before leaving the room and grabbed a city cop standing by the exit by the arm. The cop nodded and Bernie slipped out of the room.

I stepped toward the railing to follow him, unnoticed by everyone else in the room except for that cop. The video continued with a flourish of trumpets. I crouched as people do when walking through someone's field of vision and tiptoed across the floor after Bernie. As I neared the door, the cop stepped in front of me.

"Are you Jack Delmas?"

"Yes, I am."

"Step into the next room, please."

"That's where I was going," I said. "You need something?"

"Just step into the room."

"Look, Officer, I'm in a hurry."

"Step into the room! Now!"

What in the world does this jerk want? I walked with him through the door. Once into the light of the hallway, I reached to my back pocket for my wallet.

"Freeze!" He pulled his service revolver and drew a bead on me. "Move your hands slowly up over your head."

"I was just reaching for—"

"Up over your head! Now!"

I laced my fingers and put them across the back of my head, arms out and elbows straight up.

"Officer, I was just reaching for my wallet."

"Up against the wall!"

I turned around and laid my palms above my head against the wall of the hallway. I tried to look behind me to see what he was doing.

"Eyes straight ahead." He talked into his radio and called for a backup.

"Officer, I haven't done anything."

"We'll see."

A second officer came from the rear of the building. He must have been out in the parking lot. Upon orders from the first one, he patted me down.

"He's clean."

"I told you," I said. "I'm just here as a private citi—"

"Shut up!" the first one shouted. "Now turn around slowly." He squinted as if he were looking at some suspect he had cornered after a shooting rampage at a high school. The second cop shifted his eyes between the first cop and me wondering what the heck was going on.

"Let me see some ID."

"Can I lower my hands?" I didn't know what Bernie had told this guy, but I sure didn't want to spook him.

"Do it slow," he said. He directed the second cop toward me with a nod of his head. I handed the second cop my wallet and he flipped it open to my driver's license.

"Is this you?"

"Look, you two either let me go or let me know what's going on, or I'm going to—"

"Stuff it, mister," the first one said. "There's a warrant out on you."

"Warrant? Is that what Bernie told you? There's no warrant out on me."

"Put your hands behind you and turn around."

THIRTY-NINE

She was a big blonde in a starched uniform. She had short hair and was smacking pink bubblegum. "Okay, you can go now."

"And?" I asked.

"And what?"

"And we're sorry for the inconvenience, Mr. Delmas," I said. "We had no business pulling a gun on you."

"Yeah, that too."

For the council meeting the cops had set up a temporary office on the first floor of city hall, complete with a computer hookup to headquarters, so it took no more than five minutes to check me out. The cop who had pulled the gun on me wanted to throw me in the back of his squad car and take me all the way to headquarters and the city car he drove was gone. I tossed Neal's name out and threatened them with an even bigger suit than the one he popped them with two years earlier. Neal comes in handy every once in a while. The only thing that popped up was a couple of old warrants out of Louisiana that had been withdrawn, the legacy of a case I had worked on a few weeks earlier.

Out in the parking lot, the space marked Reserved for Mayor was empty and the city car he drove was gone. Bernie had bought enough time for a pretty good head start.

I thought about going back and telling the cops their mayor hired a Realtor and some white trash drunk to burn out an old, cranky Yugoslavian shrimper. But the Realtor and the drunk are both dead now, so they'd have to take my word on it. I decided that might not work.

Maybe I'd have better luck saying that Bernie used a dummy corporation, with his near-comatose mother-in-law and this same Realtor as corporate officers, to buy up Point Cadet for a casino, and then he burned out an old man who refused to sell some land they wanted. At least I'd have a paper trail. But a corporate paper trail is a real yawner for most desk sergeants. Bernie would be in Brazil by the time I walked them through that one.

Of course I could tell them how Bernie steered city contracts for waste disposal to NuCoast Enterprises and used Lennis to dump the stuff into the gulf. Now, that's something they could understand. But Bernie had brought Billy Weldon into the deal, and Weldon had to be the biggest patsy on earth. There was no way Bernie would take the fall on any of this, especially since Weldon was no longer around to defend himself.

None of this would hurt Bernie one bit, at least not in the next few hours. And I was wasting time even thinking about asking the cops for help. So I cranked up the Lincoln to go after him by myself. When Bernie sent me and those oil drums out the other night for Lennis to dump over the side, I took it real personal.

If I were Bernie, where would I go? I'd go home and get enough stuff together to get out of the country. I figured Bernie had stashed a bunch of money offshore. And nobody's going to leave town without at least grabbing a toothbrush. Not to mention a passport.

I raced through town, headed to the north shore where Bernie lived. Chances were good he'd be gone, but somebody may have seen him. Maybe his wife was there. And if I got real lucky, I could catch him right there at his house. What I was going to do once I caught him was something I'd just have to play by ear.

I doubted that it would get to a shootout. That's not Bernie's style. But I reached behind the seat and got the .45 automatic I keep there. There was one clip in it already, and I had a spare in the glove compartment that I fumbled for and found and stuck in my hip pocket.

The night was hot and clear, and when I crossed the Popp's Ferry Bridge and got out of the lights of downtown, I could see a few stars. The moon was big and had risen high enough to turn from orange to bright white. The air was still and filled with the perfume of wisteria and honeysuckle. The crickets chirped a constant symphony, and as I crossed over the bayous and marshes the bullfrogs chimed in.

I parked in the street, two lots down from Bernie's house. The house backed up to a bayou that had been dredged and bulkheaded. It fed into the north shore of Biloxi Bay. The house was a two-story on a cul-de-sac with a two-car garage facing the street. A dark Bronco was in the garage; the door was up.

The house was dark except for a mercury vapor glow from the backyard. I sneaked up the driveway and walked around to the back of the house. I crouched and scooted along the hedge beside the rear deck. I peered over the hedge and looked in the windows of the den. No lights were on in the den or anywhere else in the house.

The air-conditioning unit at the corner of the house kicked on. The night was hot and damp and the heavy air clung to me like a second skin. I wiped the sweat off my forehead and swatted at a mosquito and tiptoed up the steps to the deck.

The back door was unlocked. I stepped inside, where I was on shaky ground. If he shot me inside the house, Bernie would say he was defending against an intruder.

The streetlight out front and the security light in the backyard shone through the windows and gave the rooms a blue glow. I could see my way around, but it would be pure luck if I saw anybody lying in ambush for me. But Bernie was long gone. I knew he was. At least I was pretty sure.

The sink was empty and the trash can empty with a fresh plastic bag in it. Either the the maid had come that day or the place hadn't been used lately. The foyer inside the front door shone yellow from the streetlight filtering in through the amber side lights flanking the front door. The burglar chain was in place. I glanced through one of the side lights. The mailbox was stuffed with advertising brochures.

The stairway was narrow and dark and I eased along the wall on my way up, leaning forward to hit the deck if I had to. The upstairs was lighted only by what came through the windows. At the top of the stairs was a landing and a wide hallway from which led four doors that I guessed to be bedrooms.

Three of the rooms were dark. From the room to my right, toward the front of the house, a dim light shone, maybe from a closet or a bathroom. I ran my eyes back and forth among the three other doors as I eased along the wall. The light came from a walk-in closet on the far side of the room. On the carpet in front of the closet door lay a pair of pants, wrinkled and left in a pile. In the closet, the top two drawers of a chest of drawers were opened, and the underwear and socks inside had been tossed around like a salad. The shoe rack had been pulled out to the center of the walk-in and Bernie's clothes had been rifled. A couple of shirts, still on hangars, lay on the floor. His wife's side of the closet was undisturbed.

Down in the garage there was only the Bronco. Bernie had either switched cars, or his wife had driven him somewhere. But her clothes were still in the closet and nobody had been in the house or even dropped by to pick up the mail. I stepped down the driveway toward the lights of a car that had pulled in at the house across the street.

A young man was lifting a sack of groceries from his trunk. His wife was at the back door passenger side, unbuckling a little girl from a car seat. I was ten feet up the driveway before he raised up. He caught a glimpse of me and it startled him.

"Sorry if I scared you. I'm looking for the mayor."

"He's probably still at city council," he said. "He ought to be back any minute."

"How about Mrs. Pettus?" I asked. "Do you think she's around?"

By this time, the wife was standing and holding the baby.

"She's been out of town for a couple days," she said. The young man shot her a glance that said not to tell strangers when the neighbors are out of town.

I thanked them and walked back across the street. Maybe Bernie had taken a city car. But what good would that do? If he really was trying to run for it, surely he wouldn't take a car with City of Biloxi written all over it. He must have ditched the city car. Was it possible that he was still around here? If he saw me pulling into his drive, maybe he just ran out the back door. At the very least I ought to check.

The back door was as I left it. If Bernie was in the bushes, he was smart enough to wait until I left before going back in. I stepped to the railing of the rear deck and scanned the backyard and the backyards of the houses to either side. Under the strong, white moon and the single mercury vapor light down by Bernie's boat house, the grass looked like a field of snow and the crepe myrtles cast long shadows.

The boathouse was an open one, four tall poles and a tin roof. There was a hoist lift rigged to the underside of the roof that lifted the boat with canvas straps girded under the hull. The canvas straps dangled from the roof. The hoist lift, which normally suspended Bernie's runabout over the water, had been lowered and the boat was gone.

I knew where I'd be taking that boat if I were Bernie.

FORTY

It had not rained inland in three days, not since the edge of that hurricane skirted Biloxi and I took that near-fatal ride on the *Side Pocket*. The days were typical of the Mississippi Coast summer pattern. The sun brings the gulf to a simmer and pulls up all the water vapor the sky can hold. Thunder clouds form and drop all this water back to earth around three in the afternoon. But the big clouds had not gone inland for a while.

The thick cover of pine trees on both sides of the logging road had prevented the water in the ruts from drying. It was tricky driving in the Lincoln, but at least this time I knew the road. With a low ground clearance, I scraped the red clay several times going through some of the deeper ruts. I also had to ease to what passed for a shoulder at some of the wider mud holes so I could have at least one of my rear tires on semisolid land.

No cars had been there that day. The rain when I was there a few days earlier had wiped out all the old tracks and there were no fresh ones. I let the windows down and the sweet smell of honeysuckle in the pine trees drifted through the car. A possum made an erratic crossing in front of my headlights, paying no attention to me. It sniffed the ground as it crossed the road and disappeared into the underbrush.

I pulled to the side in the same clearing I had used a couple of nights ago. I missed my old truck, and hated to think of it in the hands of some pervert at a chop shop. I walked along the tire ruts to the top of the rise. Off to my left the bait shop was dark except for the red neon Budweiser sign in one of the windows. The weathered boards of the pier beside it glowed white-gray under the high, clear moon. Tied to the pier, pulled in snug, was Bernie's runabout.

The seaplane was at the end of the pier inside the chain link hangar. Bernie sat in the cockpit, reading a flight chart, bathed in a green glow from the instrument panel and a white dome light. He had already swung back the chain-link gate and tied it to keep it open. He stepped out to the pier and picked up his suitcase and a rifle with a scope.

Over the water, across calm air, I heard the clang of Bernie, still in his wingtips, stepping onto the hollow aluminum pontoon of the seaplane. He laid the suitcase and the rifle on the backseat of the plane.

Below me, fifty yards up the bayou from the seaplane, was the mooring where they had loaded Belter's boat. Tied to it were three aluminum skiffs, flat bottomed and square nosed and painted olive drab. The bayou extended to my right several hundred yards. The waist-high carpet of marsh grass on both sides of the bayou spread as flat as a putting green, unbroken by bush or tree except for a clump of cypress at the waterline halfway to the lake. A derelict trawler sat in the marsh close to the cypress trees at the water's edge. Its steel mast tilted twenty degrees toward the bayou and stuck up twenty-five feet.

The bayou was so straight it looked dredged. I kept low as I scooted to the skiffs, keeping an eye on the seaplane. Bernie was checking the gauges, nearly ready for takeoff. I had seen one or two seaplanes take off, spotter planes for pogy boats in the gulf. They're on pontoons but they get into the air real fast.

He couldn't maneuver around the skiff if I turned it sideways. As fast as seaplanes get into the air, he couldn't leapfrog me this close in. I paddled to the center of the bayou with a four-foot-long piece of planking that was lying on the bank. I figured the bayou was no more than a few feet deep, few bayous are, and I pushed the boat along by jamming the plank into squishy mud. It felt like I was pushing it into Jell-O.

The wind was coming straight in. The crickets and bullfrogs kept up a loud drone, but not loud enough to cover any bump I made on the bottom of the skiff. I had misjudged the depth of the bayou, or at least the depth of the mud, and was leaning over the side to stick the plank far enough down to hit something solid. I pushed hard and it stuck in the mud. I lost my grip and the skiff scooted past it. I was left with nothing but my hands to steer the boat, but I got it to the other side. The skiff didn't have an anchor, but there was a cast net. Lightweight filament, white with a ten-foot diameter.

Bernie reached toward the dome light and the cockpit went black.

"Bernie!" My voice rang out over the water, carried by the wind. "Get out of that plane, Bernie!"

I took the safety off the .45. I saw no movement from the plane, but I knew he heard me. He turned on the runway light and it blinded me for a second. At the edge of the glare I spotted his outline as he stepped onto one of the pontoons. The crack of a rifle shot rang out. The skiff shuddered as the impact of the round slammed into the side right at the bow. A second crack of the rifle. A slug hit the water two feet short of the boat, but closer to my end. He was finding his range.

I grabbed the cast net and hopped over the side. I used the boat for cover as I waded through the heavy mud to the opposite bank. I pushed the boat away from me to draw his fire. It landed across the bayou, parallel to the bank. The stern came to rest against a log half on the bank and half in the water, and this gave Bernie a good thirty-foot opening to run the plane through.

I crouched low in the marsh grass, not wanting to be a sitting duck in a spotlight for a man with a rifle and a scope, and crawled away from Bernie toward the wrecked trawler. He fired a shot at me, but it was a little behind. He fired another couple of rounds but the marsh grass hid me pretty well as I stayed down below the range of the fixed light of the seaplane. I needed a log or something to get behind, but there was nothing but the marsh grass. I had my pistol, but I decided that to shoot back would do more harm than good, since he could surely see the flash of the muzzle and get a bead on me. Besides, at that range, a .45 was no match for a rifle with a scope.

The shooting stopped and the propeller chugged to a start. The engine revved up as he pulled out from the little hangar. He maneuvered the plane into position to take a straight run down the bayou. Bernie bore down on the throttle and the engine grew loud and rose in pitch. He flipped on all the lights and the water churned from the wind of the propeller. The strobe on the top of the plane began flashing, and the blinding landing lights popped on.

The plane eased into takeoff position. He shot it to full throttle and the engine screamed and it came toward me, slowly at first, but gaining momentum at a surprising rate.

I grabbed the net. I positioned myself right at the bank and stood on a cypress knee. I bunched it up and held it at my right side. The plane roared toward me. I was now standing fully in the landing light and was blind to everything except its dazzling white gleam. The tiny waves slapped the bottoms of the pontoons as they lifted off the surface of the bayou right in front of me.

The exact instant the pontoons left the water, I hoisted the net straight up as high as I could. The plane was climbing but still barely above my head. I ducked and lost my footing on the cypress knee and fell into the marsh grass.

The propeller sucked the net in. The motor sputtered as it wrapped around the axle of the propeller. The engine choked out and went silent. The plane hurtled like a javelin and started dropping. It was ten feet off the ground when it scraped against the rusted tower of the derelict boat. The tower ripped the gut of the plane and I smelled the sweet spray of fuel. The screech of metal against rusted metal produced a yellow trail of sparks behind the plane.

It slammed headlong into the big cypress right at water level. The fuel poured out of the split gas tank and spread around the base of the tree. Back up the bayou, the sparks had set off an azure flame on top of the water beside the old boat. Cooled by the water from the bayou, the little blue incandescence, not two inches high, fanned over the area like a lawn.

The blue shimmer raced to the downed plane and circled the cypress like a film. Two seconds later, the blue lightened to yellow. There was a whoosh as it intensified to bright white, and then a shattering, deafening blast. A flame mushroomed upward in a fireball so intense it seared my cheeks.

I jumped into the bayou and waded as fast as I could across it, but the mud clung to me and sucked down my feet like I was wearing heavy weights on both ankles. The roasting heat backed me off and I could get no closer than a hundred feet. The flames, fed by the aviation gas, were so bright that it was impossible to see anything more than the outline of the plane. The fusilage had fallen to the side from the force of the blast. One wing had been ripped off, the other was curling in the heat. The nose of the plane rested against the cypress and the tail sank down into the mud.

FORTY-ONE

The lead story on the radio news at the top of the hour was a national feed from CBS. Biloxi, Mississippi, in the space of one week, had lost one of its prominent citizens, Billy Weldon, in a collision at sea, and its mayor, Bernie Pettus, in a yet unexplained airplane crash. The FAA was at a loss to explain what appeared to be melted monofilament line wrapped around the shaft of the propeller of the mayor's plane. The autopsy showed that Bernie died from trauma to the head. There was no smoke in the lungs. Since the crash was in a remote swamp, there was little hope that there were any witnesses.

A front moved in the night before, and the weather had cooled. The winds had calmed and it was a perfect morning to be out on the gulf. Joey was at the helm of the *Miss Marie*, and Sheila and I sat on the cap rail at the stern looking at the skyline of Biloxi as we passed Point Cadet Plaza. Perinovich's will had been read. The boat went to Joey, and Neal had made sure the title was transferred quickly through a document from the chancery judge.

"You never have told me exactly where this casino is going," I said.

"Can I trust you?" Sheila asked.

"That's a hell of a question to ask a man you've just invited to spend the week at a condo in Panama City."

"There never was any new casino project. At least not on the Point. That was nothing more than a decoy."

"What do you mean 'decoy'?"

"You haven't seen the plans on the front page of the paper?"

I explained that something had come up the night before. I'd had to leave the city council meeting early, and I had not seen the morning paper.

"Are you saying that after all that talk and all those options and all those tacky drawings of castles and horse-drawn carriages, the big casino isn't going to be on the Point?" I asked.

"That's exactly what I'm saying. In fact, Stash has built up a pretty good coalition down here to go to the legislature next session and try to get the Point declared a historic district."

"You mean like the French Quarter? Biloxi's going to have a Yugoslavian Quarter?"

"And French, and Vietnamese," she said. "We've got a lot of houses down there, entire blocks, in fact, that were built by the original immigrants. Those are my people. The rest of the Coast has looked down their noses at us long enough. And now we're going to have something. We'll have shops and restaurants and art studios."

"But what will happen to the people?"

"They'll live there. Just like the French Quarter. The French Quarter has thirty thousand permanent residents. We can do the same thing here."

"I don't know," I said. "You think you can pull this off?"

Her gaze was cool, level, and unflinching. "Nobody thought I could make it with my hotels down in Miami."

I smiled and held my hands up shoulder high in surrender.

"We fooled that poor Billy Weldon," she said. "We put out the word that the Point was where the next casino was going to go. So he and all the other flippers in the area concentrated their efforts down there while Stash and I went over to the strip and optioned up the land around the Silhouette."

"The Silhouette? I hear it's just about bankrupt."

"Nothing that good management won't cure. I've run the numbers. When I put my hotel there and Stash puts in his restaurant, we're going to make it the best one on the coast."

The wind had been blowing all day from the west. It was warm and held no threat of rain, but when the boat turned and we stopped heading directly into the wind, I realized that it was not as strong as I had thought, that most of it was apparent wind, and the waves were small without any whitecaps.

We were barely past the bridge and the Mississippi Sound lay blue and broad in front of us. The sun sparkled off the riffles on the water from the wind, which had picked up after we crossed out from the protection of the Point.

"So you think it was an accident?" she asked.

"No doubt about it. Your uncle Cass was a good man. Nobody wanted to see him dead." God forgives certain lies.

"Is this the place, Mama?" Joey called out from the cabin.

"This is it, honey. This is Uncle Cass's spot." She reached for my hand. "This is the place. He always said that he knew he was home when he got close enough to see us waiting for him."

Sheila had not told me what we had come for, except an inaugural ride on Joey's boat. The name would remain *Miss Marie*. One of Perinovich's strongly held beliefs was that changing the name of a boat would bring on the worst sort of bad luck. Joey had begun his job with the Gulf Coast Research Lab and he was using the boat to conduct his studies and the lab was paying him for the use of it.

The engine churned up a little higher as Joey shifted it into neutral. Then it fell back as he pulled off the throttle. The wind had died. The tides were not running, so the boat sat still without an anchor. Joey turned off the engine.

Joey emerged from the cabin with a wreath. It was round with a matrix of deep emerald greenery and at least two dozen bright red carnations. Father Carey also stepped out to the deck. He was wearing a pair of cutoffs and a Loyola of New Orleans T-shirt, but he was slipping on a black vestment and a heavy silver necklace with a wooden cross.

As he approached us, he kissed the crucifix. Sheila made the sign of the cross, and so did Joey. Father Carey had a vial of holy water that he lifted and shook in our direction, tossing drops of water across the boat, onto the wreath and onto Sheila, Joey, and me. As the drops descended in their arcs upon us, Sheila and Joey again crossed themselves.

It was a sweet service, very short, and Father Carey told a few stories about Perinovich and what he meant to the lodge and to Saint Michael's Parish. Sheila pulled down her sunglasses and dabbed at her eyes a few times. Joey stood stoically but the muscles of his throat worked as he swallowed hard a couple of times. The shadow of the sunlight caught Joey's face just right and I realized that I was looking at Mike Perinovich once again, what he would have looked like had he, too, reached adulthood. I felt the lump growing in my own throat as I pulled the sunshades down over my eyes.

Father Carey chanted the litany for the dead from memory as he approached the side of the boat and dropped the wreath into the water. Joey stepped over and handed him a small vase I had not noticed before and stepped back as the priest made the sign of the cross against the side of the little container.

"What is that?" I whispered.

"It's Uncle Cass's ashes."

I propped my glasses back on the top of my head and glared at her.

"Don't look at me like that," she said.

"He said a million times he wanted to be buried next to Marie and Mike."

"And he will be. This is just a small portion of the ashes. He said he was carrying some extra weight. That's what this is."

"Are you for real?"

"The priest said it was okay. Look, Jack, you got to admit the gulf was a part of him. I just think we ought to return some small part back to the ocean. Humor me, okay?"

Well, I thought, what the heck. Who am I to question how somebody wants to pay their respects?

Father Carey stepped to the side of the boat and tossed a few drops of holy water into the calm sea. The wind was dead and the water was flat as an indoor pool. The drops hit and sent out a series of rings on the flat surface. "Ashes to ashes, dust to dust," he said as he removed the top from the vase and bent forward to scatter a little piece of Casper Perinovich over the Mississippi Sound.

As the priest tilted the jar, from our starboard side, west toward Deer Island, a circular riffle appeared on the surface of the water, a quarter mile away and headed toward us. The ocean had started moving, not enough for us to feel on the heavy boat, not yet enough to move the *Miss Marie*. But tide had gone out earlier that morning, and the calm waters we were riding were the low point of that ebb tide, the end of the outward momentum, that stillness before the tide reverses itself and goes back in.

There was a slight movement of the water against the side of the boat, the first stirrings of the incoming tide moving toward the mouth of Biloxi Bay. The ashes landed on the water in a slow trickle, and left a slight trail of powder for a second or two. This ephemeral track of the ashes showed that they were riding the tide back to Point Cadet, and Cass was on his last ride back in.

On the shore, through the haze of the morning and thirty years, the ghosts of Marie and Mike stood in front of Point Cadet Plaza, next to their blue Pontiac Bonneville, waiting for Cass to come home. I had forgotten how pretty Marie was. Mike was still a gawky teenager full of devilment, with a mouthful of braces and not a care to his name. He was jumping up and down and waving both arms over his head scissors style. "I see him, Mama! There he is! Daddy's coming!"

Father Carey poured the last of the ashes over the side and the riffle that had been headed toward us reached the boat. The wind strengthened and made a sudden kick, a strong updraft, and blew the ashes straight up. I removed my sunshades and watched at the vortex of swirling ashes being carried up into the heavens. The sun hit them at just the right angle to make them sparkle like gold dust until they rose so high that they faded into the background of the azure sky.

And when they were absorbed into the sky, the wind, Perinovich's evil wind, which had come back to visit him one last time, died as suddenly as it came. And the surface of the water became smooth and reflected a perfect image of the bridge, the tall casino towers, and Point Cadet Plaza.

BE SURE TO READ
MARTIN HEGWOOD'S NEXT NOVEL

MASSACRE ISLAND

COMING SOON IN HARDCOVER
FROM ST. MARTIN'S PRESS

I killed what was left of my beer and leaned back in my chair. I poured myself the last of the pitcher, and a calm came over me for the first time since I found that bomb, and I decided to kick back and let Jimbo take me on this ride. I started looking around for the waitress and noticed that Scooter was walking in our direction. He got a little closer and I realized that he was headed toward our table.

"Look who's coming," I said.

"Good thing the girls went to the bathroom. Darla woulda pee'd all over herself."

"Jimbo! My main man!" Scooter broke into a big smile and slapped his hand into Jimbo's for one of those arm wrestling contests that pass for handshakes at a deer camp or a golf course.

"Scooter, I want you to meet this friend of mine. This is Jack Delmas from over at Bay St. Louis."

The man had a crunching grip; he had done some outdoor work some time in his life. "I go over to Bay St. Louis sometimes," he said. "We play the Diamondhead course about once a year."

"Been reading about you, Scooter," Jimbo said.

"Don't believe everything you read."

"You here by yourself?" Jimbo asked.

"Was when I walked in. But I ain't no more."

"I would ask you to join us," Jimbo said, "but Jack and me, we're working on a little project right now."

"So I saw. I was just on my way out and thought I'd say hi. Let me know if I can do anything for you." He pointed his finger at Jimbo as if it were a pistol and winked at him. He turned and walked back to where this tall redhead in tight jeans was standing, purse in hand, next to the service bar across the room. Scooter stuck out his arm and she took it and they walked toward the door. Most of the people in the place had stopped what they were doing and watched the couple in awe, the way medieval peasants must have watched the king's carriage as it passed through the village.

"You didn't tell me you knew Scooter Haney," I said.

"You didn't ask. Everybody down here knows him. He's been a regular at every bar in Mobile for the past twenty years. I knew him before he got rich. He ain't changed a whole lot. I kinda admire that."

"I'm not telling you how to run your business," I said. "But he's a prime suspect in a murder case your department is investigating."

"So?"

"So you think you ought to be socializing with him?"

The waitress came with a fresh pitcher. If Jimbo was ordering these things, I sure wasn't seeing it. He poured himself a glass and took a big gulp and belched.

"I know some things about this case you wouldn't have no way of knowing," he said. "Let me tell you this. Scooter Haney didn't kill nobody in that beach house or nowhere else. He ain't got it in him. He don't get into fights like he used to. He's more into lovin' nowadays. You ever heard the saying 'So many women; so little time'? Well that's Scooter's motto."

"But what about that threat he made to Kellie Lee on the telephone?"

"It's a fake, son. It probably did come from Kellie Lee's answering machine. But somebody spliced it together. We knew the second we heard it that it was bogus. But them TV folks, they got a copy of it, and they're in such a feeding frenzy right now they didn't check it out too good."

"Where'd y'all get this tape?"

"Kellie Lee's daddy," Jimbo said. "He's the one who put it together, sure as I'm sittin' here. He's this old sorry two bit con artist who walked out on Kellie Lee's mama twenty years ago. I guarantee you he's trying to work up a wrongful death suit against Scooter. Probably got the idea from that O. J. Simpson lawsuit. He wouldn't have enough sense to think it up hisself."

"But you still don't know that Scooter didn't do it."

Jimbo chugged down the rest of the glass and wiped his mouth with the back of his hand. "One time when I had just moved down here, a bunch of us went to the Dauphin Island Fishing Rodeo. Scooter was there. Now you can't believe how many people come to that thing. I'm talking maybe twenty thousand people walking around where the weigh-in station is. And it was hot, let me tell you. Well, we're over at the pier looking at this tarpon somebody had landed when we hear these tires squeal out at the street and there's this thud. Somebody had hit a stray dog.

"Poor old thing had a broke leg and was scared to death. Limped up under this cabin and was just whimpering and crying. It was enough to break your heart. Well, Scooter climbs up under there and picks it up. The dog was bleeding all over him and ruined this brand new Izod shirt he was wearing. And don't you know he puts the dog in his car and takes it all the way into Mobile to the vet. He's probably still got that dog."

Across the room, Lila and Darla were making their way back toward us. Darla had put on a fresh coat of lipstick.

"A man who'd do that," Jimbo said as he stood, "you think he'd murder four people?"

"Sorry we took so long," Darla said. "That place was so crowded you wouldn't believe it."

"Where'd Scooter Haney go?" Lila asked.

"He left right after y'all walked off. I don't think he felt all that comfortable in here."

"Does he know you two are on the case?" Lila asked.

"All I can say is when he saw us, he didn't hang around very long."

Darla scooted her chair close to me, and pressed her thigh against the side of my leg. The girl was beginning to give off heat. "I'll bet you get a lot of good cases, don't you?"

"Why don't we get away from all these people and go somewhere quiet and talk about them," Jimbo said. "Some of this stuff we don't need to be telling to the whole world. You girls can keep a secret, can't you?"

Darla reached for my hand and gave it a light squeeze. "I won't tell." She had the softest little voice.

"We'd need to tell Mike and Tony something before we leave," Lila said to Darla.

"Mike and Tony?" Jimbo asked. "You mean the Mike and Tony out at the front door?"

"Just tell them you're not feeling good," Darla said. "We can see them again any time."

Jimbo slapped his hand against his side pocket. "Uh-oh, Jack. I think the call just came in. I gotta get to the phone." He stood and walked toward the front of the hall in a big hurry.

"What call's he talking about?" Lila asked.

"I'd like to tell you," I said. "But I really can't."

We sat and listened to the band as Darla rubbed my hand in both of hers and gazed at me with her big gray eyes, her ample chest rising and falling in a steady, quick rhythm. She had a permanent, slight part to her lips. Jimbo came back toward us across the dance floor, almost trotting.

"We gotta go, Jack."

"Was it an important call?" Lila asked.

Jimbo frowned and nodded his head. He poured another shot

of Jose Cuervo and knocked it back. He made a face as he swallowed and opened and closed his eyes real hard three times. Then he smiled with his lips closed and squinted at Lila, his eyes mere slits, Clint Eastwood style.

"Can we go with you?" Darla asked.

"Yeah," I said. "Can't they go with us?"

"I'm afraid not. Too dangerous."

"Oh, *no*!" Darla looked like she was about to cry.

"Are you sure we've got to go?" I asked.

"We need to get moving."

When I stood, Darla was still holding my hand. "Y'all be careful. Please."

"I'm sorry we gotta run like this," Jimbo said. "We'll tell you all about it next time."

As we rushed across the big floor the girls sat waving at us, Darla's white, rounded Spandex top glowing under the purple lights from the bandstand. Jimbo had this grin, the same tight lipped smile that came on right after that last shot of tequila.

"What in the world did you just do?" I said as we walked across the parking lot to the truck. "I had thought up enough stories to keep those two entertained for the next month."

"Mike and Tony, those two bouncers, were going to meet them later on."

"But those girls wanted to go with *us*. Especially Darla."

"You can call her some other time."

But I don't know her last name."

"I can find it for you. Don't worry about it."

He started the truck and raced the engine twice before popping the clutch and squealing out of the parking slot.

"Are you OK?" I asked.

"Let's go have us some fun!"

We launched onto the Interstate from the entrance ramp like an F-14 catapulted from a flight deck. Jimbo stuck a Lynard Skynard CD in and turned up *Sweet Home Alabama* to window rattling pitch as we raced down I-10 toward Mobile, blowing past everything else on the road until we got to the Dauphin Island exit.

"You up for some more pool?" The wind whipping through the open windows was so loud he was almost shouting.

"Pool?" I just left a Dolly Parton look-alike who was rubbing up against my leg, and I did it for a game of eight ball?"

"I'll get you her phone number, no problem. You can pick up right where you left off. You wanna play pool or not?"

We took the next corner with two wheels almost leaving the ground, the jacked up cab of the truck leaning enough to press me against the door. Got onto this two laned road running through low marshy country, thin stands of skinny pines stretching out to either side and cattails in the ditches, and rode it for miles. There was a constant rising and falling of the buzz of locusts and a rotten egg smell from exposed mud where narrow bridges spanned the bogs and bayous.

The place we finally turned into didn't have any name that I could see. A street light on a pole in the parking light cast enough light for me to see on the front, outside wall a rectangular patch where the yellow paint on the cinder blocks was a little brighter and less sun faded. A sign or board, probably bearing the name of the place, had been there until recently. Kids like to steal things like that to use as wall decorations. Along the roof line a long strand of Christmas tree lights blinked red and green and blue.

The parking lot, a shell covered and rutted patch of hard packed sand, was covered with puddles of milky, standing rainwater. To the rear of the place and beyond the parking lot there was low, marshy ground thick with bull rushes and palmettos, the kind of muck favored by cottonmouths and alligators. This marsh circled the parking lot like a moat, stretching out fifty yards in all directions. Beyond this marsh was sparse stands of skinny pines on what looked like semi-solid ground. We stepped out of the truck and the smell of salt water was strong in the breeze.

"Smells like the beach," I said.

"That's because it's right there through them pines," he said, pointing past the back of the building. "We ain't but about three foot above sea level here."

Through the trees, I caught a glimpse of moonlight shimmering on the Gulf, and when I stood still I could hear the steady lapping of waves through the constant whirring of insects.

"You ready for some fun?" he said.

"I was ready for that back at Shirley's."

He stepped back to the driver's side door and re-opened it. The truck was jacked up so high that the door was at waist level. He reached to the floorboard under his seat and came up with a bottle of Jim Beam. "You ever read any Ernest Hemingway?"

"What?"

"Hemingway. He wrote *For Whom the Bell Tolls* and a bunch of other books."

"I know who he was."

"Back at State, I took this English course. First time I'd ever read all that much except for newspapers and stuff. This professor, he really liked Hemingway. So I got started reading some of his stuff and got to where I liked it. But the thing I liked best about Hemingway was not so much his books, it was the man hisself, his own real life."

"Has this got anything to do with Darla? 'Cause right now, I'm having a hard time getting past that."

"Hemingway, he was a lot like me. Liked to fight, liked to drink, liked women. Liked to do stuff just for the hell of it. But he had something I didn't have. He had this code he come up with." Jimbo twisted the top off the bottle of whiskey and held it out to me. I shook my head. One of us was going to have drive home. He turned it up and took a swig. "It hit me one day that I needed me a code. Far as I can tell that's what separates the good guys from the bad guys. So I come up with one. Got it written down back at the house."

I sat on the back bumper, resting my hands on my knees. A bull frog started its deep croaking over in the marsh a few feet away. I wondered what Darla and Lila were doing. Jimbo twisted the top back onto the bottle.

"One thing I put in the code," he said, "is that I don't never snake another man's woman."

"Snake?"

"Steal her away. She goes out with some man, she stays out with him for that night. Lila and Darla, they were supposed to meet Tony and Mike and go out to a movie. That's what Mike told me. Now he did say that him and Darla, they ain't all that serious or nothing. But, still, they did have a date later on."

A damned code. I would have never dreamed it, not from Jimbo McInnis of Waynesboro, Mississippi. You just never know.

"Can you handle yourself all right?" he asked.

"Usually."

"Good." He unbuttoned his shirt, took it off, and tossed it on the seat. Beneath it he was wearing a Mississippi State T-shirt with a bulldog face on it, its tongue hanging out the side of its mouth. The slogan *Dawg Pound Rock* was emblazoned beneath the dog. "What do you think?"

"Elegant understatement," I said. "I didn't realize the new J. Crew catalogue had come out."

"J what?"

"Never mind. The shirt looks just fine."

"You don't have on no Ole Miss shirt underneath, do you?"

"I'm afraid not."

"Well, this ought be enough to do the trick."

"The trick?" I asked.

"A private eye, he got to know karate and stuff like that?"

"What are we about to get into?"

"We gonna rock 'n roll a little. I noticed you ain't drinking much." He flipped me the truck keys and we walked across the lot, the gravel and oyster shells grinding beneath our feet.

The trucks parked beside the honky tonk were working trucks, fishermen's trucks, not like the show trucks back and Shirley's. In the beds of these pickups there were cast nets and trawl boards and chicken-wire crab traps. The bumpers and fenders were scratched and dented, and the paint was for the most part faded. One truck had a tag on the front bumper supporting the Hurricanes, the high school team out of Bayou La Batre. There was one Camaro, recently sanded down and unpainted except for a flat coat of red-orange primer. It had extra wide back tires and a big, black number 3 decal—the number was slanted to the left—in the center of the rear windshield. Dale Earnhart's number, God rest his soul. The only other car in the lot, a champagne colored Crown Victoria, seemed out of place because it was new and clean and free of decals or bumper stickers. At the far end of the building, the end opposite the front door, right up against the building was the dark green Plymouth Barracuda I had earlier seen around the island.

"They used to keep the riff-raff outta this place," Jimbo said, pointing at the Barracuda. "They keep lettin' the low lifes in and they're gonna lose their four star rating."

The tonk was dark inside with a low ceiling, a concrete floor, and cheap paneling on the walls. There was the customary array of lighted beer signs and posters. The bar was to our right, a rough cut, homemade counter with a top made of varnished plywood, stained by years' worth of spilled drinks and spotted with burn marks, two to five inches in length, made by a hundred cigarettes laid on the plywood surface. The woman behind it was a high mileage model with jet black hair teased up high and eyebrows that looked as if she'd painted them with a Magic Marker. She had a cigarette stuck in the corner of her mouth as she drew a couple of draft beers into clear, heavy mugs. Behind the bar, taped to the rear wall, was a sign that read "If you want to argue, go to

law school—If you want to fight, go join the damn Marines!"
Other wall decorations included an Alabama football schedule, an
Auburn War Eagle flag, and a faded poster of Bear Bryant wearing
a plaid sports coat and his famous checked hat. He was walking
across the calm surface of a pond.

We stepped to the bar and Jimbo ordered a set-up for himself
and a draft for me. At the far end of the bar, I caught Bobby Earl
Fair, the owner of the Barracuda, looking at us. He was on the
other side of this guy who was wearing dirty blue jeans and white
rubber shrimper boots. Bobby Earl kept peeking around the guy
to watch Jimbo. He and the guy in the shrimper boots seemed to
be examining a sheet of paper laid out on the bar.

"Looks like Bobby Earl's set up shop," I said.

Jimbo set his bottle on the bar, raised up on his stool, and
looked over the top of the shrimper. "You know him other than
by sight?"

"He got in my face the second day I was here and told me to
quit going around the island asking questions."

"What did you say?"

"I told him he had a smart mouth and that he was ugly. Then
a few days after that, I saw him taking bets at the Pelican Pub. I
understand Jason Summers used to bet pretty heavy with him."

"Yeah. Bobby Earl's a suspect all right. Far as I'm concerned
he's one of the front runners. 'Course they ain't asking my opinion these days. You know I said how Scooter, he wouldn't kill
nobody? Well, that scumbag down there, I wouldn't put nothing
past him. And that white trash group he's tied in with is worse
than he is."

"You think they could have planted that bomb on my porch?"

"About half of them are anti-government types who study that
shit on the Internet day and night. Timothy McVay ain't got nothing on the White Resistance. Hell, McVay might have even been
a member. Yeah, they coulda planted a bomb."

The shrimper sitting beside Bobby Earl had never looked

around. He reached into his pocket and pulled out a wad of bills and laid them on the bar. Jimbo turned his face toward me and acted like he wasn't interested in what Bobby Earl and the shrimper were doing.

"You see that sheet of paper in front of those guys down the bar?" he said. "Let me know when Bobby Earl touches it."

"Are you planning on doing something in here? You think it's a good idea to try to roust a suspect when you've been shooting tequila?"

"I'll let those tight-asses with the Alabama Bureau of Investigation worry about stuff like that. You in for some fun or not?"

Bobby Earl smoothed out the wadded bills and put them into a stack. He put the stack on the sheet of paper, pressed his forefinger down on it, and pulled it toward him across the bar. The shrimper pointed to something written on the paper and Bobby Earl started shaking his head.

"He just touched the betting sheet," I said.

Jimbo sprang off the stool. In two quick strides he was at the other end of the bar. He stabbed the bar with this buck knife that came out of nowhere and impaled both the betting sheet and the stack of money. He pushed the shrimper aside and I broke the guy's fall as he stumbled backwards. Jimbo grabbed Bobby Earl's wrist and put him in a half-Nelson so quickly I completely missed the move.

"How many times I gotta tell you gambling's against the law in Alabama?"

"Turn me a-loose, Jimbo! I got witnesses here!"

"And I got evidence. Right there on the bar."

"Hey!" the woman shouted, "read that sign back there!"

"Now just take it easy," Jimbo said. "We'll be through here in a minute."

"Aw, come on, Jimbo," the shrimper said. "Don't take my money."

"You just sit your ass over there in that chair by the pool table. And don't you go nowhere until I tell you to."

"When did the Sheriff's department start giving a shit about gambling anyhow?" the woman said.

"When these unsavory elements started moving in."

Jimbo walked Bobby Earl over to the wall and pushed his chest against it. He ordered him to put his hands against it and gave him a quick pat down. I kept an eye on the shrimper and the money and spread sheet stuck to the bar. The shrimper kept shaking his head and drawing in big breaths and blowing them out, completely disgusted by the whole deal.

Three kids who had been at the pool table eased toward the door a step or two at the time in an effort to go unnoticed. When they got close enough and had a clear shot at the door, they broke for it. Everybody else sat frozen where they were, watching the unfolding action to see if it was going to spread.

"All right, Bobby Earl," Jimbo said as he let go and stepped back three paces, "get the hell outta my sight."

Bobby Earl hitched his belt and tucked his shirt back in his pants. "You ain't got no right to be rousting me."

"The hell I don't! I heard about that threat you made the other day at the Sea House. You want a piece of me, you know where to find me. I better not ever hear no more about you saying out in public how you gonna whip my ass."

Bobby Earl gave him a venomous look. The muscles in his jaw were working so hard I could see them rippling even from where I stood at the bar. He looked at me and curled his lip and snorted before swaggering out the door at a deliberately slow pace.

"You think you ought to be rubbing his face in it?" I asked. "He looks like he'd take a sniper shot at you in a second if he ever catches you out on one of these backroads."

"Not at me, son. That White Resistance group that's done set Bobby Earl up with his territory, they all got felony records. They damn sure ain't gonna pop a cap at some deputy, not just because one of their bookies got rousted. That spells death penalty." He turned to me with that slit-eyed smile. "But *you* might oughta watch your backside for a while." He looked around the room which had become as quiet and still as a wake. "Show's over, folks!" Jimbo shouted. "It's time to party!"

"Come on, Jimbo," the shrimper said. "Give me my money back, man. It took me all night dragging them nets to make that."

"I don't know why all the sudden the sheriff cares about a little gambling," the woman said.

"Let me have one of them little garbage bags," Jimbo said.

"You done run all my customers off."

He pulled the knife out of the bar and picked up the betting sheet taking pains to avoid the corner Bobby Earl had touched. He dropped it in the white plastic garbage bag and pulled the twist tie closed. Then he folded the whole thing and stuck it in his back pocket.

"You still want a beer?" the woman asked me. "Least y'all can do after running my customers off is buy a beer."

"Come here, Tee Jay," Jimbo said to the shrimper. "Here's your money. You ought to thank me for saving you from throwing it away. I saw on that sheet where you had picked Mississippi State to get beat. Hey, give this man here a beer on me."

The shrimper smiled and the woman handed him a can of Busch. He asked her for change for the Alabama Redemption machine. The front door opened and four guys in jeans came in shouting and laughing, a loud bunch, already drunk. That seemed to lift the woman's spirits some.

"I don't know if they can lift Bobby Earl's prints off this betting sheet or not," Jimbo said. "They claim they can, but it don't seem to me like you could do something like that. Anyhow I got a buddy who can match them up with the ones they say they took off that envelope they found at your place."

"Are you telling me they have prints from that letter bomb?"

"Some. But they probably ain't the bomber's prints. They

might just be from some clerk at the store where he bought the envelope. But, who knows. Sometimes criminals slip up."

"So why is Bobby Earl a suspect?"

"He was Jason's bookie, and you never know how deep in hock Jason might have been in to him."

"You believe that's what happened?"

"It's believable," he said. "Especially when you consider that Bobby Earl Fair is a friggin' psychopath and I think he's already been in on one killing since he took over the bookmaking operations in Mobile County. You remember reading about this car salesman who was at a red light in Theodore and this car pulls up beside him and unloads two barrels of number-four shot into the side of his face? We can't prove nothin', but that guy was in to the tune of two grand to Bobby Earl."

"They killed a man over a measly two thousand dollars?"

"It's a new bunch who moved in since the old bookie retired. They don't know how to handle it. I believe they outted somebody over two grand, and sometimes Jason would lay more than that on just one game."

Over at the pool table, one of the guys who had just walked in lined up to break. He got under it with his cue stick and the ball went airborne and bounced off the bumper and onto the floor. He yelled "Shit!" real loud and popped the door of the ladies' bathroom with his fist. All his buddies laughed and hooted.

"Told you this was a fun place," Jimbo said. "Why don't you go over to that pool table and lay a quarter on the bumper?"

"I'm out of practice. I don't know how good I'll play."

"When was the last time you broke and missed the whole damn table?"

We sat at the bar, stools turned around and elbows propped on the edge, so we could stretch out while we watched. Two couples walked in and sat at a booth along the wall. The barmaid stepped around the bar and went to take their orders. The game we were waiting on took forever. These guys were really bad, or drunk, or, more likely, both.

Jimbo traded in his almost full bottle of Jack Daniel's to the barmaid in exchange for two shriveled up limes, a half-full bottle of some off-brand tequila with a miniature sombrero attached to the neck, and the free use of a salt shaker. I asked Jimbo about possible state regulations against bar patrons trading in already-opened bottles of liquor. He pointed out, with accuracy, that this wasn't exactly the Court of Two Sisters we were sitting in.

Jimbo quartered one of the limes while we waited for the pool match to end. He licked the fleshy part of his hand where the thumb and forefinger join and sprinkled it with salt. He licked the salt, took a swig of tequila out of the bottle, and bit down on the wedge of lime in a smooth three-step operation. That droopy-eyed, tight-lipped smile crept back up his face.

Over at the pool table, the winners gave each other a high five and the losers bought another round. They all chugged the remainder of the beers they already had to make room for the new ones.

"Who's next?" one of the winners shouted.

"You ready?" Jimbo said.

"We're just playing pool, right?"

"Lighten up, man."

We grabbed two sticks out of the rack up on the wall, didn't even sight down them to see if they were crooked. Jimbo set his tequila bottle on a nearby table, and we flipped a quarter to determine which team got to break. The game was eight ball. They won the toss, and their break was truly bad. The two we were playing against both worked as roofers and both had been out in the sun all day. They smelled like it. Not a strong odor, but the smell of stale sweat dried into their shirts and pants, the scent of the working man. They had light sunburns, their hands were rough and dirt stained, and one of them had a ponytail. The other one could have also put his hair into a ponytail if only he had a rubber band.

Jimbo lined up the four ball, a gimme shot straight at the side pocket. He hit it just a little to the side and it rattled against both sides of the hole before dropping in. He left himself a tough shot, the six in the corner. He had to run it down the edge of the table, but it hit a little hard and bounced away from the edge. It rolled to a spot six inches out from the pocket.

The two roofers high fived each other. "Too bad, bulldog," one of them said. He then sank the seven on a show-off shot, an extra hard pop that slammed the ball into the pocket. But he left himself in terrible shape when it ricocheted back to the middle of the table. He missed the next shot.

"Your shot, bulldog."

From back at the bar where the two others were seated came a loud, "Roll, Tide!" Jimbo's smile got a little bigger as he winked at me. These were some serious Alabama football fans, and that's a group that doesn't take kindly to criticism of the Crimson Tide or of anything remotely associated with the program, especially when they've been drinking. Jimbo bent over the table and laid his face almost down on the felt as he lined up his next shot. He made it, and walked around the corner of the table to where the cue ball had come to rest. As he walked in front of me he whispered to me, "You ready to rock 'n roll?"

"Not over a football game," I said.

He cleared his throat and looked at me, his smile looked just like Stan Laurel's of the old Laurel and Hardy comedy team. "You guys must be Alabama fans."

"Roll Tide," the guy with the ponytail said.

"What they got this year?" Jimbo studied two possible shots and decided on the come back carom to the side. "Besides probation, I mean."

"Well, they gonna kick Mississippi State's ass," this roofer up at the bar shouted. I didn't realize our voices were carrying so well that the guys at the bar could hear us.

"That so?" Jimbo pointed in my direction. "What they gonna do against Ole Miss?"

All four of them laughed to make it clear they didn't think the prospect of Ole Miss beating Alabama was worth serious discussion. I thought the Rebels were going to be pretty good, and we were playing Bama in Oxford that year. But I didn't say anything. Football talk in a strange bar, especially in Alabama, can get real tricky, real fast. I had the feeling Jimbo was trying to start a war here.

"Well, I think you boys are in for a surprise this year." Jimbo hit the ball with a soft touch and it banked off the opposite bumper right into the side pocket in front of him. "Because I been studying the situation real close. And you know what? Bama sucks."

Oh, God, I thought. This is not good. Not in some honky tonk in the middle of a swamp in Alabama. I swear, I could feel the barometric pressure going up. The two other roofers at the bar got up and eased toward us. I backed up a little to make sure nobody was behind me.

"Jimbo!" the woman warned, "you better read that sign again!"

"Can't I give a simple opinion about something?"

"Hey!" one of the pool players said, "Bama *rules*, man!"

"They used to," Jimbo said. "But they're going down. They living on reputation. I noticed they had to drop Louisiana Tech off the schedule 'cause they couldn't beat 'em."

The woman behind the bar, no doubt an expert at spotting storm clouds, picked up a telephone and started dialing some familiar number. Since the pool game started a fairly good crowd had come in, mostly kids. There were two tables of them on what was sometimes a dance floor. They were drinking pitchers of beer and eating popcorn. Jimbo missed the next shot.

"It's all yours," he said to the nearest roofer.

All four of them were now lined up at the pool table eyeing Jimbo. They tried to look grim. But their eyes showed that they were anything but angry; they were excited. And I knew then we were in for one hell of a fight. These guys had spotted their chance to make this a south Mobile County evening to remember. We were just playing out the same old familiar scripted play to its inevitable conclusion, which is a knock-down, drag-out brawl. I could delay it, but I damn sure wasn't going to be able to stop it.